While twenty-year-old  excellent living as a tattoo artist in a near-future version of Hell's Kitchen, the rest of the country is splintered and struggling in the wake of a war gone on for too long. Technology has collapsed, borders rise and fall overnight, and magic has awakened without rhyme, reason, or rule, turning average unwitting citizens into wielders of strange and specific strands of magic.

Hemingway's particular brand of magic has made him a household name. Not only is he a talented artist, but his work comes to life. Literally.

When NYC's most infamous serial killer—the East River Ripper—abducts Hemingway's best friend, Grace, he has only days to save her. Hemingway teams up with his stoic cop roommate to hunt for the killer and rescue Grace before she becomes the Ripper's latest victim. But as the duo chase clues to the serial killer's identity, Hemingway begins to fear the magic he and the Ripper share might eventually corrupt him too.

EARNEST INK

Alex Hall

A NineStar Press Publication

Published by NineStar Press
P.O. Box 91792,
Albuquerque, New Mexico, 87199 USA.
www.ninestarpress.com

Earnest Ink

Printed in the USA
First Edition
October, 2019

Print ISBN: 978-1-951057-13-8

Also available in eBook, ISBN: 978-1-951057-12-1

To found family

Chapter One

Earnest Ink

I work without speaking because that's the way I prefer it. The vibration of my machine, the softer buzz of the fluorescent lights overhead, the tap of my foot on the pedal—it's the best music in the world.

When I hit a ticklish spot, the girl I'm working on gasps, jolting in my chair.

"Don't move," I say. And then, with a salesman's false cheer: "Almost done!"

The girl is sweating down the crook of her neck. She's got silver glitter paint on her eyelids and cheeks, a new fashion trend I just can't quite get behind. Under my lights the mix of perspiration and makeup looks like a blurry constellation.

She wanted a bee inked onto her collarbone, one of those tiny honeybees you find on good tequila bottles. Easily done, and she met the cash requirement. She's eager, nervous, and breathing in and out in little puffs.

I can't remember her name, but that's fine. Customer relations is Eric's job.

There's another kid leaning over my glass counter, watching eagerly as I work. "Does it hurt?" he asks. "When the magic happens?"

The bee's fat yellow thorax wriggles from side to side as it begins to wake, fighting the pressure of my needle, hungry for life.

"It looks like it hurts," the kid says. I ignore him.

One minute more and—thanks to my peculiar magic—this bee will fly free.

I'm perched on a swivel stool, a wet paper towel in my hand to wipe away ink. It's too hot in my studio, even with the industrial fans whirling overhead and the door propped wide open. Evening light slants in through the door and the north-facing, floor-to-ceiling window panes that look out onto West Forty-Sixth. It's muggy, too warm for New York in October, and all of Hell's Kitchen is wilting, including my client.

"What does it feel like?" the kid demands. He's leaving greasy fingerprints on the surface of the glass as he strains to get a better look at what I'm doing. I study him out the corner of my eye, wiping sweat off my nose with the back of my wrist before it drips on my customer. He looks like one of the street punks who have taken to running in packs near the cruise terminals, sleeping in old, abandoned cargo containers and panhandling up and down the marina.

He's skinny and tall, hair dyed an unsettling violet and styled into spikes all over his head. He's got a silver ring in his septum and more hoops in his ears; his eyelashes are coated with purple mascara to match his hair. Green glitter paint sparkles on his lids. His T-shirt and jeans are torn and dirty, and he's got a pack of black-market cigarettes rolled into one sleeve against his upper arm.

"Tattoos hurt. The magic bit? Not so much. Now get off my counter; you're leaving streaks."

That's from Eric, working customer relations from behind the shelter of our gigantic, old-school cash register. The register's solid brass and built like a tank, and Eric keeps pepper spray and a butterfly knife in the drawer with the cash just in case. Eric hates people in general, and New Yorkers in particular.

Before the draft he was an intern at a law firm in Connecticut. He wasn't on the front for more than six months before he contracted Cascades fever and was sent home on medical discharge to die. While lying in bed one day, he saw me on TV and decided he could make good money as my receptionist and bodyguard.

Eric didn't die. He got better, found his way from Connecticut to New York, crossed the border on a military visa, and stayed. I hired him because he knows how to sell an idea, keep a tidy client book, and break an assailant's neck with one arm.

"Sorry." The kid jerks away from the countertop. I lean back over the girl in my chair. He clears his throat. "I mean, how would I know, right? I've never seen magic before. Except on TV. And you can't believe everything you see on TV. Some of that shit just isn't real."

He's got a barely noticeable accent, a strange softness to his vowels. I think he must be Canadian, and I'm surprised. Most of the Canucks still left in the city keep to themselves, living and working south of Wall Street in a homogenous neighborhood known affectionately as Little Montreal. From what I've heard, they're a close-knit, fanatically private, mostly wealthy group of people, and it seems unlikely one of their kids would take it upon himself to break with tradition and trade real family for the rat pack running rampant on Pier 88.

The girl twitches and giggles when I wipe her collarbone. A lazy breeze sneaks in through the door, along with shouts and muffled laughter. It's tourist season, and outside Earnest Ink, the sidewalks are busy with gawkers from out of town. Mostly they just take selfies under my sign. If they're stupid enough to come in without plenty of cash in hand, Eric chases them out.

I'm guessing the street punk spent his last handful of dollars on the cigarettes rolled in his sleeve, so I'm not sure why Eric's letting him linger.

"This particular 'shit' is real as it gets," Eric drawls while I smooth petroleum jelly over skin. The ointment's pleasantly cold. The girl shivers.

"Can I come closer? Just a little? I want to see." Without waiting for permission, the kid bends over the counter, resting his elbows on the glass.

Eric shifts languidly behind his register but doesn't chase him off. Bee Girl is our last appointment of the day. Eric's bored and probably hungry, and maybe that's why he lets the kid stay—for entertainment. But he doesn't really want to have a conversation. Probably he just likes the look of the kid's hair and eyes. Eric's in his early twenties like me, but he acts ten years older. I think it comes from seeing the front line and living to tell about it. He dresses like a runway model in secondhand Chanel suits and 1990s-era Givenchy. He keeps up on the latest city fashions with an eagerness bordering on obsession, and reads literary classics with equal enthusiasm.

"Okay," I answer without looking up from my work. "But maybe don't talk so much. It's distracting." I smile apologetically at my client, but she only giggles more. Cheap wine has dyed her lips indigo. I test my machine, squeezing the trigger. It vibrates under the pressure of my fingers.

"You him?" the kid asks eagerly. "Hemingway? The thaumaturge?"

I nod. Hemingway's my surname. It's what I've gone by since I escaped Ketchum, Idaho, for the big city.

"Huh." He sounds reluctantly impressed, but he doesn't take the hint to shut up. "Did you really do Arctic Fox in their hotel room before their last show?"

Eric snorts. Bee Girl blushes pink under her paint. I check my ink cup to make sure I'm not running low before working the foot pedal again.

"Matching ink, all six of the band members." It hadn't been a very exciting job. They'd been specific and unimaginative about what they'd wanted and too stoned at the end to react much when the sailors' swallows I'd inked onto their biceps spread their wings and took flight, swooping a few inches into the air, tethered by an invisible thread of magic to tattooed flesh. "Photos in the red book, there. Take a look."

I hear him open the book and flip through. The tattoo machine sends vibrations through my bones and the girl's, together.

"How much, eh?" the kid asks. "For a small one?"

"You're not old enough," Eric retorts. "Come back in a few years and then we'll talk."

"I'm sixteen!"

"Law's eighteen in Manhattan," I say over the buzz of my machine. "I never break it."

"It's a stupid law... Are you *sure* you're him? I expected someone...taller." He's so lanky he reminds me of a brilliantly plumed stork.

"License is right there in the window," Eric replies, examining his fingernails. "And rules are rules, so take off and come back when you've grown pubes."

Eric can be a real bitch, but I don't mind. Life can be a real bitch, too.

The kid takes his advice and leaves, stomping his way out of the studio and into the stale afternoon, bony shoulders hunched.

We close shop later than I'd planned. After Bee Girl we get a walk-in, a grunt with a Platinum MasterCard in his wallet looking to celebrate turning forty. He wants his badge number done on his pectoral in typically boring Gothic script. It's the sort of thing I can easily freehand, and it's not every soldier who lives to see their fortieth birthday, so I nod Eric's way, and he swipes the grunt's card. Like Bee Girl, the soldier sits sweating in my chair as I work. He flinches beneath my needle, flexing his fingers and crumpling the week-old newspaper he'd been reading while he waited for me to clean and reset my machine. His bare chest is muscular, the flesh pitted with small scars and dusted with freckles. He's not large, but he's solid after years in service. There's gray in his close-clipped beard and sprinkled throughout his buzz cut.

He closes his eyes. Eric leaves his refuge behind the counter, crosses the studio, and firmly shuts the front door. A moment later I understand why: thunder rumbles, shaking our windowpanes. A gust of sudden wind blows a funnel of flower petals along the sidewalk. The muggy gray sky splits open, and late evening becomes a twilight deluge. Pedestrians shout and scatter for cover. There are three more stories above Earnest Ink—the industrial penthouse I call home, one midsized loft rented by a geriatric busybody, plus a floor with older apartments we use mostly for storage—but I can hear the rattle of rain on the building's roof through the radiator pipes.

"Summer in the city," my client says, smiling grimly, as another bout of wind throws a spatter of rain against the windows. "Wouldn't trade it for the world."

I refrain from pointing out we're closer to fall than summer. Weather on the island in early autumn is always a crapshoot. But he's not wrong—I wouldn't trade it for the world.

The bell above the door jangles a warning just before it cracks wide enough to allow the scent of wet city— industrial soap over old piss, cut grass, ripe produce, and motor oil—into the studio. The newspaper pages blow out of the grunt's grasp and onto the floor, making him swear.

Grace slips in with the wind, ruffled and half-soaked, then pushes the door closed and puts her back against it as though to brace against the storm. Her cheeks are pink from the wind and rain; she's got a smear of yellow glitter paint on her chin.

"Jesus," she says over the buzz of my machine. "It's like the Amazon out there."

The grunt in my chair muffles amusement, making me wonder if he's seen the actual Amazon. It's possible he has, probable even. The seven-digit badge number I'm etching into his skin begins with a three, which means he's been specially trained for off-continent work, which explains how he's got enough credit on his MasterCard to afford my services.

Grace stoops to gather up the scattered newspaper and pauses as she catches sight of the headline emblazoned across the front page in a large font: East River Ripper Strikes Again!

"Fuck," she says. "Have they found her body yet?" She folds the paper, shaking her head. "I can't believe he snatched her in broad daylight. Bastard's getting bolder. Bet the shit's really hit the fan in the mayor's office."

"Client," Eric chides Grace.

The grunt in my chair starts to sit up, then freezes when I remind him: "Keep still, please."

"Sorry." But he smiles at Grace. Everyone smiles at Grace; she's just that sort of person.

"Don't you worry, miss," he promises. "We'll get him sooner or later."

Taking a good look at my client, Grace arches one brow in silent surprise. I get her astonishment. Most grunts would rather spend their reserve on black-market sweets or cigarettes or a show—costly old-school comforts, escapism. The guy in my chair is maybe one of three military I've inked since I set up shop in Hell's Kitchen.

"Sooner might be better," she says. "Like, this one's week ran out two days ago, and I bet her body is already in the river. Another couple of months and he'll be looking for his next grab."

Emotion flushes the grunt's bare chest and throat. His skin grows hot beneath my hand. He's not smiling any longer, but he keeps his mouth shut instead of rising to Grace's bait, which earns him points in my book.

"Hemingway." Grace blithely switches subjects, ignoring Eric's pointed glare. "Why are you still working? It's *Friday* night. We've got a place to be. You promised."

"Almost finished." I pause and glance up, watching fondly as she struggles to repair the damage the wind and rain have done to her elaborate updo. She's traded her day kit for a black tank, purple tutu, rainbow tights, and black boots. More yellow glitter paint sparkles on her mouth and on her cheeks.

"Don't rush," Grace says, meaning the opposite, before throwing herself onto the comfy red velvet chaise I keep on hand for visitors and afternoon naps. She takes out her mobile to check the time. Thunder rumbles. Rain on the glass makes it seem like the studio is under water. "Not like Pink Jones will play Cleo's again any time soon. And please God let the rain keep the paps away."

I look down at my client. He stares back, concerned. His irises are so dark they're almost black except for flecks of rust. He's big enough, and strong enough, to crush me into chalk if he decides I'm taking advantage. There's a lot of money between us, and at this point there's no going back. When I'm finished he'll have his own piece of real-life magic: Gothic numbers floating in the air a few inches above his skin like some sort of futuristic hologram.

"Wouldn't dream of rushing," I promise, smiling reassurance. "It's like the sign over the door promises: Earnest Ink. I take perfection very seriously."

Total BS, but he buys it hook, line, and sinker. They always do.

Chapter Two

The Ripper

When I'm finally finished and we're cashed out and closed up, it's dark outside. Eric waves a terse goodbye and makes for his apartment on Fifty-Second, head bowed against the wind, Gucci raincoat flapping. Grace is sulking pointedly without making a sound. I'm immune to her dramatics. Grace and I used to have sex before we decided we're better off as friends. We no longer live together, but we see each other almost every day. I know her moods as well as my own.

Most of the time, we're good for each other.

Grace is a theater major at AADA when she's not working her father's Chelsea art gallery. She'd sell her soul for even the smallest role off-Broadway, but she lacks the subtlety needed for that lucky break. Grace overacts everything; even her orgasms are a production. After a while it's enough to wear a person out.

It rains on us all the way to Cleo's, but luckily the club's not far. Two blocks east of Earnest Ink, we leave Hell's Kitchen for the more massive city skyline near the lower end of Central Park. Here it feels like all of Manhattan is under construction, scaffolding and blue builder's wrap covering many of the skyscrapers from top to bottom. It's late enough in the evening that the nail guns and jackhammers and generators have gone quiet, but a flock of long-necked industrial cranes loom in the rain, lit from the bottom by white security spotlights casting strange shadows over the pavement.

The sidewalk on both sides of Eighth Avenue is crowded with pedestrians heading home from work or out for dinner or to market. The shops that used to stay open twenty-four hours a day close at nine, an hour before curfew stops the subway from running. Yellow cabs inch north along the wet street, nose to tail. Their windows are mirrored for privacy. Even close-up I can't see the drivers or their fares behind the silver glass, but I do see my reflection staring thoughtfully back: short dark hair, eyes too large in a thin face. Raindrops are beading on my eyelashes and on the oversized, vintage Pink Jones hoodie I threw on hours earlier before leaving for work. The band's logo—a long-nosed, cartoonish armadillo smoking a large blunt—is reflected in reverse across my chest, its one eye closed in a perpetual wink.

I glance away. Grace, several steps ahead as usual, slows to grab my hand and tug me on, turning sideways to keep her tutu from getting squished in the crowd. She thinks I don't know she's wearing it because of me. It's a subtle reminder of things past, her ballerina princess accessory against my brooding dark jeans and black boots. Grace might mock paparazzi and autograph hounds, but she likes to show me off whenever we're out because my fame usually gets her free drinks and food.

Grace, for all her family's old money, can't keep a penny in her bank account.

Cleo's is midtown's worst-kept secret. Located in the recently renovated basement of the Plaza Hotel, the club's so new it's doubly shiny and clean in an immaculate city. The club's owner, a retired Los Angeles movie mogul, has enough clout to bring in acts from all over the country, interstate travel visas be damned. He must be greasing more than a few palms at the Port of Entry, but nobody on either end is complaining, and Cleo's keeps landing all the best bands.

At the back of the Plaza, on Fifty-Ninth Street, Manhattan's precurfew crowd has morphed into a well-behaved mob. Half of midtown has turned out to catch a glimpse of Jones or her mates. Undeterred by the wind and rain, people press up against temporary bollard barriers put up outside the club's entryway. A handful of on-duty grunts linger, wary of trouble, but the looky-loos seem content to stand in the weather, mobiles in hand, taking snapshots of Cleo's flashing sign and breaking occasionally into snippets of the band's latest hit.

Grace's fingers tighten on mine. I squeeze back, struggling to pull my hood up one-handed and disguise my face. I catch a flash of violet out of the corner of my eye: it's the street kid from earlier in the day, the one who left fingerprints on Eric's counter while he made fun of my height. He's crammed up against one of the barriers, squeezed between a group of starstruck girls wearing head-to-toe faux leather and Pink Jones ribbons in their hair, and a grim woman with a press tag around her neck and a camera in her hands.

Catching me looking, he shows me straight white teeth in a wide grin. The rain has done nothing to subdue the garish color in his hair.

"Hemingway!" he shouts, loud enough to be heard over the weather, the muted rumbling of the crowd, and the angry horns of yellow cabs one street over. "Are you here for work or to see the show? Hemingway! Are you gonna ink Jones?" He laughs at his own joke.

Curious faces turn in our direction. I dip my chin, but it's too late. A hundred flashbulbs go off, turning raindrops into tiny stars. Dazzled, I blink. Someone else yells my name. People in the crowd clap and stomp their feet. The grunts peer in my direction, mouths and eyes flat beneath their visors.

"Who is that?" Grace wants to know as she pulls me hastily out of view, down several steps off street level toward the club's recessed door. "Do you know him?"

"Just some street kid who came into the shop earlier," I answer. "Never met him before today."

Grace gives me a look but doesn't reply. Off the sidewalk, we're out of the rain. I don't recognize the bouncer watching the club's door, but he recognizes me. His eyes widen a fraction before he remembers to guard his expression. He's afraid of me, reticent as he checks our IDs and then stamps our hands for entry.

Not everyone in the world appreciates thaumaturgy. Most people are still becoming accustomed to it. And plenty more use magic as an excuse for hate.

Inside Cleo's it would be pitch-dark except for the rainbow strobes, flashing disco balls, and an eight-branched octopus chandelier suspended over the red-lacquered bar. The regular DJ, hidden in an alcove behind the stage, is playing a fine Pink Jones mash-up ahead of the opening act. The club is packed, the floor so tight it's become a single mass of people expanding and contracting like some sort of multicolored amoeba. Everyone's laughing and shouting, coming down or going up after a long week. There's a mist in the air, pumping out from above the stage to keep the space cool. Despite the press of bodies, it's ten degrees colder inside Cleo's than outside in the rain. Relieved, I push back my hood and let the mist coat my face.

Grace heads straight for the dance floor. I head straight for a drink. The bar's a cluster-jam of thirsty people, but I manage to squeeze my way through. Danny's working the left corner, and two more guys I know by face but not name tend middle and right. All three are wearing black-and-red leather to match the lacquered bar. The strobe lights flash in their eyes.

New York State lowered the drinking age when they reinstated the draft. Maybe the mayor thought allowing sixteen-year-olds alcohol would take the sting out of conscription, or maybe he assumed with the borders closed, booze would be hard to come by. He didn't count on bathtub gin or Brooklyn homebrew.

I'm solidly legal, but even if I weren't, very few people in the city refuse me something I want.

When I catch Danny's attention, I order three shots of hooch straight up, no chaser. I slam the shots back one after another while Danny smiles and shakes his head.

The person nursing a glass of red wine near my elbow grins in appreciation.

"Oh, honey," they say just loud enough to be heard over the din of Pink Jones's trademark bass. "You'll be feeling that in no time."

"Not me." I lean in close so they can see my grin. "Alcohol and I have a friendly relationship."

They're dressed head to toe in tight black satin except for a striped scarf hung loosely over their shoulders. They're cute as hell in an Eartha Kitt sort of way, all long legs and stacked heels. I'm betting when they slide off the stool, they'll be at least a foot taller than I am.

They grin back before finishing their wine in one elegant swallow. "Care to dance?"

"Love to."

I can't help glancing across the dancefloor, searching gyrating bodies until I find Grace in the crowd. When I pick her out in the pulsing light, she's already attracted a group of colorful admirers, butterflies drawn to a promising flower. She's laughing as she dances, arms above her head and long hair coming down around her shoulders. I've no doubt she's forgotten me completely.

"Nice tutu," my new companion says, following my line of sight over the edge of their glass. "You two a couple?"

"No." The hooch has hit my empty stomach hard; I'm suddenly light-headed and giddy. "Not anymore." I'm grinning stupidly, but I don't care. "I'm all yours."

It's two in the morning and long past curfew before Pink Jones calls it a night and we all pile out of the club and onto the pavement. It's still raining. I make sure Grace is safely in a cab toward Chelsea. She clings to my neck as I ease her into the back seat, whispering affectionate nonsense into my ear. But the rain's soaking through my hoodie, and I need to piss badly, so I push her off and give the cabbie her address before slamming the car door.

After Grace's cab peels away from the curb, I stand in line to wait for my own. Much simpler to walk back home, but nobody walks after curfew. The grunts have cleared the crowd from the bollards, and now they stand watchfully on either side of the cab queue. The cars pulling up to the curb are painted white instead of yellow: curfew cabs, the drivers having completed the special training needed to ensure every after-hours fare makes it home safe and sound. Like the soldiers standing guard, the men and women driving the white taxis are armed;

they wear collapsible batons on snap-chains around their necks. When telescoped out, the batons are nasty and solid as a lead pipe.

I stare up at the sky as I wait, getting rain in my eyes. There are no visible stars above Manhattan, only high-rise windows flickering from bright to dark and back again, and the spotlights illuminating sleeping machinery. In the early morning hours, when the rest of the city sleeps, alcohol is my best friend. I love how soft it makes me feel. I adore the wobble in my step as I finally reach the edge of the queue and duck into a white cab. The driver studies me in the rearview as I slide into the back of the car.

"Where to?" He repeats himself twice before I hear him past the post-concert ringing in my ears. He's trying to decide if I'm drunk enough to cause trouble. He needn't worry. I moved halfway across country to avoid trouble. I fish the stiff plastic curfew card out of the back pocket of my jeans and pass it up. He slots it into the dash and waits until the readout flashes a friendly green.

I'm a safe fare. Still, he doesn't relax. He's thinking my face is familiar. He's worrying he's seen it before, in grainy black and white, on one of the many fliers tacked to the wall in the company break room. He's worrying I belong on Rikers.

But he can't kick me out of the car; the flashing green dash says I'm good.

"Five hundred West Forty-Sixth," I answer quickly when his reflection in the rearview turns dour. I've been sitting without speaking just a little too long.

The cab lurches away from the curb. I close my eyes, seeing strobe lights and rainbow flashes against the backs of my lids. Pink Jones's dolorous lyrics and upbeat synth play on repeat in my skull. I smile, remembering Grace dancing like a mad creature at the foot of the stage, all crushed tulle and wild hair with glitter paint streaking her face. Her enthusiasm was contagious. My feet hurt from stomping, my throat from screaming.

I don't own a mobile phone. That doesn't stop me from collecting numbers. In the front pocket of my Pink Jones hoodie reside an assortment of paper scraps—corners of cocktail napkins and business cards.

People give me their digits. I don't think they really expect I'll call. I think they do it just to say they did, to pretend they're flirting with danger.

We pull up outside the studio entrance. *Earnest Ink* glows fluorescent blue above the door in vintage neon tube. The sign cost me a fortune—almost nobody bends glass anymore—but Eric found a supplier upstate willing to repurpose some old tubing and made it happen. I griped about the cost, but I didn't really mean it. I've got plenty of money, and as far as I'm concerned, Manhattan could do with a neon resurgence.

I pay the driver, and he returns my curfew card. The wind has let up but not before it blew a pile of trash up against the foot of my building, sodden hamburger wrappers and newspaper pages and torn flower petals sticking to the brick. Loose trash is a no-no on the island. The street sweepers have been neglecting our corner, or maybe the storm's blown over a trash bin. Either way, someone will pay a hefty fine unless the garbage is gone by morning.

I scuff it away from my door with the toe of my boot while I fumble with my keys. The cab squeals off into the morning. Ionized mercury gas buzzes blue over my head.

The studio's as we left it, quiet and dark, my machine sleeping, the ancient cash register a solid monster keeping watch from the counter. My head swims pleasantly as I secure the door. I'm sorely tempted to sprawl on the velvet chaise, sleep off the drink there on the ground floor instead of braving our rickety elevator to the penthouse, but I know better. I've succumbed before and woken up with a stiff neck and aching back for my sins.

The elevator is concealed behind a black curtain at the back of the studio. It's got old carpet on the floor and even older mirrors on the walls. I cue the top floor and rock on my boot heels as it rises, whistling Pink Jones and stealing glances at the guy whistling back from the elevator walls. When I'm drunk enough, I can admit he's not bad looking despite the butchered hair and narrow chin. His eyes, although too large, are kind, and his hands are graceful, and his shoulders are wide enough to be solidly masculine. The bulky concert hoodie hides any evidence of binding; his jeans hang on narrow hips.

I pass okay. Mostly no one ever looks twice. I don't close my eyes anymore when I brush my teeth in front of the bathroom looking glass.

The elevator opens onto my floor where there's yet another door for security reasons. I fumble my keys before I can fit the one I need into the lock. I lean on the wall as I bend my knees, groping along the carpet. The wall is papered with cabbage roses and rough to the touch, peeling in places. The carpet shag is so deep, my keyring is lost in plush gray fiber. Or maybe it's the bathtub gin making the distance between my fingertips and the floor seem too far.

I've almost hooked the ring between my thumb and pointer finger when Thom yanks the door open from inside. Off-balance, I fall across the threshold into our foyer, then laugh like a loon. Thom backs up. She doesn't like to touch people if she doesn't have to. She's too self-contained for anything like human contact.

"Christ, Hemingway," she complains, hands on hips. "Keep it down or you'll have Harcourt calling in a complaint."

"I won't." Thom's always worrying, but nothing ever wakes our second-floor neighbor. Elderly Ms. Harcourt sleeps like a baby, probably because she's deaf in one ear. "Anything on?"

It's my standard greeting because it's the one she responds to best. Say hello or good morning or what's for dinner and Thom pays no attention at all. Ask her about the web of string and paper tacked to the loft's northern wall and she perks right up.

"Nothing yet," she says grimly as I shut and bolt the door. The loft smells of Chinese food, which means she's ordered in. My stomach growls response. "It's been quiet."

She switches her glare from me to the old police scanner she keeps on our kitchen counter. Thom's military, but before the draft, she was aiming for a scholarship to John Jay and a degree in forensics. She's scary smart and would have made the NYPD proud if the world as we knew it hadn't ended.

Now she works the Port Patrol a.m. shift six days a week, searching boats and barges for self-evacs—refugees fleeing the volatile Eastern Seaboard—before they're allowed to dock, or dragging people out of the Hudson if they're desperate enough to jump ship and swim toward shore in their bid for the safety of Manhattan. It's physical work, and most nights she comes home exhausted and sporting new bruises and old chilblains—desperate people don't pull punches and the Hudson's cold—but it's after Thom hangs up her uniform that her real work begins.

Her brain work: the crime scene tacked up all over the brick wall. Newspaper clippings and Polaroid snapshots, "Missing" posters, names and dates and other snippets of esoteric information written on brick in white chalk, and strings of colored yarn connecting each data point. Thom's murder wall is exactly like one of those crazy collages you see in old detective movies, only the wall's large enough that she's pasted it all against a hand-sketched white chalk map of the island, allowing each data point its corresponding place on Manhattan.

Originally, I'd planned to hang something modern and colorful on that wall, but Thom claimed it the day she moved in, and I've become resigned to our gruesome East River Ripper accent wall. I even drew the map; it's some of my best work, completely in proportion.

"Too quiet," Thom continues as I kick off my boots and pad across our badly distressed wood floor and into the kitchen. "Five years, fifteen vics, and his MO never changes. He *always* drops them on the seventh day. There should be a corpse by now."

"So there's no body yet." I root out a plate from our mostly empty cabinets, snag the remnants of Thom's dinner from the fridge, and dump leftover Szechuan shrimp out of a carton. The room's still slightly off-kilter, and I'm very pleased with myself for no reason other than I've found greasy food. "Maybe, you know, that's a good sign."

I'd give Thom a grateful hug for ordering in, but she wouldn't find my tipsy affection welcome. So I grin at her instead.

Thom's taller than I am by a few inches. She's also ripped as fuck. Grunt work has made her strong, given her muscle in places I didn't know muscle grew. She's required to keep her hair cut very short for safety's sake; when she's off-duty she covers her dark fuzz with a tattered red beanie. The beanie belonged to her twin brother, Rafe Castillo. It's all of him that Thom has left. That, and Rafe's missing person's poster tacked on our murder map above the East River Bikeway.

With Thom, it's not just brain work for brain work's sake. My roommate is hunting her dead brother's killer. Has been for the past five years, two of which she's spent living with me.

"It's not a 'good sign,'" Thom says coldly. The icy inflection is more for the Ripper than for me, though I know she finds my detachment frustrating.

Serial killers are not my thing. I've seen enough violence to last me. I don't need to go looking for more. But I understand what finding and stopping the Ripper means to Thom, so I don't take offense at her glares. For Thom, it's personal.

I carry my plate over near the windows, collapsing into one of several overstuffed secondhand chairs we keep scattered about the loft.

"Maybe he's dead," I suggest helpfully. I pick out bits of shrimp from rice with my fork, one small morsel before the next. If I chew each bite one hundred times, I'll fill up quicker.

"Maybe your latest grab—" I wave my fork at the murder wall, and at the newest photograph in a collection of many. "—what's her name, Christy Spears? Maybe Christy went all batshit on his ass and he fell in the river. She's military, right? Bet Christy's got some jacked

Houdini-type skills and escaped herself before the Ripper could get to work." Going by just her picture, Christy's delicate and blonde and doesn't look strong enough to fend off a Chihuahua, but she's a trained grunt, which means looks are deceiving.

Thom's dark brows rise. "Then where is she now?"

"Halfway to Alaska if I were her. Or, you know, anywhere it's not a million degrees and raining."

"Shut up." Thom perches on the arm of my chair, a safe six inches away. Her brown eyes are fierce in the loft's mellow light, her face flushed dusky. She smells like sweat and the Hudson, even though she's changed out of her uniform and into jeans and a bright flannel shirt. "You're drunk. You're stupid when you're drunk."

I mumble agreement around a mouthful of rice. She's not wrong.

We sit without speaking and stare out the windows at the rain. Thom's a good roommate. She doesn't care that I'm still finding my way, an awkward phoenix out of the ashes, and I don't care that she's obsessed with a killer who snatches young men and women from the Upper West Side, mutilates their bodies, and dumps their broken corpses in the East River.

Okay, maybe I care a little.

Because the mayor believes the East River Ripper is the result of thaumaturgy gone wrong. It's not the first time it's happened, after all. Some people just can't handle being different. Me, I'm pretty sure normal is overrated.

Which doesn't mean I want the Ripper to keep killing. Or that I don't get stomach sick every time a new victim pops up on Thom's murder board. But I can't help thinking he didn't ask for magic any more than I did, and I can't help wondering what he was like before it found him.

Did the magic make him a killer, or did it only make him more of one? Nobody knows, least of all me. Sometimes wondering makes me feel hollow.

"You'll get him," I tell her, and I believe it. Catching the East River Ripper has been Thom's obsession for so long, I can't imagine our penthouse without the murder wall. I'm not the type of person who believes in setting goals, but not just for Thom's sake, I'm determined to see this one through. "Okay, probably not in time to save Christy Spears, maybe. But you'll get him."

Thom doesn't reply; she's too busy watching the rain fall.

I eat until my stomach stops growling, and then I head for bed. Thom doesn't appear to notice when I dump my dishes in the kitchen sink and exit our living room for my adjoining apartment. I had a door cut in the wall when I decided to combine the penthouse and the next-door maintenance room.

Despite the mass of electrical and plumbing works in one corner, my apartment's perfect—ten by ten with loft ceilings and southern exposure. There's a mattress on the floor, one of those roll-away portable hanging bars for clothes, a bin for shoes, and three more bins for tubes of paint and my brushes. Unused canvases are stacked in neat piles on the rough plank floor. A large easel near the one rectangular window waits upon my free time.

The paintings hung on the brick walls are finished: cityscapes, studies of birds or trees, people in the park, stormy gray water in the Hudson, and flowers and barbed-wire fences near Wall Street. When Thom goes rambling over the island on her one day off, I sometimes tag along, sketchbook and pencils in hand. She's looking for a murderer. I'm looking at the way afternoon light falls across a person's face as they stare out over a sea of yellow cabs and mirrored windows, or at the dimples on a sycamore trunk, its bark like silk where it doesn't fold over into darker lumps.

I've got a good eye. Almost ten years working in the tattoo business has refined my hand and my palette. Landscapes and portraits are different beasts than stencil design, but I'm not bragging when I say my canvases pass muster. I've sold several through Grace's family gallery, brokered eagerly by her starstruck father. I'm careful enough to use a pseudo, and nobody in the fine art world makes the connection. Grace's father won't spill my secret.

He's not allowed. He signed a nondisclosure. I have a good lawyer.

Unlike my ink, my paintings don't come to life, though I keep trying. They're static canvas and acrylic. I've composed a hundred different paintings a hundred different ways, tested a hundred different mediums from charcoal to watercolor to oil and back to my favorite heavy acrylics. I could paint one hundred different sailors' swallows and, unlike those I've inked across the biceps of certain famous drummer, not a single bird would take flight.

They're just ordinary paintings, and when, every so often, I get a money order with my name on it mailed from a posh address in Chelsea, I take pride in knowing I made that money on my own, through hard work.

Still, I can't help wanting more.

Chapter Three

Labor Day

I said not everyone in the world appreciates magic. Some people, they've got good reason to fear it.

The way I became famous is like this: I was in Seattle on Labor Day seven years ago when the bombs went off, and in the middle of the resulting chaos, a guy snapped a photo of me giving CPR to a toddler wearing a gauzy purple tutu and tiny white Converse high-tops. After he took the photo, he tweeted it out. And after that photo hit the internet, my life changed.

I wasn't supposed to be in Seattle that weekend, but at the last moment Don, my boss in Ketchum, decided to close Tank Tattoo for the holiday. Sad Pigeon was playing Key Arena, and Don had two tickets burning a hole in his pocket—one recently unattached because his girlfriend had dumped him for refusing to spend Labor Day floating the St. Joe River. I didn't blame him; even in late August, St Joe's is cold as ice, and in my humble opinion, his ex wasn't much warmer.

So I had a buddy with a car, some extra cash in my pocket from some simple touch-up work I'd done at the beginning of the week, and a ticket to Outcast. We drove most of the night, taking shifts behind the wheel even though I only had a farm permit and not an actual license. We stopped twice at a Denny's for pie and the bathroom, once in Coeur D'Alene and again in Cle Elum. We coasted down out of the Cascades and into the Emerald City before morning rush hour.

As we scoped a spot to ditch Don's ancient Honda Accord for the day, I watched the sun rise on the Space Needle. Sometimes I stop to think how I'm one of the last people who ever did see that.

Later I learned the seven IEDs were timed to go off all together at ten thirty when downtown would be swarming with tourists and locals, but the one buried in a trash can near Pike's Place Market went off early.

There wasn't a bang like you see in the movies or on television, just a blast of hot air and a rumble. The ground shook me off my feet and onto the damp pavement, newly hosed clean before the market opened. I remember that the concrete was cold and smelled like fish and lilies. After that everything was falling, pieces of glass and metal, fresh flowers and shellfish, people and bits of people. Part of a car tire, all shredded rubber split like two black-feathered wings, fell on my head from the sky. It hurt.

Someone screamed, and I knew it wasn't me because I was biting my lower lip so hard I could taste iron. It was an inhuman, despairing sort of howl, and it frightened me, so I crawled in the opposite direction, wanting to get away from the sound.

I ended up under an overturned table, surrounded by upended florist buckets spilling water and bunches of candy-colored tulips. A man lay on his side next to me. I knew he was dead because where his chest should have been there was a mash of black and red, and he sure as hell wasn't breathing anymore. The little girl wearing the tutu was crumpled behind him in a puddle of water. She was lying on her stomach, head turned toward the man. Her eyes were wide open and the exact shade of midday

Ketchum summer sky. The water and the pavement around her were turning pink.

My hands shook as I rolled her over. She wasn't breathing either, but I couldn't see any obvious reason she should be dead, so I did what we'd all learned in Mr. Miller's eighth-grade health class and started kiddie CPR. Her mouth tasted of those cinnamon-sugar donuts they used to sell from carts in the market.

I haven't been able to stomach cinnamon or donuts since.

That's when the guy used his cell to snap a photo. You can still find it online and also in an antique frame on President Shannon's desk. The president showed me that herself and said how she looks at it sometimes to remind herself that God works in mysterious, magical ways. I don't believe in God, and I hate to see myself in photos even now post-testosterone, but I've learned better than to scoff at mystery.

In the photo, I'm bent over the girl, hands on her tiny breastbone, my ear to her mouth. She's a fairy princess in purple tulle, her blonde hair plaited into a neat bun. Her white Converse were probably pristine when she put them on that morning, but in the photo the shoes are spattered with scarlet. It's not her blood; it's mostly mine. I'm bleeding from my nose where the tire hit me, and from the place in my thigh where a long shard of jagged metal sticks out like a gruesome alien appendage.

In the shock, I didn't feel the wound. I couldn't hear anything because of the blast, so when the guy with the phone finally put down his phone and scrambled across debris to help, I didn't get at first that he was trying to put pressure on my bleed. I would have punched him in the face for groping my leg if I hadn't been so busy saving the tiny ballerina's life.

And I did, too. The kid started breathing again just before I passed out from blood loss. These days she's a third grader in Bellevue, and at Christmas and on her birthday, her mom sends me a card. The guy with the mobile phone who took the photo and then saved *my* life is called Greg. He's a stockbroker who lost his wife, his dog, and his luxury apartment in the attack when five of the other six bombs went off ten minutes later as planned.

Don didn't make it. His name is on the plaque at the Seattle Memorial. I bring him flowers and a pack of cigarettes every year on the anniversary of his death when Washington State flies me across the country to read out the names of the dead from a podium in front of more cameras.

People come from all over the state to hear my voice and see my face, if they're lucky enough to be able to afford a ticket. But it's not just because I went viral.

It's mostly because of what happened after.

Greg's photo was everywhere for weeks: on the internet, on the television, in print. My dad clipped it out of the newspaper and threatened to hang it on the wall near the TV, but I convinced him that was in bad taste. Honest to God, I was just waiting for my fifteen minutes of fame to time out so I could get back to everyday life in Ketchum, or at least as close to everyday life as anyone was allowed anymore.

I was hardly the only Good Samaritan that Saturday. Five hundred and thirty-two people died in the bombings, but many more escaped with their lives because someone stopped to help. I figured Greg's photo would be forgotten when the next big meme came around, and I could get busy trying to forget that one of the one hundred and sixty people dead in Pike Place Market was my boss with the frigid girlfriend and an extra Outcast ticket in his pocket.

But it didn't happen that way at all. A few weeks after airspace was cleared again for domestic travel, President Shannon rode Air Force One down to Ketchum and walked right into St. Luke's, where I was recovering from surgery on my leg, and shook my hand. Then she asked me if I wouldn't like to design a tattoo for remembrance and ink it myself on her left wrist where she could always see it. I was loopy on painkillers, so of course I said yes.

Come New Year's I was set up in the Oval with one of Don's machines and more cameras all around, sick with nerves and thinking I'd rather be anywhere else in the world. The tattoo I'd designed was simple, meant to go quickly: a minimalist tulip blossom and stem outlined in black. I'm an artist—even at fourteen I had talent to spare—but when I finished up and scrubbed away President Shannon's blood with wet gauze, it wasn't my artistic chops that made everyone gasp.

It was the candy-hued flower rising in vibrant color above the outline I'd inked into the president's wrist, a living snapshot hovering just above her dark flesh, attached and yet somehow separate. Startled, President Shannon jerked away from my hand. The flower, drifting in full color above her wrist, went with her.

There in the Oval Office I smelled fish and lilies, and I tasted cinnamon sugar on my tongue. Everyone who was watching, from the members of the press corps, to the congressmen and senators and interns who'd popped in for the occasion, to the VP in his buttoned-up suit, to President Shannon herself, understood something else had changed in a world now constantly shifting.

It took me longer to catch up.

Chapter Four

Coruscation

I wake late to the sounds of Saturday in the city: sirens in the distance, foot traffic from the street below, restless pigeons squawking on the ledge outside my window, a dog barking. I roll off my mattress, stretch until my spine cracks, and then wander, yawning, between stacks of canvases to the window. I take stock of the world beyond.

The wind blew the rain away overnight. The sky above Hell's Kitchen is a cheerful blue, cloudless. Forty-Sixth Street is steaming, moisture coming off the asphalt as the afternoon warms up. The old maple tree outside the apartment is still green, untouched by the colors of autumn. It might be October, but fall has not yet arrived.

I keep an electric kettle plugged into the wall by my mattress. While it brews—tea, green, in my favorite travel mug: "Made in Ketchum"—I take my time dressing for the day. It's a ritual: boxer briefs and compression tank first before a checked button-up and black denim. It's a becoming, as I rub a dollop of gel through my short curls, styling by feel alone. The gel smells of vetiver and was a Christmas gift from Thom. The little silver tube looks expensive, and although I don't recognize the brand, I suspect she spent more for my vanity than any soldier surviving on government salary should.

I snag my steaming travel mug and take it with me into the loft. Thom and I share a bathroom. It's not a problem. I only use the space to brush my teeth and shower and for the toilet. Thom sometimes uses it as a retreat when she needs privacy or time away from her murder wall. The bathroom door has a lock. Thom sleeps on a futon in the main room and lives out of a closet near the kitchen. I can walk in on her anytime. I think it must be like living in a fishbowl. She never complains, but on bad days, she logs an hour or two behind the locked bathroom door.

After Grace moved out, I was lonely. I'd never lived solo before. Without another person around to fill the penthouse with noise and energy, I did the opposite of flourish: I wilted. I drank too much, slept too much or not at all, forgot to eat, and began to miss appointments.

Three weeks with only my own thoughts for company and I was teetering on the edge of despair, a shadow of my former self. When my hands began to shake and I couldn't tattoo a solid line if I tried, Eric stepped in.

"I've put an ad for your new roommate in the Sunday paper," he'd told me, yanking apart the curtains in my bedroom, letting light fall where I lay, listless, on my mattress. "First respectable inquiry you get we're accepting." When I'd groaned, he only pulled the blankets from my grip. "Some people aren't meant to live alone, Hemingway. At the moment, you're one of them. Maybe that will change. But for now, you need companionship."

A babysitter, I thought he meant, and that made me angry enough to cry, but I didn't, because if Eric caught me blubbering, I knew I'd never hear the end of it.

Thom had been my first respectable inquiry—a young grunt with a steady paycheck and a need for personal space. My sizable digs suited her perfectly; her admittedly eccentric temperament somehow eased my jagged edges. I know she had a hole in her heart where her twin used to live. I couldn't fill that chasm any more than Thom could eliminate my compulsion to duck and cover every time a cab backfired, but we did okay together, and two years into the arrangement, we're both less lonely.

At the moment, Thom's a lump on the futon under a pile of mismatched quilts, blissfully unaware of the daylight creeping into the loft and puddling on our floor. The police scanner on the kitchen counter is silent, shut off. The perfume of freshly brewed tea permeates the space, oozing from my room. It's a peaceful scene—if I keep my back turned to the chalk map and the photos of the missing tacked to the north wall.

After I brush my teeth and take a piss, I find my boots by the door where I left them and try to stamp them on without spilling tea or waking Thom. I grab my keys and wallet and a pair of round-lensed sunglasses off the kitchen counter. Then I tiptoe out into the hallway, locking the door behind me. Thom's not the vulnerable sort, but an unlocked door in the city, even in a secured building like mine, is just asking for trouble.

I endure the old elevator, ignoring my reflection, and let myself out into the afternoon by way of the studio. I linger on the stoop, sipping hot tea. A few tourists glance my way; a few more take unsubtle snaps with their mobiles. Nobody asks for a selfie, probably because I'm showing my teeth in a snarl. I'm never pleasant until I've finished my first cup of tea, even when I'm not suffering from a Pink Jones–induced hangover and the aftereffects of greasy Szechuan shrimp.

I chug down half my mug, scalding my tongue. Stifling a belch, I snap on my shades—protection against bright sunlight and curious glances—and start the short hike up toward Columbus Circle. The subway runs sporadically on the weekends when it runs at all, but Columbus Circle's usually a safe bet. The only lines left, though, are the A and the C, which were in the middle of a security update before Seattle blew up and Dallas fell— the Transit Authority managed to finish most of the refurb before they ran out of cable. The A is still the most reliable ride on the island, if you're willing to wait. There aren't as many people in the city as there used to be, but with only one decent subway line running up and down Manhattan, overcrowding is an unavoidable problem and security delays are always a pain in the ass.

Luckily, I'm in no real hurry. I may have rolled out of bed late, but my Saturday has just begun. I blow on my tea as I walk. Today's already as muggy as yesterday. The rain has left patches of stubborn grass in neighborhood gardens green and vibrant, but the wind tore late-summer blossoms from window boxes and planters, scattering colorful petals on the sidewalk. The bright flowers are crushed under the feet of pedestrians, leaving stains on concrete.

An old man in tights and a long, loose tunic is playing piano at the corner of Fifty-Seventh and Broadway. The upright piano is strapped to a low, wheeled platform and decorated all over with vintage bumper stickers. The pianist and his traveling instrument are a familiar sight during spring and summer, before the weather turns cold. He wears his busker's license pinned to the top of the wide-brimmed hat he uses to shade his eyes. His long fingers move deftly up and down the keyboard, his feet working the pedals, conjuring classical show tunes. He's very good, but he would have to be to afford the license on his hat.

He winks at me as I cut around the piano and wait for the walk sign. In response, I drop a few dollars into the busker's jar atop the piano. The crush of people standing with me clap and whistle enthusiastically as he segues neatly from "Memory" to "If I Were a Rich Man." That's a dig my way, but I ignore it. The pianist knows very well who I am, even if no one else has recognized my face behind my shades and travel mug. He knows I can afford to toss more than two fivers into his tip jar. He also knows *I* know he'll spend what money he earns busking on black-market Percocet. I prefer not to encourage other people's bad habits.

The piano man is called Jim. He's an uptown staple. Before he strapped his piano to rollers, he used to play for the New York Philharmonic. Now he gets his applause from people waiting on street corners for the walk sign to change. He likes to remind me, passive aggressively, that fame is fleeting and I'm still very young. I like to remind him with a sneer that my business is none of his.

The light switches to walk, and the crowd surges across Broadway, a living river split by idling yellow cabs into smaller tributaries. "If I Were a Rich Man" is swallowed by the noise of jackhammers and generators. Even on a Saturday, construction continues, new framework on old footprints. They're building higher in Hell's Kitchen than they were ever allowed to before.

They'll never fill all those brand-new, city-view apartments. Not unless the borders open, and no one, least of all the city planners, expects that to happen any time soon. Truth is, everyone knows the construction is busywork, the people in hardhats no different than hordes of street sweepers employed to brush relentlessly spotless streets, the armies of maintenance officers raking the same Central Park beds over and over again, or the leagues of safety inspectors attached in duplicate to the same square city block.

Somewhere along the line, a suit in City Hall must have decided a busy city is a healthy city—and that boredom leads to apprehension. Generally, I don't disagree. I know I'd much rather live in the moment than think too hard about the future. Besides, if you ignore the razor-wire fences around Manhattan and the stern-faced soldiers patrolling the streets, New York City has never looked more beautiful.

At Columbus Circle, I take the steps down into the subway, use my curfew card on the turnstile, then wait in line for the security pass through. The queue inches forward at a snail's pace, but nobody complains. Most people are flipping through the Saturday paper in search of distraction. I finish my tea in slow sips. By the time I pause inside one of the station's three full body-scanning machines—arms raised above my head, shades removed so the computer and the grunt monitoring the feed can make note of my face—I'm beginning to feel more awake.

The clutch of people on the other side of security disperses suddenly, feeding into a newly arrived train. They fill all three cars to bursting, packed together like sardines in a tin, before the doors whisper shut and the train rushes on. Timing's on my side today, and when the grunts wave our next group through, I end up at the front near the edge of the platform, inches from the yellow caution line painted on the floor. More grunts stand on the wrong side of the line, eyes sharp behind closed visors, alert. Fish-eyed lenses on the ceiling will catch whatever mischief the soldiers might miss.

We wait quietly, occupied with our own thoughts. A woman sings soft accompaniment to the music playing through the buds in her ears. A group of women talk in low voices over shared pages of newspaper. But mostly we all avoid any semblance of connection—New Yorkers to the core.

When the next train arrives, I find a spot in the first car and lean up against the wall, still anonymous behind my shades. The seats fill up and then the spaces between, far exceeding any safety limit. It's worse than an elevator, bodies taking up air and giving off heat. Someone steps on my foot. I pretend not to notice. The woman with the music in her ears nudges up against my front. I growl a muted warning until she edges away. It's probably an accidental bump, but even with grunts and cameras watching, subway pickpocketing is on the rise. It's not our money they want; stolen curfew cards go for thousands of dollars underground.

When we're all aboard, the doors slide closed and the train lurches forward, quickly picking up speed. I distract myself from the squeeze of humanity by counting the broken pixels in the reader board up and across from my head. Most of the LEDs in the sign are long dead, irreplaceable, but a few still flicker in bursts of seemingly random white light.

Outside the car windows, the subway tunnel is dark, but the time in between stations is short enough that my eyes don't adjust to false night. Nobody says a word as the train barrels on, even people who are obviously traveling together in couples or small groups. Nobody smiles. It's probable the camera on the car ceiling is as useless as the broken reader board, but there's no way to know for sure.

I get off at Fulton, then wait in line again to scan my card before riding the escalator up out of the bowels of the earth. Sunlight filters through the huge steel-and-prism glass dome two stories deep into the station below. The afternoon sky overhead turns the dome into a faceted sapphire; flocks of tourists snap pictures of the glass ceiling from moving escalators, threatening to clog traffic until they're waved along by station security.

Fulton's less crowded in the evening a few hours before curfew, so much so that I've sometimes spent time squatting on the station's checkered marble, trying to capture the fractured light through the dome with my pencils and sketchpad. Grace calls Fulton Station the Crystal Palace and says what I'm trying to catch on paper is something called the gloaming.

Once outside the station, I breathe easier even in the sticky air. Settling my shades again on the bridge of my nose, I cut away toward Wall Street. Lower Manhattan buzzes with cheerful activity all around. The streets are uneven beneath my boots, ancient brick warming in the sun where asphalt has cracked away in chunks and not yet been replaced with cement. There are fewer cabs this far south—the streets are narrow, closer together, and it's cheaper to walk. I can smell the East River over last night's rain. I think of Thom and her murder wall and immediately wish I hadn't.

As far as I'm concerned, it's too fine a day for homicide.

I've got a shrink. Mine's government funded, one of the dubious perks of being me. Her name is Emma, and she could be my grandmother if my grandmother lived in a

Brooklyn walk-up and drove a retrofitted electric Harley. Officially, she's supposed to be monitoring my state of mind for any post-bomb-blast PTSD. She also takes notes on my magical manifestations, which she emails once a week to Langley. I'm not supposed to know about Langley, but Emma said she prefers to be open with her patients and that keeping unnecessary secrets is bad manners.

"Besides," she'd told me somberly during our first session, "I'm sure they have more reliable ways to keep tabs on you, Hemingway, than an ex-hippy, semiretired, antiestablishment Berkeley PhD like me. I expect they put you and I together for a reason, and it has more to do with efficiency than my patient notes."

I suspect they put us together because for all her grandmotherly affection Emma's way too badass to be afraid of a little thaumaturgy. She may be a snitch, but she's also a damn good shrink, and she's done me plenty good and no harm.

These days Emma and I mostly talk about my issues with food, Thom's obsession with the Ripper, and, after bad nights, a reoccurring dream I have that I'm drowning in the Elliot Bay.

I never miss an appointment, even if it means suffering the crowded A on the one day I allow myself off each week. Not because I'm worried about PTSD or magical manifestations or even drowning in Elliot Bay, but because if I do, I've no doubt Surveillance will come knocking at my door for missing my nonnegotiable, government-ordered head shrink.

In a small, expensive café just off Wall Street, I roll hot tea over my tongue and squint thoughtfully past the top of my travel mug at the forest of potted orchids surrounding our small table. Emma concentrates on buttering a croissant. The café's part bakery, part tropical florist, and all luxe. They use real sugar in their breads and tiny frosted cakes, which means their pastries are too costly for most people in the city, which in turn means Emma and I generally have the place to ourselves. As far as I can tell the place does most of its business by way of discreet deliveries to the inconspicuously wealthy living in their glass-walled apartments near Battery Park.

Emma smiles at me before turning the old smartphone she keeps on hand in case of client emergencies facedown on the table, a signal that I have her full attention. The phone should be obsolete, the parts inside worn out; I have no idea how she manages to keep it running.

"How's the painting coming?" she asks.

Emma's not just making small talk. She's seen my paintings. She even owns one. She made a point of going up to Chelsea the last time I had a showing and came away with a view of the Hudson done in yellow and red and black. She says she's hung it prominently in her dining room because she likes the colors and the way I made the dirty water into something beautiful. It sounds like an honest compliment, but part of me suspects she's just keeping an eye on it in case the river comes to life and starts spilling out of the simple reclaimed wood frame.

"Good." I shrug. "Followed Thom across Two Bridges a few nights ago. Thought she'd caught a lead but no luck. I sketched traffic while she scoped the fence line. Headlamps on the wet pavement. I'm thinking of doing a series on coruscation."

Emma hides a grimace behind a pinch of croissant. I think she tries not to judge Thom too harshly for my sake. She's said bluntly that she finds my roommate's obsession with the East River Ripper unhealthy. I haven't explained that Thom's obsession is a personal vendetta. I'm pretty certain explanations would do more harm than good, and although Emma says she's my friend, she *is* my shrink, and I can't risk adding a wrinkle to our professional relationship.

Besides, it's really none of her business.

"Coruscation," I prompt. "You know, a sudden gleam or flash of light."

Emma nods. "Also, a striking display of brilliance or wit," she tells me. Her long gray hair hangs, braided, down her back. She's wearing a silk scarf the color of caramel around her throat, and there are heat-induced apples in her cheeks. She doesn't look seventy. Time or genetics has been kind to Emma; except for her hair and a few delicate laugh lines, she looks hardly a day over forty.

"I'd love to see them," she says, daubing up the last crumbs of her pastry. I've dutifully eaten the fruit cup she ordered for me before I arrived, but I'm sternly ignoring the cream cheese danish.

"Not yet," I hedge. "They're not ready. I'll send you an invite to my next show."

"Okay." Emma leans back in her chair. The orchids on their glass shelves almost brush the top of her head. The white blossoms and shiny green leaves are stark against the café's concrete walls. Their roots are disturbingly like fat snakes tumbling over the edges of individual square stone pots. "Anything particular you want to talk about today, Hemingway?"

It's my cue that our session has begun and I need to stop messing about and start giving my answers more thought. Emma doesn't let me get away with half-assed effort. She's paid well to do good work.

"I've been exchanging emails with that surgeon in Scottsdale." I pick up my fork, set it down, snatch it up again, and run the ball of my thumb over the tines.

"Oh, yes?" Emma prompts gently.

"I like her. She's good. Could be the one. Maybe next winter, if I can get an exit visa." Arizona's one of the six territories still abiding by the old Constitution—the other five being California, Texas, the District of Columbia, New York, and most of Maine—so travel to Scottsdale shouldn't be difficult, only very, very expensive.

The doctor in Arizona is the sixth gender-affirmation surgeon I've talked to. They all seemed good, all five of them before. Three of them are in Manhattan, within walking distance of home. But I found something wrong with each. I think it's hard to settle on one because I'm fastidious; Emma says it's because I'm afraid of commitment.

"Scottsdale's lovely in the winter," Emma says. Then she waits.

"I like her, I do." I can hear how defensive I sound, and I hate it. I try on my best pleasant smile, the one I save for nervous clients. "I think she's the one. I think I should put my name on her waiting list."

"You think you should." Emma meets my eye. "Do you want to?"

"If I say yes, will you write me a referral?"

She tilts her head. "If and when you're ready, Hemingway, I'd love to." She casts a pointed glance at my uneaten danish, maybe implying I'm not as ready as I should be.

I scowl. "It doesn't need to be you," I remind her. "There are plenty of other shrinks in the city who would write me a referral, just because it was me who asked."

"Maybe not so many as you think. But you're right. It doesn't have to be me. So why is it?"

She hasn't asked me that before. It's like pulling my own teeth out one by one to make the words come.

"Because you don't care how I choose to live my transition." I drop my voice a little even though we're the only ones in the café other than the barista behind the industrial counter and about one hundred blooming orchids. "You're only here to keep tabs on my magic. The rest of it—it's no skin off your back if I get top surgery or if I don't." There's a lump in my throat, and I cough to clear it. "Yet."

"Or ever," Emma agrees. "But, you're right. My only concern is your magic."

She buys me a potted orchid on the way out, something she's never done before. I bury my face in the white blossoms, touched by her kindness. She squeezes my shoulder before she pulls on her motorcycle helmet, obscuring her face. I stand on the sidewalk, balancing Emma's gift and my tea, people passing behind and around me, and watch as she guns her bike over old brick and broken asphalt, barely avoiding an oncoming delivery truck. The driver shoots her the bird, and Emma returns it with enthusiasm before streaking around the corner.

I'm so surprised by the wave of affection that hits me as I watch Emma disappear that at first I don't notice the jab of something solid and sharp in the small of my back. By the time sentiment dissipates and my head catches up, it's too late: he's got his hand on my upper arm as well as his knife against my spine.

I bobble my travel mug, and it falls to the sidewalk, spilling tea. Nobody pays it any attention, not even the on-duty grunt standing idly on the other side of the street.

"Pretty flower. No, leave the cup. Walk ahead, now, magic man, nice and steady. Don't do anything stupid or I'll cut you, eh?" He pinches my arm painfully. His friendly Canadian accent has gone cold and flinty.

Pickpocketing in the subway is expected. Pickpocketing in broad daylight in the open city is definitely not. One panicked word from me and the grunt across the street will be on us both. I can't help myself; I twitch.

"I said: nothing stupid." His knife has punctured my flannel and is working on my skin; I feel the trickle of warm blood under my shirt, but shock keeps the pain distant. "Unless you want to spend the rest of your life in a wheelchair. Walk."

I walk. We could be a couple going for a stroll he's so close, curving protectively over me, all hard angles and angry, biting blade. I clutch Emma's orchid in both hands; the stone pot is heavy and reassuring. The white blossoms tickle my chin and mouth and give off a sweet, spicy scent.

"If it's my curfew card you're after, just take it."

"If I was after your card, it would already be gone and you with no clue. Shut up."

He herds me west and then south, toward the Charging Bull. We pass soldiers on every corner, but I can't bring myself to shout. The knife is a promise against my spine. The streets and sidewalks are thick with wealthy tourists too engrossed in their own experience to notice mine. His breath is warm against the top of my head. Just before we reach Bowling Green and the high, chain-link fence that protects Arturo Di Modica's bronze statue from vandals, he shoves me abruptly off the sidewalk and into a narrow alleyway between two prewar buildings.

It's more of a crevasse than an alleyway, with just enough room between stone facades for an obsolete air-conditioning unit and a humming electrical box. The street punk crowds me out of sight and up against the electrical box, yanks me around, and in doing so manages to move his knife from my back to my front, settling the tip beneath my navel. We're chest to chest, but he's got at least ten inches on me and I'm looking at his collarbone. He's very pale where the baggy white T-shirt he's wearing has exposed his skin. Since last I saw him, he's swapped green glitter paint to silver. His violet hair stands up in angry spikes.

If he doesn't want my card, I can only assume I'm in big trouble. Could be he hates magic. Could be he's transphobic. Could be he's just mad I won't give him a tattoo.

I decide I'll bash his nose in with Emma's potted orchid before I let him hurt me further.

"Listen," he begins gruffly, forehead wrinkling. The pressure of the knife blade against my front falters slightly with his concentration. It's like he's stumbling for what to do next, which makes no sense to me at all. It's also like he's not quite so proficient at assault as he's pretending.

I take advantage of that brief hesitation to wrench sideways across the front of the electrical box and away, out of his grasp. The knife slices my flesh, but I'm free. He swears and lunges after. He's all arms and legs, and there's no way I'll make it past him to the relative safety of the street. He grabs at my elbow. I smash him over the head with my orchid.

The pot shatters. Soil explodes over my front. But he goes down, onto his knees, blood on his face.

"Asshole!" I snarl. Dropping the remains of the ruined plant, I dodge around him and run for the street.

Not fast enough.

He lassos my ankle with one hand. I hit the ground front-first, scraping my chin. It's a solid fall, and it slams the breath right out of me.

"Nice try." Suddenly he's on my back, knees on my shoulder blades, fingers in my hair. The knife's disappeared, but he doesn't need it. I'm small, he's heavy, and I'm still seeing stars, struggling for air. "Jesus fuck!" He spits onto the gravel. "If you cracked a tooth, you're paying for the dental. You'd better be worth it, Hemingway."

My tongue tastes of dirt and iron. "Get off me!" It's more of a wheeze than a threat. I buck my hips, but he's a boulder on my spine. He pulls my hair, hard. My eyes sting with unshed tears.

"Listen." He leans forward and growls into my ear. "You're wasting valuable time. The electrical box only provides cover until the nearest grunt gets bored and decides to do his job and check the blind spots."

My lungs are finally working, but my brain is slow to come back online. Involuntarily, I roll my eyes in the direction of the humming box.

He yanks my hair again. I think he likes the feel of my curls in his fingers. I think I'd like to punch him in the nose.

"RF interference," he explains into my ear. "No cameras here. Blind spot. We're invisible. I could break your neck right now and walk away, and no one would pin me."

I know a thing or two about blind spots myself because at one time Thom thought the Ripper might be using them to slip through the city unnoticed, and spent an entire afternoon explaining to me exactly how close-contact radio frequency interference works to jam some CCTV cameras—but I see no point in telling my assailant I've been schooled.

It's occurring to me that he keeps threatening, but I'm still alive and relatively unharmed. And he's not wrong; blind spot or not, the alley is on some grunt's patrol. Whatever he wants with me, he's being stupidly slow about it.

"What the hell do you want?" I bluff courage, bucking harder against his weight.

He leans in close. His breath smells like apples. "I've got a message for you, magic man. From a friend in need of your particular...talent."

Hysterical laughter bubbles up before I can rein it back. "Tell your friend to make an appointment like everyone else. Better yet, tell your friend to bite me. I'm not interested."

He shifts on my spine, dropping something in the dirt by my shoulder. I get an impression of paper, folded several times.

"Open it somewhere private and out of doors," he tells me. "You've got three days. After that, the offer's no good. Don't be late. Seraphine hates late."

He springs up off my back, the weight on my hips released. Gravel crunches as he retreats to the end of the alleyway. I lie still until I'm sure he's gone.

Chapter Five

Floater

When I think it's safe again, I wobble to my feet. My chin and knees hurt from rough contact with the ground. My head is fuzzy, and my hands are quivering. I inch my way out of the crevasse onto the street, pausing only to pick up the piece of paper and shove it, unexamined, into the front pocket of my jeans with some vague idea of showing it to Thom as evidence of assault. I pat absently at my shirt and discover I've lost my shades in the scuffle.

I think I might puke—the evening sunlight seems too bright on stone and glass—so I lean against a street post and stare stupidly at tourists passing in front of the Charging Bull. Fearless Girl stands several feet in front of the bull's lowered head. She's small, bronze, daring—and also surrounded by chain-link fence.

"Hey." It's a grunt who's come at last, fifteen minutes too late. "Sir. You're bleeding. Do you need help?"

I can't glimpse the soldier's expression past his visor, but he sounds annoyed rather than concerned. The badge on his uniform says he's a veteran on the streets. He's probably seen his share of unsettling things. I don't suppose I'm more than an irritating blip on Saturday's radar.

"I'm fine!" I swipe at my bleeding chin. My hands are still unsteady, but now the shake is more anger than fear.

It's a delayed reaction and not one I expected. At least I no longer feel like I'll heave up half-digested tea all over the clean sidewalk.

"Here." The grunt passes me a small first-aid packet: gauze, emergency sealant lotion, latex gloves. "Seal up or I'll have to fine you for bodily fluids." He doesn't ask me what happened, and I'm glad. They're trained to read faces, catch deception.

Thom's told me I have an easy face to read. I'm not sure I can bluff my way out of the afternoon's strangeness, and the last thing I want to do is end up downtown at Central giving a statement. At least not until I'm ready.

I use the first-aid packet to clean up and seal up. The lotion numbs the pain even as it leaves a protective, stiff gel layer over my scrapes. The grunt observes without speaking almost until I'm finished, but then, late again, he cottons on.

"Hey, it's you," he says. "No way! My wife's a big fan. She's been saving up pocket money, you know, these last few years for a half-sleeve or maybe one of those creeping roses like you did on Samantha Miller's ankle before the last Inaugural Ball—"

"Thanks," I interject and hastily leave him talking to himself about Samantha Miller and DC fashion. Samantha's a sweet lady, but she has a very low pain threshold and was frankly a bitch to tattoo—and I mean that in the nicest possible way.

Thom's going out as I'm coming home. We almost run each other over in the hallway outside the elevator, both of us lost in our thoughts. Mine are sour. From the scowl on her face, Thom's aren't much sweeter.

"Hemingway." She narrows her eyes. "What happened to your chin?"

I open my mouth, but the string of expletives and explanation dies before it's born. I'm not exactly sure why. Maybe it's the piece of folded paper in my pocket, still unexamined. Maybe it's the stinging shallow cuts on my back and on my belly, and delayed shock setting in. I'd marched home in a rage with the sole intention of telling Thom everything I could remember about the punk and his ugly little knife and the Bowling Green blind spot. I expected Thom, my pragmatic roommate who daily faces much worse than what amounted to nothing more than a strange back-alley mugging, to put me right with a few acerbic but well-meaning insults and then help me file a report. I'd marched home expecting Thom to make everything right again.

But now I'm reticent. I fiddle with the paper in my pocket and stutter abbreviated nonsense about running into a wall. Thom's regard sharpens further.

"A wall," she drawls doubtfully, brow furrowing. She's wearing her uniform, which means she wants to appear official; but she's also wearing her beanie instead of her helmet and visor, which means she's not on duty.

Which together means she's caught a lead.

"Oh shit," I say. "They've found her?"

Thom nods, chin up chin down, an economy of movement. "Just got the call. Floater came up against Four Freedoms, has all the signs. No official ID logged yet. I'm on my way now before Port closes the scene."

I make sympathetic noises.

"Grace stopped by looking for you," Thom adds, wrinkling her nose. "Shrieking about the City Center." Thom adjusts the beanie on her head, pulling it lower over her forehead as if to protect her skull from memories of Grace's enthusiasm. "She landed that part she was after at the City Center. What was it—Sarah?"

"Mary." *The Secret Garden* is a City Center classic this time of year, and Grace has been after the starring role ever since I first met her. She's really too old for the part, but the draft has severely reduced the number of young people in the theater, and the City Center's not as discriminating as it once was. "She must be over the moon."

Thom dips her chin again. "She's looking for a celebration. Signals, tonight, midnight showing. She told me to tell you: you're buying." Although Thom's expression hasn't changed, I can tell she's silently laughing at me—something about the way her eyes widen just the tiniest bit and the corners of her mouth crease. "As usual."

"Shut up." But I grin before sighing. "No sleep tonight if it's Signals. And you're coming with." Heavy socializing isn't Thom's thing, especially when Grace is involved.

Thom holds up both hands in protest. "I've got a corpse—"

"Yeah, yeah." I wave her toward the elevator. "Midnight's hours away still. I'll come with you now— make sure you don't get lost in that head of yours." And maybe, if I catch a minute when she's not distracted by murder, I'll show her the note in my pocket and explain the road rash on my face.

She looks at me doubtfully. I don't blame her. We both know the Ripper isn't my cup of tea. On those occasions that I keep Thom company at a crime scene, it's with colored pencils in hand.

Maybe it's because the Ripper and I have something in common. Central's put their best detectives on the case, and they all agree; whoever or whatever is snatching young men and women from the streets and later dumping their horrifically disfigured bodies into the river, all without so much as a shred of usable evidence, is too strong, too quick, too *unique* to be typical.

Thom's already on the elevator, holding the doors. "Hemingway! Are you coming or not? Port won't wait around all night. Even Ramos and Gerzy can't put off the coroner forever."

On the elevator, I poke gingerly at the sealed scrape on my chin. Watching me, Thom scowls.

"That's some gash. It's going to need cleaning. Was the wall you 'ran into' by any chance covered in gravel? Because it looks like you've got bits still stuck in your skin."

"I gave as good as I got," I reply blandly, thinking of shards of orchid pot peppering the street kid's garish hair.

The floater's a bad one, but from what I understand, they always are.

It's obvious even to me that what's left of Christy Spears has been in the water for a couple of days. Port's scooped her out of the East River onto the rocky shore just outside Four Freedoms Park. The park's closed to tourists and locals now, as is most of Roosevelt Island. Port uses the finger of land as a base for search and rescue, the East River's answer to the Hudson's Pier 55.

Two grunts in black-and-gray Port uniforms escort Thom and me through a gate in the island's razor-wire-and-concrete safety barrier, down a flight of shallow cement steps, and onto the beach. The sun's almost set on Saturday; we're all carrying standard-issue Maglites for visibility. Fingerling waves lap up against the shore, stirring clumps of seaweed. I hear the growl of barges patrolling the river for evacs boating over from Connecticut and New Jersey and sometimes as far as Delaware. The barges have gone dark for night work. I can barely make out their flat, shadowy forms. They use sonar to keep from ramming into each other and to scan the river bottom for suspicious activity.

Civilians aren't meant to wander about on Roosevelt Island, much less wander about Roosevelt Island with the intent to examine a corpse. But Thom, despite her gruffness, is well liked by her fellow Port grunts. They respect her, although I haven't managed to work out why. She barely says a kind word to any of them, and she certainly doesn't waste her time on small talk.

They like and respect Thom enough to flag her first when a specific type of floater turns up in the East River, and to look away when I tag along.

"Ramos, *que tiene para nosotros*?" Thom demands, squatting on the rocks for a closer look. She sweeps her Maglite over the corpse. I wince when her light touches wizened features.

The naked body is twisted out of shape, curled in upon itself, shrunken. In her picture Christy Spears radiated energy—a young women in the prime of her life. Not anymore. The Ripper's sapped the life from her body until it's more a mummy than a corpse. Her skin's gone the color of dirty concrete, and shrunk tight and thin against her bones. Her hair's turned completely white— what's left of it. Except for a few stubborn remaining hanks, her head's bald. Her delicate features are shriveled to a ghoulish smile.

Thom likes to say the Ripper's like a spider, desiccating ill-fated flies before he cuts their throat ear to ear and dumps them in the water. Thaumaturgy gone bad, no shit.

I swallow and look away. I've no trouble with the snaps of dead bodies on Thom's murder wall, but the real deal is different.

"Spears, Christy," Ramos reports while her partner glares at me from beneath his raised visor. "Just like we thought. DOB: November 29, 2011. Current place of residence: Morningside Heights. But her card hasn't logged there since last Thursday morning when she left for work. She's Port—made fleet captain just last year."

I look over at Thom, but she's bent over the dead girl's withered hands so I can't tell what she's thinking. She knew all this already. Ten out of the Ripper's last fifteen victims were military, which only makes sense; somewhere near 75 percent of the city's able-bodied kids between the ages of thirteen and twenty-one are conscripts. The military and the Ripper have something in common: they're both chasing youth.

"Guessing she's been underwater these last three days," Gerzy tells Thom. "Maybe caught against a pylon or tangled in some trash. Rain yesterday must have brought her up." We all look down at Christy's pitiful, fish-nibbled remains—three baby grunts not old enough to make detective and a trick-of-fate millionaire pondering her final shame. I'd hate us, if I were her. "Coroner will confirm, but I say three days in the water. Throat cut and neck broken—I believe she fits the pattern."

"Obviously," I grumble. Gerzy sounds like he was born with a stick up his ass. "What clued you in, the mummy bit or the choice of location?"

Gerzy growls. He shines his Maglite into my eyes, making them dazzle. Gerzy hates me. Gerzy thinks I'm screwing Thom, and he'd rather be doing that himself. I haven't set him straight because I like to see him squirm. Thom hasn't set him straight because Gerzy's temper is barely a blip on her radar. Also, I've never known her to spare a thought on whom I take home to bed.

"Show some respect," Thom retorts, reminding me that once not so long ago it was her twin lying mutilated and degraded on a similar riverbank. Gerzy's light keeps me from seeing what she's doing, but I can hear the click of her mobile going as she snaps photos, recording what's left of Christy Spears. "Central's on their way; they'll tag next of kin. Ramos, got a bag? Nails are broken—she struggled. I want scrapings."

"He'll have scrubbed her clean before he dumped her. Just like all the others."

"Yes," Thom agrees. "Do it anyway."

"Coroner's here," Gerzy warns, switching off his light. "He'll confirm. She was dead before she hit the water, and we've got vic number sixteen."

"The clock resets," Ramos agrees, resigned.

Three victims a year for the last five years. Snatched, held exactly a week, dumped. Which gives Thom and every other grunt on the island fifteen weeks to find the Ripper and get him off the streets before he chooses another victim. Ramos is right—it's like clockwork; he never changes his MO.

The coroner's van is a gas guzzler with a diesel engine beneath its hood, the kind no one except military and government officials can afford to drive these days. It pulls to a stop on the other side of the fence, idling loudly, high beams turning our circle of rocky shore bright as day.

Suddenly I can see Christy Spears a whole lot better than I'd like.

"Mother Mary," says Ramos from where she's knelt by the body, sealing evidence into a plastic bag. "Grab the tarp, Gerz. Poor thing doesn't need everyone on the river seeing her bits."

Spears is lying on her side, the orange straps of the sling Gerzy and Ramos used to drag her body ashore still looped beneath her torso. With the help of the van's headlights, I can see the discolored skin around her fingers and toes is waterlogged, beginning to slough away.

She's curled almost nose to ankles, spine compressed, arms drawn up and tight beneath her chin. Fetal position, but cranked too far, as if when the Ripper sucked the vitality from her body he also shrunk her muscles and tendons one size too small.

"Ugh," I volunteer helpfully.

Gerzy smirks. He's barely eighteen and looks it, fresh-faced and self-important in his uniform. He puts a notch in his leather belt every time he pulls an evac from the river, and he's got quite a record going. Gerzy thinks the world owes him accolades for his service. I think he's a ruthless dick.

"Take a walk, Hemingway," Thom suggests, handing me her Maglite. She produces a pair of sterile gloves from one of the many pockets in her uniform. "Give me a few." She bends thoughtfully over the corpse's gaping mouth as she gloves up, grimacing absently at the smell.

I don't need to be told twice. I leave the circle of light, passing the coroner as I escape. He gives me a friendly salute.

"Hello, Hemingway." The coroner's called Doc Torres, and like Ramos and Gerzy, he tolerates my presence for Thom's sake. "What happened to your face?"

"Bark," I reply cheerfully. "Walked right into a goddamn Bowling Green tree this morning." I'd forgotten all about the attack in the excitement of Christy Spears's literal resurfacing, but the lie brings my aches and pains rushing back.

"Goddamn city trees." Doc wags his bearded chin. "More trouble than they're worth. Their roots are growing down into the sewer, you know, busting all the old clay pipe, useless. My decision, I'd cut 'em all down before it's too late and all of Lower Manhattan backs up into one giant shithole."

Before I can formulate a reply, he's left me for Christy Spears and is making eager noises as he joins Thom by the body. I respect a man who loves his job, but Doc Torres's enthusiasm for the grotesque strikes me as a little too close to zeal. I walk faster so I don't have to hear him exclaim over lividity.

The uneven shore makes moving treacherous, even with Thom's light to keep me from taking a bad step and falling into the river. Pieces of broken glass, crushed aluminum cans, and old plastic shopping bags litter the rocks; sweepers don't work the wrong side of the border fence. The East River is mucky with trash and things worse than trash; the one time I've known Thom to fall in, she was sidelined for a week with a nasty cough and a skin rash that only cleared up after a series of penicillin shots.

The water stinks, too, maybe worse than the dead. I breathe through my mouth as I edge along the rocks. To my right over the river, I can see the lights off First Avenue, white and blue windows checker-boarding the high-rises, and the red blinkers at the very top of the tallest buildings, a warning to pilots who may have lost their way. To my east, Queens is a more subtle glow. The

Midtown Tunnel is somewhere far beneath the water, twin tubes closed now at both ends, impenetrable. The Transit Authority filled it end to end with a line of obsolete buses, each neatly packed to bursting with Murray Hill garbage, before they dynamited the tunnel exits on the principle that no landfill space should be wasted.

I think of all those empty buses filled with rubbish, and all the junk floating in the river, and Doc wanting to cut down the last of our trees, and I shiver.

Alone in the dark with only my flashlight for company, I retrieve the folded paper from my pocket.

Open it somewhere private and out of doors.

The tip of Roosevelt Island's not exactly a blind spot, but outside the barrier with only the East River at my front is about as much privacy as I'm going to get anywhere out of doors. So long as Spears keeps Thom and the rest of the grunts distracted, there's no one around to pay me any attention. Even the soldiers patrolling the waterway are too far distant to spare me a thought; by now they'll have heard the coroner's tag over the radio, and if they notice my light at all, they'll assume I'm connected to the investigation.

I tuck the Maglite handle against my shoulder to free up both my hands, then turn the square packet this way and that. It's a piece of lined paper, college-ruled, folded into a square about the size of my palm, edges sharp enough that they might have been pressed with a ruler. It's bright in the beam of my flashlight, smudged where grit from the alley left a faint mark.

It reminds me of the notes Brian Bobbet used to pass me across his desk when we were sixth graders at Adam's Elementary School, after I'd kissed him once behind the janitor's shed, only minus childish sketches of hearts and flowers—an innocuous relic of a less complicated time.

I unfold the piece of paper carefully, one square at a time, revealing a perfectly normal piece of notebook paper, torn along one edge where it's been ripped from, I assume, a perfectly normal spiral notebook, the sort you can still get at office supply stores or even your corner grocery. There's faint blue writing across the middle margin, made fainter by the glare of the Maglite, and I adjust my stance, squinting to make out the scrawl.

CAXU3056743
Tues Noon

A string of letters and numbers, a day and time, and beneath that a surprisingly elegant illustration of a tiny feather. I frown. Together they make about as much sense to me as Brian's hearts and flowers had to my much younger self, a secret code I never managed to crack. Eventually Brian had taken my confusion and withdrawal for coldness, and he'd grown angry, calling me a freak in front of the rest of the class.

Like the feather, the handwriting is graceful, letters and numbers evenly spaced. There's an artistic flare to the slant of the A, X, and N, a subtle flourish on the tail of the S. It's not quite classic calligraphy, but it's pretty. And not a computer font, either. I pride myself on knowing pigment, from the vegan Kuro Sumi I use in my tattoo machine to the Lascaux Acrylics I use on my nonhuman canvases.

The owner of the rich handwriting used a cheap blue gel ink rollerball pen to go with the basic college-lined notebook paper. My aesthetic sensibilities bristle.

The feather, though—the bitty, pen-and-ink plume—belongs on a museum wall. I adjust the Maglite beneath my chin to better see the miniscule barbs, the curving rachis. Even the cross-hatched down sprouting at the base of the vane looks soft; the silk fluff almost seems to move, shivering soft blue on white paper, when I exhale.

Entranced, I scrape a thumbnail over the illustration, and the feather immediately kindles, the dull gel ink turning gas-flame blue. The drawing erupts off the paper and hovers in front of my nose, vivid in the dark. I smell smoke. The notebook paper is burning in my hands, shedding cobalt sparks onto stony ground.

"Crap!" I drop what's left of the note, stamping on blue sparks. Papery black embers curl, light as air, and drift toward the water. The feather is expanding before my eyes, growing larger as it burns brighter, gone from teeny to about the size of my forearm in a matter of seconds.

"Hemingway!" It's Thom, furious as she steps around my shoulder, then stiff and disapproving. "You promised!" Her thick boots smash escaping embers. Gerzy and Ramos are right behind her, mouths agape. "No *horseplay* when we're on duty!"

She's wrong. I never promised because there's never been a need. My "horseplay" stays sedately within the perimeters of flesh and ink, regardless of my ambitions. It's much safer that way.

"Look out!" I warn an instant before the feather stops expanding and explodes, a small firework at its pinnacle, dissolving in a shower of blue flares.

Ramos yelps, slapping at her uniform. "What's this?"

Gerzy just glares, a blue spark simmering on the edge of his upturned visor.

"It wasn't—" The muscle bunching behind Thom's jaw makes me reconsider. "Sorry. Sorry. It was an accident. Won't happen again."

"I warned you he was dangerous," Gerzy finally grits out, a doleful Cassandra. He shakes his head at Thom, then smiles at me. It's not a nice smile. "You belong on Rikers with the other one, Hemingway. A nice concrete cell and out of sight, out of mind, where you can't do anybody any harm." Hatred makes him quiver. "You're just lucky Thom can vouch you're not out grabbing girls and boys off the street every fifteenth week."

I launch myself in Gerzy's direction, but he sidesteps and Thom yanks me back.

"Shut up, Gerzy. Don't be an ass," Ramos says, but she's staring at a flotilla of cobalt sparks where they float on the edges of the river, unquenched by water, and she won't look at me.

"Come on." Thom clutches my elbow and pulls me around. "Time to go."

"Freak!" Gerzy says under his breath but just loud enough to be heard over the murmur of boats and barges and Thom's angry breathing.

Just like Brian Bobbet.

"I thought you said you couldn't get it to work," Thom says when we're seated in the back seat of a white cab, pressed thigh to thigh. She's staring out the window at the city lights, still breathing hard. Her fists open and close restlessly on her knees.

"What?" I lean the back of my head against the sticky bench seat and close my eyes. Blue feathers burst over and over again behind my closed lids, a celebration.

"The...you know..." She's furious but hushed, perfectly aware that if the driver's not listening, the state mics in the white cab are. "The thing you *do*. I thought it only worked for tattoos. You *said* it only worked on skin. You haven't figured out how to make *it* work anywhere else."

"Oh." I muffle a sudden yawn. I feel as if I've been awake for a year. Without opening my eyes, I poke at the sealant on my face. It's peeling around the edges, beginning to itch. "It doesn't. I mean, I can't. Get it to work. Only on people. My paintings are still just paintings."

"Then what did I just see?" Clearly, she doesn't believe me. "Hemingway, Gerzy and Ramos will keep it shut, but Doc was looking pretty pissed off when we left. He doesn't owe me any favors; I can't guarantee he'll keep *whatever that was* out of his write-up."

"Stop talking in italics. It makes you sound like a dick."

"Stop picking at your face." Thom bats my hand away from my chin. "You're making it worse. I *am* a dick, but I'm not an idiot, Hemingway. I know road rash when I see it. Also, you've got a knife hole in the back of your shirt and dried blood on your pants. What's going on?"

When my eyes fly open, we're nose to nose, her teeth shining in a white smirk. The cab driver is fingering his baton nervously, looking over his shoulder at us when he should be paying attention to the road. He doesn't need to worry. Thom's concern always looks like thunder before a summer squall.

"I need you to write something down," I decide. Then, to hedge my bets: "Please. Before I forget. I think it's important."

To Thom's credit she doesn't argue further. She gives my scraped face another searching look, then resumes her seat. She extracts her casebook and a pencil from a breast pocket and flips to a clean page, pencil poised.

"Go."

I don't have perfect recall, but the day has made an impression on my brain, and I'm pretty sure I've got the letters and numbers in the right order. The date and time is easier. After Thom's written everything down in her decidedly inelegant but professionally precise scrawl, I take the book and pencil from her and add a sketch—my own version of the miniscule feather.

When I'm finished sketching, it's a damn fine copy of the original as I remember it except for the fact that my feather, pretty though it is, doesn't catch fire even when I scrape my thumbnail encouragingly over graphite and vellum.

"So?" Thom takes her casebook back, frowning. "What is this?"

Don't be late. Seraphine hates late.

"Could be," I muse, picking at itchy sealant, "some douchebag is trying to make an appointment. Jump the waiting list, bully his way to the front of the line. Could be somebody wants me bad."

Thom's eyebrows jerk. She makes a moue of disbelief.

"Seriously? For a tattoo? Hemingway, you're not that special."

I've got a message for you, magic man. From a friend in need of your particular...talent.

"You might be surprised"—I toss the eavesdropping driver a crooked smile—"what some people will do for a brush with fame."

Chapter Six

Signals

Signals isn't Cleo's. It's a dark and dingy establishment beneath a decrepit east side tenement. The draw isn't the location. It's the space—large enough to seat upward of one hundred people without clogging the air space, and far enough away from the center of town that the mayor's inclined to ignore a few broken laws, so long as the requisite hush money is paid on time.

It's not really my first choice when it comes to a night on the town, but Signals is a favorite among the theater crowd, not just because the bathtub gin comes in tall glasses decorated with fancy little umbrellas, but because what Signals sells is media, and except for shoddily printed and heavily biased paper news, media is a rare commodity on the island of Manhattan.

There are fifteen small televisions running in the basement and two forty-six-inch Retina screens. The big screens are the real jewels of the outfit, and the four ancient analog antennae on the roof of the tenement are what make those jewels shine. The small TVs are hooked up to recycled DVD and VCR players, running old movies or television shows on loop—endless chattering homage to the good old days. But the two big screens run off the analog antennae, and some nights they pick up actual real-time broadcasts from places like Hartford, Scranton, and Ithaca—or even the White House.

Private citizens aren't supposed to hijack the city airwaves, but that happens too. A tailored broadcast from the District of Columbia might be interrupted at any time by a pirate station coming in from Brooklyn, replacing milquetoast news with real statistics smuggled back from the front line or coded personal messages from evacs caught in Jersey sent to their loved ones on the island—anguish relayed over the airwaves in pieces of poetry or blurry mobile phone snaps.

The pirate stations don't last very long before they're shut down, but there's always another broadcast springing up, hope reigning eternal.

The theater kids come to Signals to watch old movie stars do their thing on recorded television and because the place feels dangerous enough in the middle of the night that it's easy to forget real-time troubles. Other people come to Signals, too, for a drink with a fancy umbrella and a chance at hope, the possibility that maybe they'll see a family member's face stretched on a screen, or hear something they recognize in a line of bad poetry.

Neither Thom nor I are looking for lost family, so we take a small booth away from the larger screens near a small black-and-white RCA showing a grainy episode of *Dark Shadows*. We sit side by side because it seems less lonely and because Grace will take up extra space just by breathing. Thom orders a late dinner and tucks in while I down two shots of gin and we wait for Grace to arrive. There's a flame burning in a small white votive at the center of our table. I scoot the votive my direction and pass my finger back and forth above the wick, thinking of blue cobalt.

"How can you eat anything?" I demand as the second shot burns its way down my throat. "After that?"

"That?" Thom blinks vaguely between me and the television screen, where Barnabas Collins is, as per usual, finding himself in deep trouble. "You mean the crime scene?"

"I mean Christy Spears and Gerzy and Ramos and...the whole thing." I lay my head back against the booth seat and scowl at Signals' dirty ceiling. "It makes me sick, the way they looked at her like she was a puzzle to be solved and not someone's, I don't know, daughter? Friend? Girlfriend?"

"She wasn't seeing anyone," Thom says through a mouthful of fried okra. Signals specializes in faux-Southern food, and okra is about the only thing their cook doesn't ruin. "At least as far as I know."

I shoot an accusatory stare her way. "So you did know her."

"In passing," Thom agrees. "She was Port. There are fewer of us on the water than Central or Surveillance has on the streets. We know each other, at least by name. She worked the night shift, but farther up the Hudson." Thom hesitates, staring past me at something only she can see, a forkful of okra suspended in the air above the table. "She was a good person. Knew when to speak up and when to keep her mouth shut."

"Keep her mouth shut?" On the television screen Collins is being gloomy. Across the bar several people at a large table are looking my way. I slouch lower in my seat. "What do you mean, keep her mouth shut?"

Thom sighs. "Knew when to look the other way," she qualifies. Then she pushes her plate of okra to the middle of our table and points at my utensils with her fork. "If you're busy eating," she says, "they might not come over and ask for an autograph."

I dare the okra, taking tiny bites. Across the room my audience returns to their own dinners. Thom smiles, pleased.

"Shut up," I mumble around a mouthful of fried vegetable. Thom just laughs. When she laughs, she forgets to be stoic, forgets the world is a dangerous place, remembers Rafe's death is not her fault.

In the candlelight her eyes are luminous. This close I can see freckles on her cheeks, dark constellations on her skin. Not for the first time, I wish she'd let me paint her.

"Something wrong?" my roommate inquires, brow wrinkled.

"No." I wonder if I dare order a third shot of gin. It's dangerous stuff, but tonight I could use the buzz. "How about you?" The question slips out before I can stop myself or think too hard about why I want to know.

"Me?"

"Yeah, you. You seeing anyone lately? Dating, I mean? Gerzy's practically tripping all over himself to hit that."

"Hit that?" Thom drawls. "You're not serious."

If I slouch any more, I'll slip beneath the table. But maybe that wouldn't be a bad thing.

"Because we both know Gerzy's a clod, and if you refer to my lady parts as 'that' ever again—"

"Sorry! Sorry!" I signal the waitress, making the universal sign for another round, stat. "It's my Ketchum coming out."

"Well, put it away again, immediately." Thom sets aside her fork, puffs out her cheeks, and blows air in a gusty sigh. She's blinking like she thinks she can use her eyelashes to take flight, a sign that she's thoroughly discombobulated.

"Listen, Hemingway," she says haltingly. "You should know by now I don't do that sort of thing."

"Date?" It's true that in the time we've lived together, Thom's never brought anyone home, but she's usually out when I'm asleep and asleep when I'm awake. And it's also true she spends most of her free time hunting the Ripper, but although I've wondered plenty, there's no way I can be certain she's not painting the town red in between working, sleeping, and chasing a serial killer.

"Sex," clarifies Thom. "I don't like it."

"Okay." I mean to tell her it's all good and really no business of mine anyway but instead what slips out is: "Have you ever tried?"

Her expression clouds, and I'm certain she's going to get up and leave. Then she leans forward, dangerously close to the smoldering votive, and I'm sure she's going to dump okra in my lap.

"To like it? Or do you mean the act itself? A few times," she says in a tone I've never heard her use before, all seduction and smoke and promise. "Just to make sure. And I'm good at it."

"Jesus Christ." Seductive Thom is so unlike the pragmatic friend I'm used to that I have to grit my teeth to hold back an uneasy giggle. Luckily, the waitress delivers my two shots of gin right on schedule. I down the first, but before I can get to the second, Thom tips it into her mouth, swallows, and smacks her lips.

"But I don't like it," Thom continues, leaning back, freeing me from her leer. "And I don't expect I ever will. So please don't tell me I just haven't met the right person."

"I wouldn't!" It's my turn to be affronted. "Come on. I may be a hick, but I'm not an ass."

"Really? Because it seems to me you just were. A complete ass." Her jaw clenches as she looks down at her lap. "I expected better of you."

"I'm sorry!" Suddenly I feel lower than the crumbs sticking to Signals' floor. Thom's right. Of all the people in her world, I should know best how painful it is to have your choices questioned. "Shit." My shoulders slump. "I really am."

Thom softens. "I know. You're a good person, Hemingway. Maybe the best I know. Even though you hide it really well."

"Thanks." I sigh. "I think."

It's after 1:00 a.m., and Grace still hasn't shown. Thom's cut off my bar tab, which means we're drinking flat water and sharing a bowl of stale popcorn. A crowd of theater kids are gathered at the foot of one of the big TVs, listening to something out of DC. President Shannon's face looms large in technicolor, but the volume's turned down so I can't hear what she's saying.

"That one there," Thom tells me, continuing a quiet conversation we've been having while we wait. "Self-evac. He's here for news. I remember him. He came over from Jersey four, five months ago, on half a raft made out of those pool noodles. Him and his wife, together. Water was rough as usual, and they'd been swimming a long time. Wife was exhausted, starting to go under when we caught up with them. He let go and swam for it. Stupid, really. What was he going to do, climb over the razor wire at Battery Park? There's no way. He'd never make it."

The man's sitting two tables away by himself, baseball cap pulled low. He's tall and blond and has the look of the Midwest about him, like he enjoyed a life of hard work and sunshine before everything he thought he knew fell apart.

"So how'd he end up here?" I wonder out loud. "On the right side of the razor wire instead of on a boat back to Jersey?"

"Me," Thom replies smugly. "I pulled his wife out of the water, and then I went after him. He didn't make it far before he gave up. And then he was eager enough to climb aboard."

"So?" I prompt. "How'd he escape processing?"

"Me," Thom says again. "With the help of a few others. People like Christy Spears, who knew when to look the other way. People willing to do something about injustice, when we can, where we can. And now, thanks to the Ripper, there's one less Good Samaritan on the river."

Understanding raises the hair on my arms. "You'll end up on Rikers if you're caught."

"Yeah." Thom meets my horrified gaze. "But at least I'll be able to live with myself until I die—know I did what I could to reunite a few families, save a few lives."

"How many?"

"Not enough," Thom says, peeking sideways at the man in the baseball cap. "Never enough."

We wait as long as we can, until we've eaten more popcorn than any two people should, until the televisions are shutting off one by one and Thom and I and the refugee in the baseball cap are the only ones left in the bar. Still Grace doesn't show.

"She's the most self-centered brat," I complain as I toss money at our tab. "She never thinks about anyone except herself."

"You don't mean that," Thom says firmly, even though we both know Grace is not her favorite person. Grace is pageantry wrapped in drama. Thom doesn't have time for either.

"Ha." Outside Signals I scan the street for a curfew cab. "You don't even like her."

"True," Thom says as a white sedan slides around the corner. "But she was a good friend when you needed one. For that I'm willing to try."

Chapter Seven

Ailurus Fulgens

I half expect Grace to stop by Earnest Ink the next morning to apologize for leaving me hanging at Signals, but she doesn't.

I lost my Ketchum travel mug during the altercation in Bowling Green, and drinking takeout tea out of a paper cup from the café across the street reminds me that my chin hurts and Thom had insisted on cleaning and sealing my—admittedly shallow—knife wounds when we'd finally made it home. It's another uncomfortably muggy day, and all things considered, I think I'm allowed a sulk. Eric clearly doesn't agree, reminding me with pointed looks every time I start to slump that I'm expected to be polite to our customers.

It's a Sunday, but I'm booked six months out, and despite the shuttered shops on Forty-Sixth, my Sundays are no more or less busy than the other days of the week. I've only ever had two clients cancel a booking—one because we discovered she had a severe allergy to the lichenoides found in my red ink, and the other because he was hauled away to Rikers for an indefinite stay.

I endure small talk about the weather and the upcoming borough elections while I work away beneath my lights. Some people like to pepper me with questions from the chair—about the Labor Day bombing, about my life as a celebrity, about how it feels to be an oddity in an increasingly incomprehensible world. Others chatter about the cost of my services or laugh nervously over the buzz of my machine.

But they all go quiet when the ink comes to life, even if it's only a small piece of a larger sleeve, like the one I'm doing when Thom strides through the front door just before noon. My client goes googly-eyed as the koi fish I've just finished changes from two-dimensional to dynamic, rising above his skin and moving in sleek circles around his wrist above unfinished water lilies and scattering drops of opalescent water onto my floor.

"Wow," he whispers. "It's better than television. It looks so real." He pokes at the koi tentatively. The fish nudges around his finger and continues circling, unaware. The water droplets linger for a second on the floor tiles before vanishing as if they'd never been. "Thank you."

"You're welcome," I say. "Same time next week, okay?" I'm a bit googly-eyed, too, but only because Thom's never stopped by the studio during a workday, and she's brought sandwiches.

I strip off my gloves and help Water Lilies out of my chair because he's too awestruck to remember how to work his feet. They almost always are. His senses will come back to him as soon as Eric presents him with the sales slip.

Thom dumps the sandwiches without ceremony on the counter next to the register.

"Fantastic," Eric purrs as Water Lilies counts paper bills into his hand. He's looking at the sandwiches, not the cash. "Extra mayo?"

"You got it." Thom's carrying a small black knapsack over her shoulder and a compact, portable ladder in one hand. She props the ladder against the counter, drops the sack next to the sandwiches, unzips one end, and begins rummaging. "Hemingway, yours is the chicken on whole grain. Turkey and olives is mine, hands off."

"You knew she was coming?" I demand as Water Lilies exits the shop, still paying more attention to the ink on his wrist than his surroundings. If he's lucky, he'll cross Forty-Sixth without getting run over by cab or messenger bike.

"She called ahead for my order." Eric shoves a sandwich my direction, then unwraps his own and happily tucks in. "And she was cheerful about it, unlike other people I could name today."

"Give me a break." I unwrap my chicken on whole grain. The scent of toasted bread drowns my tongue in saliva. "It's hellish hot outside and my face hurts." I scowl at my roommate. "What are you doing here, anyway? Aren't you supposed to be working?"

"Special circumstances," Thom says around a black-handled screwdriver now clenched between her teeth. "Swapped a shift." Ignoring Eric's protests, she locks the studio door and flips the Open sign to Closed.

"Hemingway," my receptionist sputters, "you've got a 12:20. Geckos on the Californian ambassador's wife. She scheduled months ago—"

"This won't take long." Thom unfolds the ladder on the threshold. The ladder has cleverly hidden telescoping legs and narrow canvas steps that pop taut as Thom snaps latches into place. By the time she's finished assembling the thing, I'm reluctantly impressed. What came into my studio as hardly more than a step ladder now tops a sturdy five feet.

"Eric vacuumed the ceiling just last week," I point out mildly. "If you're looking for spider webs." Eric shoots me a dirty look over the top of his sandwich.

"Different kind of bug altogether." Thom climbs the ladder, and she's nose-to-lens with the CCTV over my door. She begins unscrewing the bulbous black fish-eye, expression serene even as the camera records her vandalism.

The badge on her uniform is clearly Port and not City Surveillance. Her last name is stitched in yellow beneath. And I doubt anyone in Surveillance owes Thom a favor so large she'll be forgiven CCTV tampering.

Lunch suddenly tastes like ashes in my mouth. I set it aside.

"Don't worry," Thom says without looking around. She's focused on the innards of the camera box, working the screwdriver. "I'll think of an excuse by the time the interruption logs."

Eric huffs. "Good thing they're not wired for sound." He licks mayo from his fingers, appetite unaffected. Eric's got balls of steel. Even criminal vandalism doesn't put him off free food. Of course, it's not his ass on the line.

The camera, unscrewed from its housing, falls into Thom's hand, trailing red and white wires. Gracefully she switches the screwdriver for a small, wallet-sized box. She attaches the box to the camera by way of a FireWire connection. On the box, a screen lights up, and she pushes a toggle with one thumb. I get an impression of light and shadow flitting across her stark features as she scrolls through CCTV imagery, but I'm too far away to get a good look at the recording.

"What are you searching for?" asks Eric. "Hemingway, you haven't had a break-in, have you?" It's his turn to look like he's just tasted something foul. "Oh, Jesus, your face—you told me you tripped over Ms. Harcourt's cat—"

"Not a break-in," I interrupt hastily, trying to stem Eric's growing tide of outrage. At the same time, Thom, balanced atop her ladder, tilts the light box so we can see the grainy image frozen on the screen.

"You recognize this kid?" she questions Eric.

I should have guessed from the beginning what Thom was after; I should have known the moment she went all cold and tight-mouthed when she patched up my knife holes.

Eric walks around the counter, standing on the toes of his vintage Tom Ford loafers for a better look.

"Oh, hell," he sighs. "Yeah, I remember him. Friday afternoon, he blew in out of the storm. Asking stupid questions, wasn't he, Hemingway? But I let him stay because I liked his style. All that purple hair and a heavy hand with the glitter paint—it worked." He sighs again, biting his lip. "Also, kid had an expensive watch on his wrist, a chronograph, the sort you can't hardly find anymore. I thought maybe he had money. You know, some of them do."

Eric's got a thing for watches I don't understand. He spends more each year on old-fashioned timepieces than he does on rent. I like to tease him about wasting money on time, but he doesn't think I'm funny.

"Some of them?" I ask. "Some of who?"

"Street kids," Eric explains. "You know, the punks hanging out on Pier 88. Most of them are living hand to mouth—my church takes meals out there every Tuesday, and plenty of those children need the help. But plenty more are willing to do whatever it takes to make a living—

you know what I mean." His couture-clad shoulders slump. "It's my fault. I should have chased him out the moment he stuck his nose through the door."

"It's fine," I assure him, bemused. More than five years working for me, and I had no idea Eric went to church. He just doesn't seem the loaves-and-fishes type.

"What's he done?"

"Assault and battery." Thom disconnects her box from the camera and begins the process of putting the CCTV box back to order. "Ms. Harcourt doesn't have a cat."

Eric's accusing stare scorches me.

"It was no big deal." But my protest sounds weak even in my own ears. I grit my teeth and paste on my game face, a surly sneer that convinces most people I don't give a damn. "It's Manhattan. Muggings are a dime a dozen."

"Not lately. Not with two grunts on the street for every fifteen civilians." Eric returns his attention to Thom, who is calmly shrinking down her ladder, screwdriver, FireWire, and light box safely stowed back into her pack. "Who is he? What's this about? Money or magic?"

I know Thom's remembering unnatural blue sparks floating on the East River, but she doesn't let on. "Could be either. Or neither." She slings her pack over her shoulder and tucks her ladder again under one arm. "I've got a few friends down at Central Command. I'll send the punk's picture around, see if it hits. Meanwhile, don't do anything stupid."

I'm not sure whether Thom means Eric or me, or the both of us.

She flips the Closed sign to Open on the way out the door, hitting the street without so much as a wave goodbye. It's as if I imagined that lingering moment of connection last night, as if hours spent together in comfortable companionship meant nothing at all.

Heat blasts into the studio before the door shuts behind her.

Eric waits a beat and then swings my way.

"Hemingway, in order to keep you safe, I really need to know—"

"Stop. I'm not in the mood. I pay your salary; I decide what you need to know." His expression turns dark, and I suffer a twinge of regret. It's true I cut the paycheck, but we left the employer/employee relationship behind long ago.

As far as I'm concerned, Eric's family. I'd like to think he feels the same way about me.

"Prick." But he says it fondly. "Just be careful. And let me do my job."

"Whatever." I rub my nose to hide my smile. "Asshole."

After that we both sit in silence, staring uneasily up at the CCTV until the Californian ambassador's wife arrives in a cloud of expensive, contraband perfume.

By midafternoon I'm looking in vain for Grace in every passing pedestrian outside my windows. Eric's got his nose buried in a worn copy of *Wuthering Heights* like it's just a normal Sunday between appointments. But I've seen the appointment schedule, and I know we're finished for the day. My wallet is that much fatter, and if it were a normal Sunday, Eric would have already said his goodbyes and sauntered off toward home.

I'm occupying myself with cleaning and putting away my equipment in between looking out the windows for

Grace. Water's beading on the outside of my panes, which makes me hope it might be cooling off outside.

"Go home." It's not a suggestion. "I'm almost done here."

Eric doesn't even look up from his book. "I'll wait."

"The door's locked." I refuse to raise my voice, although I want to. The thing with the street punk is just too strange. I want some time alone to think, but neither Thom nor Eric seems willing to just let me be. "I'm not worried."

"You should be." But Eric closes his book, marking the page with one finger.

"I need to borrow your phone." Changing the subject is easier than arguing.

Eric keeps his mobile in the register next to his pepper spray and a butterfly knife. He pops the drawer and passes it my way. It's a new-this-year, vintage-style, Texas-made Motorola, heavy in my hand. The orange stamp on the back of the case says it has passed state inspection.

While Eric observes, I flip the phone open and dial Grace's number. The line makes clicking noises until the call connects. I can hear distant, unintelligible voices behind the static: analog interference. Then the call rings through on the other end. It rings and rings, and I'm about to hang up when a man answers. I know him, but I'm surprised. Grace's phone is her entire life. I can't imagine her handing it over willingly to her hypervigilant father.

"Hello?" he repeats over the line when I'm too startled to reply the first time around. He sounds irritated and out of breath.

"It's Hemingway," I blurt before he can hang up. "Sorry. I was expecting—can I talk to Grace?"

"Hemingway!" Grace's father has game voice just like I have game face. He's a salesman; he's good at it. In an instant, he switches from exasperated to ingratiating and makes me almost believe he's been waiting around all day just to catch my call. "How are you?"

"Just fine, sir."

Eric's brows draw down in consternation. I don't usually do polite, but that doesn't mean I'm incapable of it. I went to a Catholic school in Idaho where corporal punishment is still legal—I learned early on how to mind my Ps and Qs to avoid a paddling.

"Good, good. Glad to hear it," Grace's father replies heartily.

Frances Miller has worn tailored three-piece suits and shiny gold cufflinks every day of his life. He waxes his silver mustache and puts pomade in his hair. He comes from old money made in real estate and still retains most of it by reinvesting in the local art business, and even though—or maybe because—he knows I'm worth his portfolio four times over, he expects a certain level of respect.

"Good," he repeats. "Fantastic! Still puttering around on Forty-Sixth, son? You know you'd do well in Chelsea. Anytime you'd like to pull up stakes and set down roots, you just let me know."

"Yes, sir. No, sir, I'm not ready to move quite yet. Mr. Miller, can I talk to Grace?"

"She's not around, I'm afraid. In fact, I was hoping you were her. Your call, I mean." When he chuckles, it sounds dry and forced.

"But..." I lick my lips. Eric's studying the ceiling, mouth pursed. "Isn't this her phone?"

"She left it behind," Miller reports. "Yesterday morning. I sent her on an errand to the peddler, you see. My arthritis, you know, it begins to plague me this time of year." He sighs. "I'm low on aspirin, and Grace said it was a lovely day for a walk in the park and she'd just run out and see if Miksail had any in." He sighs again. "She's so excited about her play—she's told you, yes? What foolishness! She must have lost her head. Left her phone behind, and I'm still low on aspirin."

I blink, trying to process. "You mean Grace hasn't been home since yesterday morning?"

Miller's huff of fond despair rattles down the phone line. "You know Grace, my boy. Always head in the sky, getting distracted at the worst times, leaving her poor old father in a spot. I suppose I'll have to send to the zoo for the aspirin myself; the arthritis is plaguing me something fierce. I imagine she's out celebrating with the theater crowd and won't show until she runs out of friends willing to buy her drinks."

The friend who buys Grace drinks is me; it was me she was supposed to be celebrating with last night. But I can't see my way to telling her father she didn't show. Arthritis isn't the only thing plaguing Mr. Miller. He also suffers from a dangerously unreliable heart.

"Miksail, you said? In the Park Zoo?" The Bronx closed their zoo last year for lack of patrons, and Prospect Park's was struggling before I moved onto the island. As far as I'm aware, Central Park Zoo is the only one still running, and that's mostly because it's a thriving hangout for black-market peddlers. "I can go, if you like, sir. No need for you to be out and about in this weather."

"Yes, yes! Miksail—red-panda exhibit!" Miller's effusive response is loud enough that Eric cocks his head in amusement. "Hemingway, you're a gem! Tell him it's my usual dosage I'm after. And if you see Grace, son, you tell her I'm not pleased, not pleased *at all*. That child needs more discipline in her life. Why, sometimes I think it would have been better if I'd not payed off her draft." And he hangs up.

I take Eric's mobile from my ear and stare dully at the backlit buttons.

"Miksail, I know him." I shrug, resigned. "Nice day for a walk in the park."

Eric transfers his butterfly knife from the register to a discreet pocket in his trousers. "You're not going alone."

I set his mobile precisely in the center of my counter. "I haven't needed mothering since I was eight years old. I wish you wouldn't start now. I'm perfectly capable of finding a peddler in the zoo."

"Don't worry, darling." Eric winks without humor. "Mothering's not my thing. Keeping you out of trouble is. I like a steady income, and you're it. I also like your face, and lately it's looking a bit worse for wear."

It's been a long time since I've been to the Central Park Zoo; I've almost forgotten how much I hate it. Once inside the gates, it all comes rushing back. The place is much too crowded, for one thing, with tourists and young families and elderly couples enjoying the cooler air. Sweepers work the paths and picnic areas; grunts walk patrol. The attendant who takes my cash in exchange for two entry passes explains that the sea lions are about to be fed and that I'd better hurry if I want to catch the action. He also asks me to sign a park brochure for his son.

"As proof," he babbles, fumbling my change. "That I shook your hand, Mr. Hemingway."

"Just Hemingway." I force a smile. I can't stand big crowds. Even before Seattle they'd made me nervous. Now they make me feel like I'm drowning; with so many people around, the air seems thin and useless. My lungs struggle to work properly.

I sign his brochure with a black Sharpie, wishing I hadn't lost my protective shades. The people who aren't rushing to watch the sea lions nosh pause to stare in my direction. I duck my chin and stride deeper into the park, shoulders pulled up around my ears, and practice the deep-breathing exercises Emma recommends for anxiety.

Inhale, exhale.

As I walk by, people mutter and point. I'm used to it. Almost eight years since Seattle, and I'm still that celebrity everyone wants to bump into on the street. Once I'd thought that would change. By now I've realized it probably never will.

A few people turn away in disgust. I'm used to that, too. The fear of crowds, the hitch in my stride, the whispers and the rubbernecking—it's all part of being me.

I can't see Eric in the press of people. I wonder if he's still within shouting distance. I don't need mothering, but I could use a friend.

He appears at my elbow, a baseball cap in one hand. The cap is emblazoned with the zoo's logo. More than half the tourists are wearing them. Eric claps it on my head and adjusts the brim to hide my eyes. Then he hands me his own blue-tinted glasses.

"You look like a deer in headlights," he scolds. "Act natural. You're making the grunts nervous. Walk."

I don't tell him I've forgotten how to act natural, just like I've forgotten exactly how the Space Needle looked during that last sunrise. Instead, I choose a random path and concentrate on putting one foot in front of the other. Eric trots behind, whistling softly. We leave the crowds behind. A sign up ahead says Temperate Zone in green letters.

"This is dumb," I mutter. "I should have let the old man get the pills."

Eric hums agreement. "Why didn't you? The Hemingway I know isn't usually so accommodating. Far from it."

"Shut up." Being angry is easier than being afraid. The hitch in my lungs eases some. "It's Grace's dad—he's old. He has a bad heart. Besides..." I lower my voice. "I can't find Grace. She's missing."

Eric has very expressive eyebrows, and he knows it. Usually he bounces them to show disdain or dismay. Now he arches one in disbelief. "Missing?"

"We had a thing last night. Not a date." Had sharing a table and a candle with Thom been a date? It had felt like one, looked like one, but now I'm not so sure. "A thing. An important celebration in her honor, and she didn't show. Grace never skips anything about her."

"Missing," Eric drawls, his mouth turned up in amusement. "Hemingway, she probably just started the celebration too early and is sleeping it off somewhere."

"Miller sent Grace for his pills yesterday *morning*. He hasn't seen her since then." I shake my head. "She left her phone behind. She would have gone back for it once she realized. She can't live without it."

"Oh, look, lemurs," Eric coos, scanning the exhibits ahead. "I love lemurs. So, what, you thought you'd find her *here*?"

"No," I reply automatically, although maybe, crazy as it sounds, I did. I'm not sure whether Eric likes Grace. I'm never sure if Eric likes anyone other than me and my bank account. Eric and Grace cross paths in the studio several times a week, and Eric's either cordial or snide, depending on the day, while Grace is always a little bit nutty. "I just thought I'd do the man a solid and get his pills, and maybe by the time I deliver them she'd, I don't know, be home again. From wherever she's...sleeping it off."

Eric rolls his eyes. They're a foggy gray, the color of winter sky.

"Miksail usually sets up by the red-panda exhibit," he tells me, jerking his thumb at the sign ahead. "Come on. Let's get this done."

Red pandas are adorable. They have fat teddy-bear faces on fuzzy, tawny feline bodies, and ringed tails. Their stubby legs and button noses make them look more like raccoons than bears. I'm not much for cutesy, but I can't help wishing for my sketchpad and Fineliners. Any other day I wouldn't mind sitting a few hours in the slim shade of the bamboo trees capturing red-panda antics on paper.

Inside the dome, comfy wooden benches are set around nooks and crannies for easy animal viewing. Most of the benches are empty. Apparently, everyone in the park is on their way to watch sea lions feed. But the enclosure isn't deserted. Apart from six red pandas climbing high up in the trees, several people stand clustered around one of the wooden benches. They're not paying attention to the animals. As Eric and I approach, I see they're listening intently to a middle-aged man who sits squarely in the middle of the bench, a collection of small cardboard boxes arranged to his left and his right. I can't hear what he's saying; his voice is raspy and whisper-low.

There are things you can't easily find in New York, not since the borders closed and the United States fractured. Basic items—luxuries I never thought I'd have to live without. Real sugar, for one. Coffee and cigarettes and aerosol hair spray. Perfume and room deodorizers. Aspirin, most narcotics, tampons, contact lenses, some brands of soda. Guns, obviously, but also pepper spray like the small bottle Eric keeps in our register, and certain varieties of knives. Jailbroken phones. Fluoride toothpaste. Chewing gum.

I miss chewing gum. But not enough to pay the two dollars per stick Doublemint goes for on the sly.

The group around the bench turn as we approach, shifting minutely to give the guy holding court a better look at us. He must see something in Eric he likes, because he makes a gesture with his fingers and the cluster around the bench parts farther. Me he ignores, heavy-lidded gaze skating over my hat and shades before darting back Eric's direction.

"Hello there." He greets Eric with a wink and a sly smile. It occurs to me that what he likes the look of is Eric's expensive clothes and shiny loafers. I wonder what the peddler would think if he knew Eric's got a butterfly knife hidden in his striped Versace trousers.

Then I wonder if maybe they've done business before. It's not impossible; Eric probably doesn't get his vintage clothes and books down at the local department store.

"What can I do you for?" Miksail's a bony sort of Saint Nick, seated cross-legged on his garden bench peddling lost artifacts from cardboard boxes to people like Eric who won't give up on past luxuries, or people like Miller and Piano Jim who have more basic needs the state won't meet. "Columbian, Kenyan, something local? I've got a robust little Hawaiian Arabica at thirty per pound. You won't find a better deal this side of Broadway."

The thing about the black market is it's complicated. Most grunts on the street will turn a blind eye so long as the dealer sticks to inoffensive commodities, and so long as the local precinct gets a healthy cut of any profit made. Coffee's innocuous, which might explain why the peddler is sitting unrepentant in front of six red pandas and at least three hidden cameras.

"I prefer tea," Eric says. He ignores ensuing throaty chuckles and marches forward until he's looking straight down at the man on his bench. I follow in his footsteps, cautious.

"I'm looking for aspirin. Also a girl," Eric continues, while I furtively examine the contents of the boxes. "Yesterday's customer."

"I have a lot of customers," the peddler replies. He peers around Eric, again dismisses me as inconsequential. "People come, they know where to find me, they know I like to sit and watch the *Ailurus fulgens* after breakfast." He shrugs narrow shoulders. "Aspirin I've got, plenty this week."

There's a veritable pharmacy nestled in the boxes among bags of coffee, small glass vacuum-sealed vials, and sterile syringes wrapped in plastic. Brown child-proof pill bottles and plump dime bags filled with white powder.

"Sugar," the peddler says, catching me peeking. "Pure cane." But he slides a cardboard lid over the box, hiding its contents.

"Tastes vary," Eric agrees. He discreetly slips a hand under his blazer. "Listen up. Our friend—Chelsea bohemian chic. Petite. Big brown eyes, lots of dark hair, rings in her ears and in her nose. Filthy mouth and lots of ruffles."

"Gracie Miller," the peddler says at once, making Eric and I exchange a look. His head wobbles on his neck when he nods. "I know her. Her papa sends her for the aspirin, yes, and every once in a blue moon for a bottle of Merlot. Real California Merlot. Hard to get these days, but papa can pay." He grins. "She likes to feed my *Ailurus fulgens*."

"Have you seen her? Yesterday morning, maybe?" Eric's got a small stack of cash in his hand, a lot of it, held in place by a rubber band. It's mine, one of four identical stacks the ambassador's wife used to pay for my magical ink. I bite down hard on dismay, swallowing angry protest. "On an errand for papa's pills?"

The peddler's mouth twists in amusement. "Might have," he says, then taps his head. "Memory's not what it used to be, I'm afraid. Boys, do we remember? Did sweet Gracie Miller come visit the red pandas yesterday morning?"

There are six of them, to match the six red pandas, but they're not nearly as adorable. Sallow-faced with sunken cheeks and glassy stares, and I don't think it's coffee they've been mainlining. Two of them are wearing sweepers' dungarees. The other four are wearing jeans and dock boots—from the overabundance of glitter paint, I'd say they're either sex workers, street punks, or Wall Street interns.

"Nah," one of the sweepers offers. "Chelsea usually don't come this far up—they see Fiennes on the Highline."

"Boys. Here, now. That won't do. Step up. This gent's a paying customer." He accepts Eric's bribe with dignity, rising from the bench just long enough to take the cash before settling down again between his boxes. "Think hard... It was a busy day. Lots of sad souls desperate for a little comfort. Sometimes, when I'm swamped, the boys help me out with the easy customers."

Five of the "boys" shake their heads, but the last wrinkles his forehead in concentration. "Maybe." He squints at me from under caked-on green glitter paint, then takes out a pack of cigarettes from a pocket and taps one out. "Yeah, boss, maybe. In between that lady looking for turmeric and the guy with the hair-loss problem." He lights his cigarette with a match, shakes out the flame. "Yeah, sure, now I remember. But she didn't come alone, that's what threw me off. It was her and two guys. Sold Gracie the aspirin and a coupla pieces of organic chocolate, and her boyfriend wanted a pack of Marlboros." He stabs the air with his own cigarette, triumphant. "Their shy friend with the glasses didn't want nothing—he just stood around looking uncomfortable."

"Boyfriend?" The word shouldn't feel like a punch in the chest, but it does. I know Grace has been seeing other people since we split—I've gone on a date or six myself—but I thought they'd all been casual hookups; she's never mentioned anyone serious.

It's not that I'm jealous. I'm really not. It's just that Grace and I share everything important. At least, I thought we did.

"Shit, I don't know." The punk backs off a little, eyeing me nervously. "Street kid, colorful hair? He was all over her. The other boy definitely gave off third-wheel vibes."

"You sure?" Eric says while I stand frozen in dismay. He scowls at Miksail. "Three of them here, yesterday?"

Miksail rubs a thumb over the bills in his hand. "I remember now. Plenty sure, and Robbie there's not lying. Gracie Miller was here yesterday morning with a couple of young beaus, and she left with her papa's aspirin, right as rain, so whatever trouble you've got going on, it's nothing to do with me or mine."

"Right." I clench my teeth to keep from snarling. I'm thinking: street kid, colorful hair. And remembering a knife against my spine. "Perfect. Thanks for that."

I manage, barely, to keep from erupting until the zoo gates are behind us.

"Christ, Eric! What the hell?"

Somehow, he looks suave even dodging sticky-fingered toddlers. "Calm down. I'll make it good."

"You stole—"

"Borrowed." He walks faster. "I said, I'll make it good."

"Yeah." I sneer. "Because you just happen to have twenty-five thou lying around at home. Man, what the hell?"

Eric whirls. "You want information? A man like Miksail, you have to buy it, just like anything else he keeps in stock." He taps manicured nails on his thigh. "Oh, stop looking at me like that. We both know it's not the money bothering you." He sighs, passes me his phone. "Try Grace again. Maybe this time she'll answer."

She doesn't. The line rings through, uninterrupted, ignored. The small hairs on the back of my neck rise. There's a sick feeling in my stomach, and Eric's right: it has nothing to do with the twenty-five thousand dollars he took without permission from my till.

Chapter Eight

Tremblay

I promise Eric I won't start needlessly panicking, that I'll go straight back home and wait for Thom to get off shift.

"There's no reason at all to think it's the same kid," he tells me. "Description could fit half the punks in the city, Hemingway. Don't jump to conclusions, and don't do anything stupid. Promise me."

The only reason he's not walking me back is because he knows me well enough to know I might fire him on the spot if he insists.

"I promise," I lie. Eric's mouth flattens to a straight, doubtful line, but he doesn't press the issue. Like he said, he needs that steady income.

I leave him standing outside the park on Fifty-Ninth and walk west a few blocks before I change my mind and turn abruptly south toward Chelsea. The wind off the Hudson brings with it a squall. The sky opens up, and rain pounds the pavement. I walk beneath the Highline, sheltered from the downpour. I can't help thinking somewhere above my head a peddler called Fiennes is doing business. After the Highline terminates, I'm forced to brave the downpour or grab a cab. I choose the cab.

By the time I climb out at Chelsea Market, the rain has softened to a drip. I walk in aimless circles around the market but can't work up enough enthusiasm to go inside.

Although most of the restaurants that once filled the old space closed long ago, a slew of tea shops and book boutiques and antique stores quickly blossomed in their absence. The Market remains busy; in the city, tea is serious business, printed books are all the rage, and antiques like oil lamps, manual typewriters, and hot rollers are useful again.

I'm delaying because I'm afraid I'll reach Grace's house and find out she's still not home.

There's an art shop in the back of the market, almost hidden between a tea sampler bar and a place that sells old movie posters. The shop carries good paper, fine synthetic brushes, and real acrylic paint, the kind you can't get most places anymore. The owner knows me, and he's kind enough to pretend I'm just an average customer. Sometimes, if the shop's slow, he'll brew up a pot of chocolate-mint tea, and we'll chat about perspective or color or the way shadows change across the city when the sun moves across the sky.

We never discuss the state of the world beyond our borders. I don't ask about the burn scars covering his hands and neck, and he doesn't comment when, after an hour or three, my leg forces me to sit instead of stand. The shop's called Chiaroscuro, and after Earnest Ink it might be my favorite place in the world.

Today I don't stop in. Restlessness takes me in circles around the market a few times before I move on. I've been on my feet for most of the morning; I'm cold and wet and worried, and I could do with a hot drink. There's a tea barista on every other corner, but I pass them by. I tromp on through the drizzle, ignoring passing cabs, until I reach my destination.

The sign hanging on the gallery door says Open. It's a twin to the sign in my own door, black block letters slanting capriciously to the right. Grace made both signs on the day Earnest Ink opened. The one in her father's door was a first attempt gone wrong. She said she didn't like the shape of the O. It does look a little wobbly.

Miller hung the sign anyway. He said it was the only artistic endeavor Grace had ever put any honest effort into, and so it was worth displaying. That pissed Grace off.

"Papa, theater *is* art," she'd said. "And maybe you'd know if you came to a show sometime."

But she let him have the sign with the wobbly O for Finch Gallery, and I really believe he's proud of it.

I shake water off my coat before I climb the stoop and shove into the old brownstone, and then I stamp it off my feet on the mat just inside the door. A bell over the door jingles, announcing my arrival.

Finch Gallery is a large open space divided into four smaller, airy rooms. The walls are painted white to better display the art hung alone or in groups. Soft spotlights shine from the exposed ceiling, illuminating paint on canvas. The floors are made of planks the color of honey, and the whole space smells vaguely of sawdust and glue. Miller makes and sells specialized frames from a hidden space in the back.

Just inside the gallery there's a large metal sculpture of an emaciated dog eating its own tail. It's disturbing to say the least, and very much not my taste. As I stand there grimacing at the sculpture, Miller comes rushing out of the back room, clutching a sheaf of papers.

He stops in place when he sees me, chagrin turning to joy. "Hemingway! You're here! My boy, come in, come in! No, no, don't mind the rain. Come, come!" His expression turns rueful. "I thought you might be Grace. She's supposed to work the front Sundays, but of course you know that..." He trails off, frowning at me absently.

"I've brought you your aspirin." Eric had remembered the pills at the last moment, and I'd had to peel more cash out of my wallet before Miksail would let us leave with the small brown bottle. "Sir—I'd sort of hoped Grace would be home by now."

Grace and her father live in an apartment above the gallery. It's totally luxe, but barely big enough for the two of them, which is why Grace spends most of her free time anywhere else.

"Not yet. You know Grace. Her mother raised her to be a free spirit." He tucks the papers beneath his arm, takes the pills from me, and then pumps my hand in gratitude. "Thank you, my boy. So very kind of you to do me the favor, especially with this weather." His round face brightens as he herds me across the studio. "And here I am, being remiss. Come, come, see where I've put you! In the very best light, of course."

He reminds me of a cattle dog, the way he guides without touching, using words to prod me ahead. He hounds me into one of the side salons and reintroduces me to three paintings hanging on an otherwise stark white wall.

The landscapes are a set, a triptych: square canvases done in winter gray and brown except for a flash of white and orange on the East River where the sun is rising over Long Island. I'd sat in the weeds beneath the base of the Queensboro Bridge sketching the dawn while Thom took pictures of what later turned out to be the Ripper's seventh victim—a young sweeper out of Sutton who had disappeared after leaving a bar near Ninety-First and turned up a week later caught in flotsam near the foot of the bridge.

"Some of the best you've done," Miller enthuses. "There's a poignancy to your use of *impasto* that strikes me right through!" He pats my shoulder: little, nervous taps of appreciation, like he's worried whatever it is that makes me *me* might rub off on his fingers. "Twice a day I think to myself: 'Frances, before you know it, this boy will be a household name!'"

He pauses, then laughs. "Of course, you already are, how silly of me."

"Yes, sir." I stick my hands in my pockets. "Sir, aren't you at all worried? About Grace?"

He turns somber, squeezes my shoulder. "I can see you are. Relax, Hemingway. Grace can look after herself. Besides, Manhattan's never been safer." His gaze flicks to the small CCTV camera watching us from a ceiling corner; then he lowers his voice. "How much trouble can she get into with eyes on every corner?"

"Yes, sir." But I can tell from the force of his fingers on my shoulder that Miller's trying to reassure us both. "I'm sure she'll be home soon. Tell her I'm looking for her, will you?"

"Of course, of course." Miller releases me, clapping his hands together without making a sound. His cufflinks wink under the spotlights. "Hemingway, fantastic to see you. Bring me something new soon. These will be sold by next month, I guarantee it."

To my surprise Thom's waiting for me under a tree outside the gallery, arms crossed. She's in full uniform: rain jacket over armor, padded black pants, and heavy boots. Drizzle is beading on the top of her helmet and streaking her open visor. I can tell by the purposefully blank expression she's wearing that something's wrong.

Two grunts I don't recognize are standing behind her, resting against the hood of a sleek black sedan. The badges on their uniforms have Central's spread-winged eagle and balanced scales. The insignia on the car's driver-side door matches.

"What are you doing here?" I demand. I'm afraid to hear the answer. Thom never skips a shift, and this makes twice in one week. My hands go suddenly clammy, and my stomach cramps in distress. "Who are they?"

"Anderson and Carroll are here to talk to Grace," Thom says. "I'm here for you." She nods. Anderson and Carroll push off the car and start toward the brownstone before I can explain Grace isn't home. The soles of their boots slap on wet concrete. The bell over the door jingles when they let themselves into the gallery.

"What's this?" Any other day the gleaming sedan parked alongside the curb would make my mouth water like a kid in a candy store. Miles of black steel and mirrored glass, it's a machine made to be admired. "What's going on?"

"Get in first." Thom opens the car's back door and points emphatically at leather seats. "Explanations after."

I slide in. She climbs in, slamming the door shut. The back seat's large enough for four people. I shimmy across leather, giving her space. Up front the driver's playing with a control panel that doesn't resemble any dashboard I've seen before, as full of lights and buttons as an airplane cockpit.

In a city hungering for lost technology, the console's an illicit feast.

"Card, please," the driver requests, extending a gloved hand. He's no cabbie; he's dressed in full military gear. He takes my card, runs it through the computer, then hands it back when the light turns green.

"Hello, Hemingway," he says once he's sure it's me. "Welcome aboard."

"Thank you." I glance sideways at Thom. "Whose car is this? Why aren't you on the river?"

"The car belongs to my chief," Thom answers, staring straight ahead as the sedan pulls away into the street. "He wants to meet you. We need to talk. The street kid pinged."

"Yeah?" The leather seat is soft under my nervously drumming fingers, luxurious. I wish I had Thom's trick of keeping my face unreadable. "About that..."

But she's watching traffic out the window, not really listening, mouth twisted in disgust. "Name's Jonathon Tremblay. Age: seventeen years, nine months. No residence listed. Been picked up multiple times for petty larceny, disturbing the peace, loitering. River piracy. Nothing out of the ordinary. Mom's a captain, infantry, listed as overseas. Dad's MIA." She shrugs. "Record's not flagged for any other assault or for thaumaturgy."

I'm surprised, although I guess I shouldn't be. "Do they do that? Flag magic?"

"Your record is flagged." She says it matter-of-factly, like it's no big deal that in the mayor's eyes I'm no better than your average sex offender or black-market peddler. "According to my buddy, the numbers on the note are probably off a cargo container. If your dickhead lives on the docks—and all evidence suggests he does—maybe he's given us his address."

"Okay." I exhale. "And it's not just me he's been dogging; he's been hanging around Grace. Is that why those guys were at the gallery?"

Thom swivels my way. The leather seat squeaks as she shifts. "Grace tell you that?"

"Nope." Sitting there in the fancy government sedan, there's no way in hell I'm going to explain that Eric and I have been shopping the Central Park underground for information. The tempo of my fingers on the leather increases. The driver's watching me through the rearview mirror. I bet he's trained to sniff out guilt. Carefully, I rest both hands on my thighs. "Definitely not."

From the quirk of the driver's mouth, I assume he thinks we're idiots. I don't disagree. I lean my forehead against the window and breathe; the glass clouds in bursts of fog. We ride the rest of the way without speaking.

Thom's chief works out of a squat, three-story, new-construction cement building in Lenox Hill. The building's blocked by permanent waist-high barricades on three sides and an old brick high-rise on one. A forest of bollards and a small army of grunts make a second, more adaptable blockade outside the first. Unlike most grunts, the soldiers walking Port's perimeter carry guns: small ceramic pistols in holsters on their belts and compact submachine guns in hand.

The back of my neck prickles. Ketchum is a hunter's paradise. I grew up around guns; my dad taught me rifle safety when I was eight. But the sort of artillery the grunts are carrying aren't for bagging dinner—they're for keeping desperate people in line.

"Out," Thom orders when the driver brakes. Yellow cabs dodge around us. One of the armed guards pulls open my door and ushers me through a maze of bollards toward the front of the building. Thom slides out of the car and has a word with the driver before catching up.

I'd probably be pissing my pants if the car had dropped us at Central, but Port administrates the waterways and the evacs caught within. My citizenship is in order, and although I've spent plenty of time near the East River with Thom, I haven't so much as dipped a toe in it.

But I'm sweating through my T-shirt even though the rain is coming down again and the air is finally cooling off. I remind myself that Thom is my friend, and fiercely loyal. She wouldn't walk me into actual danger without warning me first.

"Oh, hell." As we pass into the building through two sets of sliding polymer doors, a thought occurs to me, and I turn Thom's way. "The camera?" I mouth even though that makes no sense either. If this had to do with the equipment she'd dismantled in Earnest Ink, surely we'd be visiting Surveillance and not Port.

Wouldn't we? I wish I'd paid more attention to jurisdiction, but law has never been my thing.

"I told you," Thom growls, inscrutable beneath her open visor, "the kid pinged."

The armed guard leaves us in the lobby next to a bank of elevators. The lobby's seething with grunts. It smells like disinfectant. There are mirrors everywhere, which only makes things worse. President Shannon's portrait hangs below a giant clock on the lobby wall; the mayor's portrait, much smaller, looks down on us from above the elevators.

Thom presses buttons. We ride the elevator up to the top floor without speaking. I don't know what she's thinking, but I'm wary of the mics I'm sure are hidden behind the elevator's padded walls.

On the third floor, we step off and walk side by side down a narrow hallway lined with nondescript doors. The hallway's empty of anyone but us. I can hear the muted hum of many voices, but it's impossible to tell from behind which door it's coming; maybe from behind them all.

Thom knocks on the last door on the left, then immediately hurries me through. The room beyond is a boring mix of beige and industrial gray. A white-haired man in uniform sits in a swivel chair behind a large desk. Beyond him a large television cycles through views of the Hudson, East River, and Upper Bay, which are spotted with soldiers in barges and storm-whipped whitecaps. The desk is clean except for a few documents and an old fax machine.

The man behind the desk has more medals pinned beneath his Port badge than one person should ever deserve.

"Castillo," the man says, addressing Thom by her surname. "Good. Come in. Take a seat. And you're Hemingway."

"Chief." Thom removes her helmet and cradles it under one arm. Her short hair has gone sleek with sweat or rain.

There are two beige chairs in front of the desk, but Thom ignores them. I follow her lead even though I'd dearly love to sit.

"Thank you for coming." He rises from behind the desk to shake my hand. He's not a big man, but his grip is strong, a challenge. He studies me openly, eyes lingering longest on my scraped face, before he lets go. Unlike me he hides his conclusions well, but not well enough. I glimpse aversion, a flicker quickly concealed.

Maybe I only catch it because I've been seeing the same expression on faces out of the corner of my eye ever since I was a kid. Usually it has nothing to do with magic and everything to do with bigotry.

He must have read my records; he knows my history. At best, he thinks I'm a girl playing dress-up. Possibly, he thinks I need to be cured.

"I've seen your work on the news," the chief says, outwardly affable. "Amazing. How do you do it?"

"Christ knows." I smile, all teeth. "President Shannon believes I'm an honest-to-God miracle."

Nothing makes a bigot madder than religious jargon out of the mouths of the damned.

"Hemingway," Thom warns, reminding me where I am. "I'm sorry, Chief. Sometimes I think all the attention's gone to his head."

"You're young yet," the chief tells me, as if age is an excuse for who I am. "I understand. Youth is a dangerous thing." The medals on his chest rise and fall with each breath he takes. "When I was your age, I was fighting a losing war in Kabul, and I thought we'd all live forever." He sits down again, shuffles documents into a neat stack. "Hubris is forgivable, young man, but given the trouble we've had with thaumaturgy in this city, now and in the recent past, you have to understand why we all find you of special concern."

"I'm not a serial killer, and I'm not Rutch." I enjoy the way the medals on his chest hitch when I say that name. "I have zero interest in politics. I just make tattoos that move."

"Did you ever meet him?" the chief asks. "Rutch?"

"No." It's my second lie that day. I'd been part of Rutch's audience, once, and watched magical-healing turned political ministry. I'd never told anyone after, not even Grace. I think I'd hoped he would notice me in the audience, acknowledge me somehow. He didn't.

"I've met him. The two of you are nothing alike." The chief selects a document from the top of his pile and slides it over the desk in my direction. It's a grainy photograph, enlarged until the edges are warped. "As for our serial killer—I understand you've had a run-in with Jonathon Tremblay."

A familiar face glowers up at me from the desk. In the photo, his hair is shorter and dyed scarlet, and he's wearing a nasty black eyeliner instead of glitter paint. He looks more vulnerable without makeup, fresh faced and scrubbed clean, almost innocent, the ostentatious gold watch too big on his thin wrist.

"Is that his name?" I ask warily. I'm positive Thom's kept my secrets, but I'm in no way certain Gerzy or the coroner or even Ramos hasn't been telling tales of blue fire on Roosevelt Island. "It was a mugging. In Bowling Green."

"In a blind spot." The chief steeples his fingers, regarding me over their tips. "I pulled what tapes there were. You go into the alley together, come out separately, the both of you worse off for it. I've got nothing more than that." He clears his throat. "Wanted your card, did he? Your wallet?"

Something in the way he stares at me over his fingers tells me to pick my words carefully. "I'm not sure. He stuck a knife in my back, walked me into the alleyway, and then I hit him over the head with a flowerpot. We tussled. He ran."

The chief's eyes narrow. "Bold of you, I must say. Tremblay's no amateur. He's got a sheet a mile long.

Disturbing the peace. Quite a lot of marauding, which is how he came to my attention. B and Es. Destruction of state property. He's been a thorn in our side for a while, but up until recently we wrote him off as mostly harmless, no more of a threat to citizens than any other street rat." He unfolds his hands and lays them flat on his desk, palms down. "Turns out we were wrong."

He takes back Tremblay's rap sheet, reshuffles it back into his pile of documents, slides out a second, larger photograph. "Take a look at this."

The snap's black and white, warped around the border, probably a frame snipped from longer footage. It's a street view—I recognize the entrance to Morningside Park. From the slant of the light it looks like early morning, just after sunrise. Trees obscure much of the pavement below the camera, but not the two figures caught center shot.

"Christy Spears," the chief says, poking his thumb at the shorter of the two people. "Just off night shift and heading home." In the photo Spears has changed out of her uniform into a tracksuit; her long hair is caught up in a high ponytail. "And there, just coming up the path behind her..."

"Tremblay," says Thom while I stand and stare at the snap, speechless.

There's no doubt in my mind it's him. His lanky form and jagged haircut are as distinct as a fingerprint. The camera's caught him several strides behind Spears, his longer legs eating up the pavement as he works to catch up. She hasn't noticed him yet. She's got headphones in her ears; I can just make out the wires. She's got her music turned up too loud, and she's not paying attention to her surroundings. Could be she's exhausted after a long night on the water. Could be she's anticipating breakfast and a day with friends before work begins again after dark.

"Hemingway," Thom prompts, making me jump. I realize I'm pressing my hand to my front where Tremblay's knife sliced my flesh.

"Shit. You think it's him. I mean, you believe that kid's the Ripper?" I think I'm meant to be afraid, but instead I'm furious, a rising tide of outrage.

"That's the last record we have of Captain Spears before she turned up dead," the chief replies. "There's a blind spot just past those trees, and there we lose them both. Surveillance has been working round the clock for the past ten days and nothing." He clears his throat. "You say Tremblay knows blind spots, used one to his advantage in your case."

I've stopped listening. "Thom!" I wheel away from the desk and the old man's concern. "He's been hanging around Grace. And now she's disappeared—no one's seen her since Saturday morning."

For the first time since she showed up on my doorstep with rent check in hand, I can read my roommate's face like an open book: sympathy, concern, regret, and remorse. She already knows about Grace. It's why she picked me up in a fancy sedan and delivered me herself to the chief. Not because she thought I needed protection.

Because she thought I needed a friend.

"It would be a break in pattern," she says, but she's nodding her head. "He followed the two of you from Earnest Ink, Friday night, all the way to Cleo's. The cameras catch him waiting outside until well after midnight. I spoke to her yesterday morning, so we know she made it home after the concert. But his interest in the two of you is concerning."

"You need to understand it's probably not chance, Hemingway. He knew exactly who you are." The chief clears his throat. "Maybe the change in MO has to do more with who you are than with your friend. With thaumaturgy."

"Okay." I look toward Thom for rescue. "What am I supposed to do with that? How do we help Grace?"

"You, nothing," the chief says before Thom can speak. "Be vigilant. If this kid is the Ripper, he's extremely dangerous. He's changed things up; he has an agenda. I'd like to arrange for increased surveillance. A few extra grunts around your studio, a man by your side at all times. Just for safety's sake, until we find him." His fingers flex and relax on the desktop. "As a heretofore inviolate citizen of the state, you do, of course, have the right to refuse—"

"Yeah," I cut in. "Thanks. I refuse. I don't need any more surveillance. I can take care of myself. It's Grace who needs your help now." I show my teeth again. "What are we going to do to find her?"

Medals rise and fall as the chief breathes. From the crease in Thom's brow, I've said exactly the wrong thing. On the television behind the desk, grunts in a raft bob up and down on angry waters. Either rain or the old monitor turns the skyline gray.

The chief neatens his papers once again, then nods. "Leave your friend to us. You'd only be in the way. Believe it or not, we're very good at what we do." He flicks his gaze in Thom's direction. "I'll be in touch when we know more."

Chapter Nine

Alizarin Crimson

Thom stomps her way down the hallway to the elevator bank, then jabs the buttons. I can almost see waves of temper rolling off her back. It's nothing compared to the fury boiling in my blood.

"You should have told me first thing," I say, fists clenched.

"Shut up, Hemingway," she retorts, stepping into the elevator. "Not here."

I bite the inside of my mouth to keep from shouting while the elevator drops more than three floors, past 3, 2, G, and then a level marked B1. At B2 I shoot Thom a puzzled, angry stare. She ignores me. We coast past B3 and B4. At B5 the car stops, vibrating gently in place before the doors part.

"This is not where we came in," I point out coldly.

Thom doesn't answer. She strides off the elevator, shoulders back, chin high. I storm after, trailing her down the cement corridor.

Halfway down the hall she wheels around. For the first time since we left the chief's beige office, I get a good look at her face. Her dark eyes are round and distressed, her face blanched. I'd assumed she was angry—I was wrong.

She's frightened.

"You should have told me!" She's the one doing the shouting. Her voice bounces off cement, ringing on the floor. "You should have told me something was up with Grace and that kid! You should have trusted me *with all of it*! You should have let me help!"

"I didn't know!"

Thom's never frightened. The fact that it's the Ripper and *Grace* breaking her cool makes me want to howl and punch the wall.

He was all over her. Street punk, colorful hair.

"She didn't tell me! I didn't know until this morning! Jesus, Thom, I had no idea!" For some reason, Grace's silence feels like a betrayal, and it stings more than Tremblay's nasty little knife.

"Listen," Thom says, blinking rapidly. "I get that you don't want Surveillance hanging around—really, I do. And I get that you and Grace keep secrets—"

I make a noise of outraged dismissal, but Thom motors on.

"But this is different. And this is about the Ripper, Hemingway. Which makes it my business, too!" She scrubs her hand through her hair, evaluates my scowl, then groans out loud. "Come on." She turns, waving a hand. "This way."

"What is this place?" It's cold on B5—too much cement—and the air tastes recycled. I can't help wondering how far beneath Lenox Hill we are. Manhattan's an island; dig too deep and one's bound to hit water.

I shudder, imagining the East River pressing against concrete walls.

"Training level," Thom snaps back. "Barracks, gymnasium, classrooms." She tosses me a sideways glare.

"Every grunt drafted into Port division begins here in Bunker Five."

"Feeling nostalgic?" I can do angry sarcasm, too. But Thom doesn't reply. I look around with grudging interest as we walk.

The corridor branches once, then again, and then again. Like the third-floor hallway, there are doors on every wall in regimented increments. They all look the same: industrial steel and numbers stenciled in red. Large fans in the ceiling circulate air through round metal grills. We pass an archway, swinging doors propped open. The room beyond looks like some sort of cafeteria: rows of benches and tables topped with napkin dispensers. It's empty.

"Where is everyone?"

"Day shift is on the water," Thom explains. "Night shift is still sleeping for the most part. It's better this way, with no one around."

"What are you talking about?" Immediately suspicious, I slow my pace.

"I mean it." Thom keeps walking. "This is my business now. It's a lucky break Tremblay let you go without anything worse than a battered face and few pokes. You know I don't like to rely on luck. Next time—if there is a next time—you need to know how to protect yourself with hands and feet. In case you're short on flowerpots."

"Funny," I retort, eyes narrowed. "Very funny."

Thom ignores my sarcasm. "It's time I teach you how to fight back."

"I can take care of myself," I say sourly. "Small but mighty, that's me."

Thom doesn't dignify this with a response. She's busy flicking an impressive collection of light switches on the wall inside the door from off to on: *click click clickclickclickclick*. Commercial can lights buzz awake one row at a time as she flips each switch. They warm slowly from blue to white, flooding the space beneath.

It's more a torture chamber than a gymnasium, and I have immediate flashbacks to middle school PE.

"I'm not climbing that," I say, eyeing the thick length of rope hanging from a ceiling beam. "Or that." Next to the rope, wicked-looking hooks anchor a net ladder to the floor and to the ceiling, stretching it taught.

"This isn't about strength training," Thom replies. "This is about self-defense." She crosses the warehouse-sized room to a really impressive collection of blunt instruments arranged by size and shape on a rack, boot heels leaving temporary divots in the blue and red training mats covering most of the floor.

The room is rectangular with high ceilings. The long walls are mirrored. My face in the glass is white and strained. A weight station, complete with elliptical machines and two treadmills, takes up the space along one short wall. Yellowing posters displaying what look like hand-drawn martial arts poses are tacked around the wide door we've just entered. I can't read the writing on the posters—the characters are all Chinese—but I admire the elegance inherent in those balanced postures.

"Right. Can you teach me that?" I pause before a drawing of a figure caught midkick, their opponent collapsed to all fours in defeat, awaiting the final blow. I imagine myself poised over Tremblay's bowed form, fists raised, ready to deliver the justice he deserves.

"No." Thom returns to the center of the room, a baton in hand. It's several inches longer than the collapsible version she wears on her belt and those employed by cab drivers. "Hung Gar is meant to be practiced for a lifetime. You don't have that much time." She beckons me close.

The training mats are less spongy than I expected; I doubt they provide much protection against a solid fall. Resigned, I take off my coat and toss it out of the way.

"My dad taught me how to punch and kick and bite when I was a kid," I confess. "I'm not as helpless as you seem to think."

"Tremblay is not a backwoods Ketchum bully." Thom rolls her helmet after my coat. "Go ahead. Show me what you can do." Then she springs without any warning at my face.

It's like trying to defend against a whirlwind. Immediately, I know I'm up the creek. I bring my fists up in front of my face the way I've been taught and do my best to dance out of the way, but her blows land around my shoulders and ribs, a flurry of taps more mocking than punishing. When I give up on blocking and attempt attack, I can't manage to land a single strike, and I let down my guard in the process. Quick as a snake Thom taps me on the forehead, chin, and chest. I swing at her belly and overreach. I'm already off-balance when she sweeps my feet out from under me with one swift kick.

I wasn't wrong. The training mats don't do much to cushion my landing.

"Jesus Christ." I lie on my back, struggling to catch my breath. Thom looms over me, a grim smile turning her usual stoic expression wicked. "Listen, that was fucking amazing, but I'm the one who met him in an alley and that's not how Tremblay fights."

"Really?" Thom offers a hand. "How does he fight?"

"Dirty," I say, and yank her over on top of me. She makes a noise that sounds suspiciously like a squeak when she topples. Her weight across my chest knocks the air out of my lungs again, but not before I've given her closest ear a solid wrench.

Thom yelps and rolls, trying to escape my gauging fingers. I roll up onto my hands and knees and scramble away, struggling to regain my feet. A shadow stretches across red and blue mats a second before Thom's on my back like some sort of feral tiger, arm locked around my throat, not quite tight enough to strangle. She's heavy, but for my size, I'm no weakling, and this time I'm ready. I manage to keep to my hands and knees, back arched. My ears are ringing. I turn my head and bury my teeth in her bicep, deep enough to leave a warning mark without drawing blood.

I guess she didn't believe me about the biting because she loosens her hold, surprised, giving me just enough room to throw my head back in a reverse headbutt, the sort every kid in Ketchum learns eventually. The back of my skull connects with her forehead. We both yell. I'm seeing stars, but it's worth it, because Thom drops to the mats, hand to her nose.

Fighting back is easier than I should be comfortable with. The rage that's been lodged in my gut since Tremblay knocked me down in the alley boils up and over. Violence feels good, feels like a solution to fear.

I grab my chance and stagger toward the weapons rack. Along the way I scoop up Thom's helmet and lob it hard through the air in her general direction. It misses her by an inch, bounces on red and blue padding.

"You little...!" It sounds suspiciously like she's laughing.

"Listen, sweetheart." The weapons rack is baffling—too many choices and none of them sharp. I grab the heaviest-looking baton I see. It's about a foot long. The handle's coated in something that looks and feels like rubber but is probably a synthetic. "I was the only openly trans kid in my high school, and I got tired of lunchtime ambushes real quick. Believe it or not, I know how to do some damage."

It's not my roommate I want to pound until my knuckles bleed. It's Tremblay for taking Grace, and the bigoted chief upstairs, and the asshole who killed Don with his IEDs in Seattle, and every other monster walking the streets of our fucked-up world.

Somehow, Thom's moved across the room without making a sound, and when I turn, we're standing face-to-face, the baton in my hand half an inch from her chest. Her nose is bleeding sluggishly, and she's panting. Her hands open and close at her side, clenching and relaxing. She wants to fight.

She has more control than I do.

"I'm not your enemy, Hemingway." But she's grinning from ear to ear like she's just accepted a box of chocolates instead of a bloody nose. "You're more capable than I thought." Her gaze drops to the baton in my hand. She's still holding its twin. "Do you know how to use that?"

"It's a stick. Stab and thwack." It's not really long enough to add to my reach, but it's reassuringly heavy in my palm. I close my fingers tightly around the handle.

"No." Slowly, so as not to be seen as threatening, she extends her baton, reverses it neatly in her fingers. "There's an impression on the butt end, see? Like a button."

I feel with my thumb because I don't want to risk looking down and away, and I find the concave divot quickly. I nod.

"Press it." Thom does. The end of her baton lights up. Electricity sizzles, arching from two tiny metal stubs hidden on the end of the stick. The hairs on my arms stand up in reaction.

"Exactly," my roommate says. "Modified CEW. One push charges the nodes; hold the button down to keep it powered on."

"Taser." I raise my eyebrows, intrigued. "I didn't know."

"Port doesn't use them on the water, of course," she says. The flare of electricity reflects in her eyes. "And there's not been much need for crowd control, not in the last few years, not since the border fences went up. So, no—" She blinks at me. "—you've probably never seen one used." She releases the button and the electricity dies. "Causes brief incapacitation but no lasting harm. Try it, if you like. I can handle it; we go through training." She puffs out her chest even as blood drips from her nose onto her shirt.

"No, thank you." But I look at the baton in my hand with new respect. "Cabbies, too?"

"Obviously not. CEW is military grade and not the sort of weapon I usually carry, but I've requisitioned one, for *backup*." Although she can't say it out loud, I know she means *for you*. "We'll pick it up on the way out."

I sigh as I carefully set the baton back in the rack. She's crazy if she thinks I'm going to shoot up even my worst enemy with electricity. "Are we done here?"

"Not at all," Thom says. "Even if you're right about Tremblay, your size and your bad leg are still a liability."

She sounds cheerful about it. "I want to show you a few basic blocks."

By the time she's satisfied, we're both bloody and bruised. I'm swaying on my feet, numb, anger drained away to a low, nervous buzz in the back of my skull. I think she takes pity on me because she brings me a warm, clean white towel and a cup of something fizzy and sweet-smelling from a nook behind the weight machines, then shows me how to use the heated compress against my sore spots. She's remarkably gentle when she wipes fresh blood from the healing scab on my chin.

"Sorry about that," she says. "Honestly, I was trying to avoid your face. Drink that; you'll be glad of it tomorrow."

I swallow obediently, grimacing at the taste. "What is it?"

"Ibuprofen," Thom replies. "And electrolytes."

She daubs at her own bruises while I drink, and I can't help thinking that she's beautiful in a fierce way, like Emma's nimble motorcycle or lightning over Rockefeller Center, or the first squeeze of Alizarin Crimson on my palette before I've smudged it with my brush. Efficient, self-contained, dangerous, and rare.

"I wish you'd let me sketch you," I say without thinking.

"Shut up, Hemingway," she retorts, then tosses our towels into a shoot and grabs her helmet and my coat.

On the way out of the building, Thom picks up a new baton from a stern-faced woman behind a stark desk. She waits until we're sitting again in the chief's fancy car before she sets the weapon on my lap. If the driver notices the exchange, he gives no indication.

"Wait," Thom says when the car drops us off outside Earnest Ink.

The rain's let up again. Watery sunlight peeks through high clouds, bouncing off sign posts and glass. The outside of my building shines, granite freshly polished by the storm. A lone sweeper brushes up debris washed into the gutter by the rain, transferring paper, leaves, and soil meticulously into a wheeled bin.

"What now?" I just want to go upstairs and shower, get my head back together, and figure out how to save Grace.

"Door's unlocked," Thom explains quietly.

It's not the kind of thing just anyone would notice; the door's closed and innocuous looking. But Thom isn't just anyone, and we've lived in the old building for years. We know, for instance, exactly how the door panel doesn't quite fit the frame, how there's a narrow gap between the door and the lintel, and how when the door's locked, the bronze patina of the ancient deadbolt is just visible through that crack.

It's not visible now. Thom's right. The door's unlocked.

"Eric," I suggest, but from where I'm standing, I can see through the studio windows. The front room's empty, lights off, the sign in the door still flipped to Closed, my giant cash register a shadow. From the outside looking in, Earnest Ink is sleeping.

"I locked it this afternoon on the way out," Thom says, as if I didn't know she's compulsive about securing our home. She motions my way—*stay back*—then turns the old brass knob and slowly pushes the door open.

The door creaks loudly. The sweeper pauses in his work to watch as Thom and I freeze on the stoop like two idiots expecting the worst. I grip my new CEW in one hand. The baton feels smooth and solid in my fingers, reassuring even though the thought of Tasering a living creature is repugnant.

"Eric was supposed to oil the hinges weeks ago," I complain lightly. I'm too worn out to be afraid—in fact a new burst of adrenaline is turning me giddy. "Ten points from Gryffindor."

Thom makes a face, unimpressed by my false levity. Then she surprises me: "Really, Hemingway. Gryffindor? Eric's definitely Ravenclaw."

We step together into my studio, wary as mice out of a hole. The door creaks again as it closes. Nothing else happens. The studio is quiet, cool, empty. Motes of dust hang in the air, caught in silvered sunshine through the windows. The old register gleams.

I glance around the space, taking quick inventory. As far as I can tell nothing's been disturbed; every tool and miscellany is exactly as I left it.

Thom throws the deadbolt behind us, locking the rest of the world out, but not before she pauses to examine the strike plate with the light from her mobile.

"No scratches," she murmurs, forehead creased. "It's a solid old lock, not easy to jimmy. Even more difficult to pick today, what with Fitzsimmons watching." She sighs. "Had to be a key."

"Fitzsimmons?"

"Sweeper," Thom says. "Well. I say sweeper..."

I goggle out my windows at the man industriously cleaning the sidewalk.

"I said I didn't want surveillance."

"Fitz isn't Surveillance. He's a friend." Waving my protest away, Thom slinks around the counter and through the curtain toward the elevator. She discards her helmet neatly on the floor, unclips her baton from her belt, then summons the car.

The elevator doors open immediately. It's been waiting. Thom steps in. I stay out, blocking the doors open with an arm and a leg.

"You think someone's up there. Tremblay—the Ripper? Waiting. To...what?"

"How should I know?" she says quickly and under her breath. "Magic you into a corpse? Pass you another love note? Give you Grace's head on a platter?"

She's right. Nothing makes sense. Tremblay had me and let me go, only to take Grace instead. Was the note meant as some sort of ransom demand? Did he take Grace not to kill her, but as assurance I'd come looking? It seems a slim hope, but I'm one I'm willing to grasp with both hands.

The elevator begins to buzz, confused by my interference.

"Ms. Harcourt has a key," I say.

"Ms. Harcourt is afraid of needles," Thom replies patiently. "She only ever goes out the back. My key is here." She touches her breast pocket. "Your key is there." She indicates the carabiner clipped to my jeans. "Wait down here if you want." And that sounds suspiciously like a challenge.

Shaking my head, I slide the rest of the way into the car. Freed, the elevator doors close, and the car jerks upward.

It seems to take forever for the elevator to rise two stories. Thom passes her baton from hand to hand, gearing up for battle. Clutching my own baton, I try to remember everything Thom's said about the Ripper. No one knows whether he ravages his victims from a distance with a look or a word, or from close up with a touch. He's killed each of the sixteen with a knife slice to the throat;

I've seen that much with my own eyes. Honestly, it's always seemed like overkill, but now I wonder if it's some sort of sick mercy.

"Ready?" Thom whispers as the elevator car jerks to a halt.

I nod and grit my teeth and think of Grace.

Thaumaturgy bursts to life the moment we set foot outside the elevator: a large blue flame feather burned into the outside of my door. The magical graffiti takes up an entire pane, showering the shag carpet with sparks, threatening to consume my home.

Chapter Ten

Thaumaturge

I wasn't the only one who became magical seemingly overnight.

There was a woman in Galway who popped up briefly on YouTube soon after I took over Twitter. Suddenly she could turn flat water into beer and Perrier into champagne simply by sticking one finger into the drink. There was an ex-solicitor in London who claimed he could dream the future. He proved it by winning an astounding series of Lotto Max draws; his face and winnings record were on the cover of the last issue of the *Daily Mail* we ever had out of the United Kingdom. A family in Kyoto reported that their youngest daughter woke up at dawn the day after Tokyo went black, walked into their backyard, and sang the sun up with the birds—literally, in inhuman, piping song. For a short while, the family posted their daughter's pictures all over Facebook: a tiny, dark-haired figure covered head to shoulders with pigeons, doves, and cuckoos, a goose squatting at her feet. I remember the captions read like some sort of bizarre fairy tale: *Airi and the birds share supper. Airi dances with the swan. Airi swims with spot-billed mallards.*

I also remember that in the pictures, Airi looked miserable. Later the family closed their Facebook account. A few months after, I read somewhere that Airi, robbed of human language in exchange for birdsong, had become a wild, angry creature better kept in a hospital than at home.

The ex-solicitor gave his Lotto winnings to Oxfam and then stepped off Beachy Head in East Sussex. I'm not surprised that whatever he saw in his dreams sent him over the cliff's edge. If I'd known ahead of time what the end of 2020 would bring, I might have done the same.

The granny in Galway opened a pub, called it the Miracle, and was on her way to amassing a healthy fortune before an electromagnetic pulse loosed above Dublin put an end to her YouTube Channel and news stopped coming out of Ireland altogether. Granny looked tough as nails, though, and I like to think she's still at it, turning water into alcohol while the world burns.

In January 2021, there were rumors of a strong man out in Fresno, California, and a kid who could talk to ghosts in Missouri, and another who could spit spider-silk on command, but by then borders were going up across the nation as states seceded or disappeared altogether, and thaumaturgy, as President Shannon hastily labeled our new strangeness, was a far less pressing issue than water rights in California or airspace over Dominion Surry.

My own unusual ability seemed the most frivolous of talents when many of my contemporaries were marching off to war. Tank Tattoo closed in March. In April I bought a fake ID from a forger working out of a truck behind the local Kmart, and over my dad's faint protests took myself three counties over to Idaho Recruitment.

I think my dad knew they wouldn't take me even though the false ID was prime. I didn't look the sixteen I pretended to be; I was small even for my age. I had iron pins in my leg and still walked with a limp. I suffered from dreams of drowning almost every night, and it showed on my face whenever I steeled myself to glance in the bathroom mirror.

When the recruitment officer called my first name and looked from me to my paperwork, I could see from the set of his mouth that I wouldn't get away with it.

"Aren't you that kid?" he said, frowning. "That one I've seen in all those pictures from Seattle?"

"No," I said through a faltering sneer. "I live in Ketchum."

He sighed, shook his head, and passed my paperwork back over the counter. "You know fingerprinting is part of the process, right? Come back when you're sixteen, and bring a doctor's note with you or there's no point. You may live in Ketchum, but I remember your face and the metal sticking out of your leg—Idaho won't draft without a physician's clearance."

I tried Montana next, then Wyoming, but I was too well known. By the time I left Cheyenne, my bad leg was a constant cramp from too much time spent on a Greyhound bus. I was beginning to accept that maybe the draft wasn't for me.

When I walked back through our front door, tired and hungry and sore and heartsick, my dad was reading a week-old addition of the *New York Times* over his dinner. He got up to fetch me pot roast and a glass of red wine, setting his tablet down near his chair. I took his place, rubbing the ache in my thigh, close to tears, and stared dully at the screen. The headlines were all bad, but beneath the wartime bulletins, in a much smaller font, a caption caught my notice: Mind over Medicine! Midtown Youth Heals Hundreds!

"Magical healing," my dad said, setting a plate in front of me and a hand on my head. "Isn't that something? Maybe God's not given up on us after all."

Two days later I purchased a travel visa with my false ID and left Ketchum for Manhattan.

Grace collected peculiarities like I collected art supplies: with unending appetite and an eagerness approaching mania.

"Here's a new one," she'd proclaimed one morning just after we'd moved in together. We were nestled shoulder to shoulder on the floor of the loft I'd just leased on Forty-Sixth, basking in scant winter sunlight through the open windows. Grace's stockinged feet were nestled in my lap; the hardwood floor was uncomfortable beneath my tail bone. Grace was hiding from her shift at her father's gallery. I was busy imagining a future with her at my side.

I was using the paper to shop for mattresses. Grace was using it to track aberrations.

"He's called the Ripper," she said. "They think he might be a serial killer—his victims are starting to pile up." Her shudder was appreciation instead of fear. "God, I love true crime."

"Why makes you think it's a guy?"

"Ninety percent of serial killers are men, you dolt." She rattled a newspaper page. "Also, so far all his vics are in the prime of life. Like, he's got to be strong. He grabs people off the street, cuts their throats, and dumps them in the East River."

"That's not magic; that's just murder." I used a bold red Sharpie to circle an ad for recycled mattresses. I was getting tired of sleeping on a pile of quilts. "And also, 'Ripper' is a stupid name. The real Ripper tore people apart in London alleyways—literally."

"So you *do* know something about true crime." Grace tossed me a swift grin, making me flush right up. "This one turns them into mummies before he dumps them. Like, sucks them dry or something. What's that about? Got to be magic, right? And no one ever sees him do it." She sounded grudgingly impressed. "So far they think it's mostly teenagers, girls and boys. Maybe we should be worried." She nudged me in the ribs with her foot. "If I were the Ripper, I'd think you're a juicy snack."

"Funny. It's still a stupid name." Pausing in my search, I reached for the mug of tea steaming on the floor next to Grace's elbow. "I think I'll need a receptionist. Do I need a receptionist?"

"I think you need a working studio first." Grace removed her feet from my lap and rolled onto her stomach, propping her head on her arms, eyes closed. "You ask me, the pit downstairs doesn't inspire confidence."

"It will," I promised, "when it's finished. People will come from all over just to watch me work."

"I bet that's what the other one said, that healer." Grace wrinkled her nose. "You'll need to be smart, Hemingway, smarter than him. Take the money, do the job, keep your mouth shut. You start spouting off about government interference, and one day you'll wake up on Rikers. I guarantee the mattresses there suck big-time." She sighed. "Take the money, do the job, keep your mouth shut, and we're golden."

Grace knew what she was talking about. The midtown healer my dad so admired—a dramatically inclined, scrawny teen who was called Rutch—hadn't lasted more than four months before he'd been declared a danger to the state and hauled off to prison. In a live, televised statement, the mayor had cited malignant thaumaturgy as the reason for Rutch's imprisonment even though the kid had made a name for himself healing everything from cancer to broken bones to serious war wounds.

It wasn't Rutch's magical healing that got him in trouble; it was his open disdain for the state. Crowds of people attended his laying-on-of-hands in search of a miracle, and Rutch didn't disappoint. But while he performed, he preached. He preached against the grunts patrolling city streets as he fixed an old man's crooked spine. He preached against the make-work policies that kept Manhattan immaculate while he healed a young woman of her lymphoma. He preached against curfew cards and white-painted taxis and the mayor's insistence that we all turn a blind eye to atrocities happening in Jersey while he put an ex-grunt's shattered arm right again.

He thought his newfound fame made him invincible. He was a fool. One day Rutch was all anyone could talk about; the next, no one would say his name for fear of being overheard by the wrong person. Overnight he went from savior to ghost, and no one said a word in protest.

Not long after his disappearance, there was a knock on the studio door. Earnest Ink wasn't in business yet; Grace and I were still putting the place to rights. When I opened the door, I was splattered with paint, irritable from the fumes, and in no mood for interruption.

The woman standing on the sidewalk had long gray hair, an easy smile, and a motorcycle helmet dangling from the fingers of one hand. She was wearing faux-leather pants under an embroidered tunic. I was pretty sure she was old enough to be my grandmother.

"Hemingway?"

"Yeah."

She held out her free hand. "I'm Emma."

"Okay." My hands were covered in paint, so I just stood there.

"Your government-appointed therapist," she said pleasantly. Her eyes darted as she took in my appearance and the state of the construction in the studio behind me. "Emma Thurston."

Grace, struggling with a roll of painter's tape, wandered over to see who was at our door.

"Wow," she said, blinking at the cycle parked on the street outside our door. "Nice ride."

I shook my head, confused. "I have a therapist." I needed a gender therapist to get a prescription for T. I'd looked one up first thing, even before I'd found a place to live.

"You can keep Dr. Brown if you like," the woman on my front step said, meeting my eye again. "I do have some experience in helping patients transition, but my primary function is to monitor your state of mind regarding the Labor Day bombing and any resulting thaumaturgical issues."

"I—" It sounded like nonsense to me. "What?"

"Jesus, Hemingway, you're dense," Grace said. "She's a spook, obviously. They're keeping tabs in case you go rogue like that Rutch guy. Or, you know, do something even worse."

"Yes," my new therapist agreed calmly. "That's right. May I come in?"

Chapter Eleven

Pier 88

Monday morning looks much the same as Saturday and Sunday except the air through my window is twenty degrees cooler and Chopin's rising dramatically from the street below, dispelling dark dreams of saltwater and suffocation.

Groaning, I knuckle sleep from my eyes. Then it hits me.

It's not just Monday. It's Day Two. Two days since Grace went to the Central Park Zoo in search of aspirin and then just...disappeared. And if the chief is right and Jonathon Tremblay's the East River Ripper—

Grace is running out of time.

I jump to my feet, dash across the room, and look down on the street.

It's still early enough in the day that the shops haven't opened, so foot traffic below is light: people on their way to work, heads bowed over their mobile devices, and a few small families hurrying toward the daycare three blocks up. The kids drag their feet and gape at the rolling piano set up directly beneath my window. He's not supposed to be there. His territory is north and west. From their scrunched noses and tears, the kids don't like the change in routine. I can't say I blame them.

I don't make any noise, but Jim immediately switches from opus no. 27, no. 2, to Dire Straits. I like the Knopfler brothers fine, but not when their lyrics are exploited at my expense. I might be a millionaire, but "faggot's" always going to be fighting words in my book. I don't care if the song was written forty years ago and on the other side of the pond.

I slam the casement wide open and stick my head out into thin air.

"Hey, shithead, you're disturbing my peace! Go back to Broadway!"

Jim's back is to me; his piano is blocking the sidewalk. I can see the top of his hat, and the busker's license bobbing in time to the music. His fingers dance along the ivories while his bare feet work the pedals. He's wearing a striped cardigan over his tunic in deference to the change in temperature.

"Broadway's closed to through traffic, haven't you heard? Broadway and Eighth and all the way west to Eleventh. Lockdown, something to do with a chemical spill on the A." Jim doesn't stop playing, but he does drift into something quieter in a gentler key. I don't recognize the music. It makes me think of childhood and carousels. "Closed all day long, I hear. Don't imagine you'll be getting much business today, Hemingway. They've put up bollards. Saw your receptionist stopped at the checkpoint. Suppose it will be a while before he convinces them to let him past."

"How'd you make it through, then?" The cool air is as good as heaven on my scraped face. I close my eyes and breathe it in, fighting for calm.

"I have my ways." He stops playing, pausing to crack his knuckles. "Thing is, I won't be getting any business, either. Not with the streets shut down. Yesterday was slow. Sunday and all." He sounds pained. "A junkie like me's got needs."

"You're kidding. You set up under my window because you need a fix?" I remember Miksail and his cardboard boxes full of sealed vials.

He doesn't deny it. "So would the rest of the lot if I didn't keep them off. Every tweaker, crackhead, and huffer this side of Madison Avenue. Crying and screaming and begging for a handout or an old-fashioned magical healing. I do you a solid, kid. I keep the riffraff away. Now do me a solid in return."

I squint down at his upturned smile. "That sounds an awful lot like blackmail, Jim." He might be lying. Hell, he's probably lying, but what if he's not?

Until last night, I naïvely assumed I was safe in my home, protected by fame and fortune. I'd been living in a bubble of my own making. I'd worked hard to build that bubble, foolishly assuming acquired wealth would protect me and mine from the life's little atrocities.

I'd been so stupid.

"Jesus Christ, Jim, get some help." But I leave the window and find my wallet where I left it in yesterday's jeans. I lean back out the window and empty the billfold. Twenties flutter in the air like oversized confetti. Two preschoolers stop and point. A woman with a briefcase in hand and headphones clamped over her ears grabs one of the bills casually from the air before walking on, unfazed.

The other five belong to Jim. He rescues them from the pavement as gingerly as if they were glass instead of synthetic fiber.

"Nice doing business with you, Hemingway."

I slam down the casement on Gershwin's "Rhapsody in Blue."

The main room's deserted, and from the state of it, I guess Thom's still on shift. She was reluctant to leave me alone, but I assured her I'd be just fine.

Tremblay's feather last night was an impressive display, and also creepy as shit. I stamped out sparks while Thom cleared the apartment and then hustled out mugfuls of water which we used to douse the magic flame before it set the whole building ablaze. As for Tremblay, it seemed he'd left the way he came: completely unnoticed.

The apartment still stinks of smoke and singed carpet. No wonder I dreamed I couldn't get enough air.

Thom's futon is neatly made, her uniform missing from its hook on the wall. The unwashed dishes in the kitchen sink are all mine. I spare my overworked roommate a second of pity before I strip off my boxers and make for the communal bathroom, intent on washing the reek of flame from my hair and skin.

I like my showers hot and sweet-smelling, exactly the way I like my tea.

I lock the door, cranking up the water pressure until the small room fills with steam. Then I stand under the showerhead and let the water pound my neck and shoulders. If I slit my eyes just right and look at my toes, everything else blurs—the white tile, Thom's scarlet loofah stuck to the shower wall by way of a clear plastic suction cup, the chunk of mud-colored organic soap we use for body and hair, my small breasts, and beneath my chest, the more masculine planes of my abdomen and thighs, a product of four years on T, a lifetime of obsessively counting calories, and a regular exercise regimen.

The scar on my left leg where metal pierced my muscle, cracked my femur, and almost took my life is in the shape of a star, ridged and white.

I watch the water splashing around my toes until the shower runs cold, then scrub myself all over with peony-scented soap, carefully avoiding the tender knife punctures in my front and back, before toweling off. I have to wipe fog off the mirror with the palm of my hand before I can shave. My shave oil is vetiver to match the gel I put in my hair. I guide my razor carefully around the new-forming scab on my chin and decide I can do without sealant. I brush my teeth with enthusiasm, spitting three times for luck before I wrap myself in a towel and exit the bathroom, chased by a cloud of flowery steam.

My gut's full of acid, but I force down a bowl of cereal and milk and a wedge of apple for the sake of healthy calories. Emma would be proud. Standing in boxers and my compression tank at the kitchen counter, I chew each bite carefully, and stare across the room at the faces of the dead tacked to Thom's murder wall.

There's no way in hell I'm going to let the Ripper add Grace to his collection.

I finish breakfast, add bowl and spoon to the pile of dishes in the kitchen sink, and get dressed. I slide the CEW baton up my sleeve. It's awkward, but it's safe from prying eyes. A military weapon is not the sort of thing any private citizen should have. The fact that I'm flagged for thaumaturgy makes carrying the baton doubly dangerous.

Before I leave the studio, I take Eric's pepper spray from the drawer of the register and slip it into the pocket of the black faux-leather jacket I've thrown on for warmth. I hesitate over the butterfly knife but leave it behind. The stolen pepper spray he might forgive, but the knife belonged to a war buddy, and Eric has a sentimental attachment to it.

I'll be in enough trouble as it is when Thom gets home and realizes I've lit out despite enduring fifteen minutes of stern admonitions the night before to stay put.

On the one hand, I hate to break a promise, but on the other, I don't have time to waste.

For camouflage, I make do with a pair of funky blue-lensed shades one of my clients left behind and a nondescript knitted cap pulled down over my ears.

It's a beautiful day outside. The heat wave of the past few months has finally broken. Overnight leaves have turned from green to gold, and a thin layer of early morning frost sparkles on windowpanes and the tops of A/C units. The nip of fall should be exhilarating; it's my favorite time of the year. But instead of stopping to admire fresh autumn flowers planted before dawn by an industrious sweeper, I put my head down and walk fast.

When I reach Twelfth, I can smell the salty Hudson and see the roof of the old cruise terminal. I head north, backtracking. Pier 88 is easily detectable for the multilevel concrete parking deck, reams of sagging chain-link fence, and the large, faded letters proclaiming: Manhattan Cruise Terminal.

The mayor closed the waters off Manhattan to cruise ships about the same time our rivers became a refuge to evacs trying to flee New Jersey for safer shores. Too many people were killed in the crossing, sucked into turbines as the gigantic ships tried to maneuver into port, or swamped in their massive wake. Manslaughter isn't good for business. The cruise lines soon stopped scheduling travel along the Eastern Seaboard, but I think most of that had to do with Coastal Virginia's pirate infestation and the unpredictable cannon fire off Myrtle Beach.

Sea travel just isn't as safe as it once was. Plus the cost of arming cruise ships priced tickets completely out of the average tourist's budget.

The fence surrounding Pier 88 is there to keep vagrants out. It's ten feet high and topped with razor wire, but it's also chain link—a cheap solution to an expensive problem. Chain link can be cut or climbed or torn off metal posts. I think the fence was meant to be a temporary fix while the city was still regaining its feet, but by the time Manhattan was more or less under control and the city planners came for the Pier with jackhammers and demolition equipment, the street punks were well established in their cement warren near the water, and no one, not even the mayor and a small army of grunts, could manage to dig them out.

Maybe if they weren't children, it would have been different. Maybe the city would have gone ahead and dynamited the old parking structure. Paved it over, mixing corpses with cement, a monument to futility. But for the most part, Pier 88 is run entirely by street rats: local kids displaced when one or both of their parents went off to fight along the Continental Divide, and teenaged draft-dodgers who would rather battle the mayor than die away from home. They're wily and dangerous and loyal only to themselves, but they're children, Manhattan's children.

By unspoken agreement the city agreed to let Pier 88 be. The chain-link fence has slowly fallen into disrepair, beaten into submission by the comings and goings of its young inhabitants, only to be reinforced from the other side as the street punks work to keep the rest of the city out. They've lined the chain link with salvaged cardboard and plywood, tacked up stolen builders' wrap, hung plastic shower curtains from the top. No one walking Twelfth can see behind the fence, not even the soldiers whose duty it is to stand across the street and keep an eye out for mischief.

As I approach the corner of Fifty-First Street, a cold wind blows off the river, rattling the fence, making shower curtains billow. I shiver, pulling my jacket tight. The two grunts lingering across from the terminal wear weatherproof jackets over their vests and black balaclavas around their necks, another sign that autumn has finally arrived. They're sharing a cigarette with a lanky figure wearing jeans and a bulky wool sweater, passing it in a circle, puffing eagerly.

I know that lanky figure. I remember the painful squeeze of his hand on my shoulder, the prick of his knife against my spine. I've seen his shadow behind Christy Spears on a CCTV snap. And he haunted my dreams overnight.

I stop walking, but too late. The ongoing blockade Jim mentioned means that Twelfth Avenue is empty except for me, a kid digging in sweepers' bins for aluminum cans, and an orange cat watching the sidewalk from atop a parked car.

The grunts turn my way. Tremblay swivels to look, cigarette hanging from his mouth. When he sees me, he stops slouching and straightens to his full height. He says something to the soldiers before dropping his cigarette on the pavement, grinding it beneath the heel of his boot. Then he heads my way, long legs rapidly eating up sidewalk.

I think about running. I know retreat is the best choice. My heart leaps into my throat. My knees feel like rubber. I'm terrified and I hate it.

Instead of running away, I slip my hand into the pocket of my jacket and palm Eric's pepper spray. The CEW baton is a solid reassurance under my sleeve. I clench my jaw to keep my teeth from chattering and widen my stance for balance the way my dad taught me when I was thirteen and finally ready to teach Brian Bobbet a lesson about bullying.

Tremblay's tall as houses and corded with muscle and probably the city's most infamous serial killer, but I'm not going to let him knock me over ever again.

He slows to a stop about four feet away, too far away for a fist to the nose but within pepper-spray range. I paste on my fiercest smile.

"What are you doing here?" Cigarette smoke makes his voice rough. Today his glitter paint is pink and orange, a rosy blushing sunset that doesn't quite manage to cover the purple bruise down the right side of his face.

Emma's orchid did me proud.

"I'm looking for Grace," I answer coldly, fingers wrapped around the pepper spray. Despite my backwoods upbringing, I've never shot anyone with anything before, and up until now I've been proud to say so. I'm ready to make an exception for Jonathon Tremblay. "Where is she?"

"I'm sorry? Grace? *Je ne te comprend pas.*" He leans toward me, a sapling bending the wrong way against the wind. He's all sharp angles, with a proud nose he hasn't yet grown into over a petulant mouth. "Today's Monday—" He turns his wrist, looking dramatically at the watch Eric assumed meant wealth. "—my note said Tuesday. You're a day early, magic man."

"Your pathetic doodle on my door says otherwise, *Jonathon*," I reply, still showing my teeth. "You wanted my attention, you've got it. Now take me to Grace, you colossal psychopath, before I kick your scrawny ass."

The knife is in his hand again like he plucked it from thin air. The blade glints. Just the sight of it makes me feel sick. I bite my tongue to keep from flinching, take my hand from my coat pocket, and aim Eric's pepper spray at his face.

"Try it. I'll pump your eyes so full of this crap, you'll be blind for a month."

The grunts take notice. They meander slowly our direction. I suspect they've shared more than a few friendly smokes with Tremblay. I wonder if they could possibly know what sort of monster he is. It seems unlikely.

"You're a sensitive prick." His brow crinkles in disbelief. "You mad I roughed you up some? Shit, Hemingway, I'd say you evened the score with your stupid flowerpot." He snorts, flips his little knife from one hand to the other. Flame licks along the blade, wreathing metal in cobalt. He's showing off. "Relax. I was just doing my job."

I let loose a burst of pepper spray a few inches to the right. It splatters on the sidewalk. Tremblay winces. He steps back. The grunts walk faster, calling out.

"Sir! The use of aerosol products is prohibited—"

I squeeze the trigger again, hard. This time the spray wets both Tremblay's boots and the pavement in front of the soldiers. Swearing, the grunts reach for their weapons. Heart pounding in my throat, I shake my sleeve and let the butt of the CEW rest in the palm of my hand.

A shrill whistle splits the air, startling all four of us. The sound comes from the kid collecting cans with the grocery cart. The soldiers turn their heads. Tremblay and

I don't. We're engaged in a game of chicken, both of us refusing to blink. I don't know what he sees on my face, but I'm almost certain the curl of his mouth is confusion, and that only makes me madder.

"Tremblay," the kid warbles. "Seraphine says quit messing around and bring him in."

"He's early," Tremblay retorts without breaking eye contact. "The note said Tuesday, noon." His smile stretches. "Or can't you read, *toton*?"

The final burst of pepper spray surprises him. Maybe he didn't think I had the balls. The liquid catches him midchest. He recoils, covering his bruised face with his hands, spitting French profanity. He's startled, not hurt. The chemical hasn't touched his skin, not yet. I mean to change that, but before I can take better aim, the first of the grunts piles on, wrestling the canister from my hand and wrenching my arms behind my back. I stand rigid in one soldier's grasp while her partner pulls a zip tie restraint from her belt.

"Listen." I squirm, keeping the baton up my sleeve and away from grasping hands. "You don't understand. He's a killer! He's the honest-to-shit East River Ripper, and he's got my best friend! Let me go!"

I try the reverse headbutt move I used on Thom, but the grunt slithers away before the back of my skull connects with his helmet.

"Sir," she tries again, breathless with exertion, "the use of aerosol products is prohibited in the state of New York." Her partner tightens the plastic around my wrists. "Personal self-defense merchandise is prohibited in the state of New York. The use of force with intent to harm is—"

We're interrupted again, this time by the scrape of metal on cement.

A gate in the fence line is opening, a panel on rusty wheels. The wheels drag instead of roll, making an unpleasant racket that echoes in the quiet street. The panel opens just enough to let a single figure through.

It takes me a second to realize I know her.

It's Bee Girl, my giggly client from Friday, but she's not laughing anymore.

She's holding a 12-gauge shotgun in clearly capable hands, pointing it our way.

"Thank you," she tells the grunts, sweet as black-market sugar. "I'll take it from here."

Chapter Twelve

Seraphine

The gate rattles as it closes behind me. A boy in dirty sandals, sagging shorts, and a grunt's helmet secures it to the fence line by looping one of those old titanium bike locks several times through chain link and snapping it. The helmet's way too large for his head. It keeps falling over his forehead while he works.

"Hello, Hemingway," Bee Girl says. She cradles the shotgun against her chest one-handed with the ease of someone comfortable with firearms. I've seen my father in the same pose plenty of times. Her face is wiped clean of glitter paint; her copper-colored hair is pulled back in a knot. She's swapped the fashionable kit she wore in my chair for a long, loose dress covered all over with an eye-popping geometric print.

Without all the face paint, she looks closer to fifteen than eighteen.

"The curfew card I gave your receptionist was jacked," she confesses calmly, reading the dismay in my eyes. "Sorry about that, but I needed to see for myself if you could do what you promise." She tilts her head. "Tremblay, cut him free."

Tremblay glides up behind me. I can't help snarling. He ignores me, efficient with the knife, careful not to touch my flesh. The zip ties fall, and he steps quickly away.

I massage my wrists, making sure the CEW is safely out of sight while I take a slow look around. My pulse is still beating in my ears, adrenaline pumping.

"We expected you tomorrow," Bee Girl continues, watching me closely. "Or I would have been outside to greet you myself."

Tremblay's moved to stand protectively behind her. His shirt is wet where I nailed him in the chest with the pepper spray. I hope it's soaked through, that his skin is burning underneath. He grins at me, showing even, white teeth. It feels like a threat. It *is* a threat.

He grabs people off the street, cuts their throats, and dumps them in the East River.

I look away.

Pier 88 is a multi-terraced cement village at their backs. An elaborate shantytown sprung up where not long ago cars and trucks parked while awaiting their owners' return from adventures in cruising. Nylon tents, refrigerator boxes, plywood lean-tos, and narrow compartments with stained mattresses for walls crowd the ground and second levels. Blankets and more shower curtains hang in places from above, presumably to provide some measure of privacy or to keep the weather out. A makeshift network of rope ladders and construction scaffolding runs the length of the pier and then from top to bottom, providing a complicated, suspended footpath between levels.

An assemblage of street punks cling to the rope ladders or balance on the scaffolding, blatantly observing my entrance. More kids peer down from the third level, where cargo containers are stacked one atop the next, four high, and pushed wall to wall until they form a mountain so imposing I worry the parking structure might collapse beneath the weight of all that metal.

"If you needed a touch-up," I say at last, trying for nonchalant, "I only do those in studio. You'll have to make an appointment with my receptionist."

Tremblay snorts. Bee Girl shushes him. More punks are emerging from the shadows of the pier, gathering on the sun-drenched pavement—fifteen, then twenty, then twenty-five. I try to count heads on the levels above, but there are too many. The place is crammed with kids.

Another cold gust rolls off the river and through the parkade, making the ramshackle village rustle and moan.

"Will you come inside?" Bee Girl inquires politely. "It's finally turned to autumn, and I prefer to do business out of the wind."

"I'm waiting for a battalion of soldiers to blow through your front gate," I retort. "You kidnapped me off the street in broad daylight, in view of at least six cameras, and carrying an actual shotgun. By now those two grunts will have alerted every person who matters between here and the mayor himself."

"Oh," she says with what sounds like honest regret, "those two work for me. As does the surveillance captain in charge of logging the cameras you saw, and also five more CCTV focused on our front door that are, naturally, hidden from street view." She puffs her cheeks, then exhales. "No witnesses, I'm afraid, and no battalion of soldiers storming my front gate."

My heart has stopped thumping, but adrenaline is making my hands shake. I'm equal parts terrified and furious, and I know neither emotion looks good on me.

"Jesus, look at that, he's gone white as pudding," Tremblay scoffs. "I told you he wasn't worth our time. This is no hero, *ma chérie*. This is a coward. It's clear as day on his face. Send him off." He flaps a hand like he's shooing away an exceptionally obnoxious mosquito.

I scowl, affronted. "I'd rather be a coward than a murderer. That's some nasty bruising on your own mug, asshole. Matches your ugly-ass hair dye."

Tremblay puts a hand to his swollen cheek. He starts forward, furious, but Bee Girl deftly blocks his way. For a moment, the only sound on our side of the fence is the wind off the Hudson. Then, high up on the scaffolding, someone laughs. It's a little kid's giggle, unexpected and endearing.

Honest joy is the rarest of all scarce commodities in the city, and you can't buy it on Sunday from a black-market peddler, no matter how much cash you carry. I stare upward, a knee-jerk reaction, and I glimpse grudging smiles on more than a few young faces.

"I think you deserve that," Bee Girl tells her fuming companion. Then she shoulders her shotgun and turns toward the pier. "Come inside, Hemingway. There's no point in running—you won't get far. Besides, we have so much to discuss. Max," she orders a lingering child, "run ahead. Have Livvy dig out tea...or, no, root beer. My friend," she beams at me around the gun, "do you like root beer?"

Without waiting for my answer, she waves me ahead, following close on my heels, directing me across the tarmac toward a row of shipping containers set up on the north side of the parkade. They're on ground level, and I'm grateful, because as we approach the pier, the network of rope and scaffolding attached to the building begins to seem less clever and more intimidating. Kids of all ages hang from the structure like spiders on a web. Some of them look much too small to be walking, let alone climbing. Others are obviously verging on adulthood— draft-dodgers or deserters or, like me, people excused from service for reasons mental and physical.

It was the shrapnel in my leg that exempted me from the front lines. Grace escaped by way of indefinite deferment thanks to her father's money and a few well-placed family connections. Thom had nothing so convenient as a bad leg or old money to give her an out. Most New Yorkers don't.

Unlike their smaller companions, the older kids aren't smiling. I can feel the weight of their distrust as they gaze down at me from on high. Their faces are inscrutable, glitter paint camouflaging emotion. They're a motley crew, dressed in anything from leather and lace to denim kilts and cotton tunics, tight satin bustiers and tatty cotton pajamas. They remind me of the flock of Monsanto-engineered peacocks I met walking the White House lawn: suspicious, unfriendly, and unnaturally colorful.

There's plenty of illicit hardware on display for my benefit, mostly in the form of bright blades and knuckle-dusters. One girl on the ground level has an actual sword strapped to her back. She glowers from beneath a fringe of pink hair as we pass, then follows a few paces behind.

It's small comfort, but the only gun I see is the 12-gauge propped on Seraphine's shoulder.

The outside of the nearest cargo container is rusty but clean. A group of ankle-biters are playing in a bucket of water outside the door. They goggle at me and whisper behind their damp hands, game forgotten. As we step up into the container, I notice the string of number and letters stenciled on metal above their heads: CAXU3056743.

Inside the shipping container, there's real root beer in three brown glass bottles, A&W labels still attached, set out on an unsteady card table covered in a cheerful paisley sheet. I haven't seen honest-to-goodness soda since before I left Idaho. I hear Dr Pepper's still manufactured in small batches out of Texas, but the average Manhattanite can't get it down at the corner shop anymore. It's not just the skyrocketing cost of sugar pricing it out of reach; it's the impracticality of shipping large quantities of anything cross country since the Midwest descended into anarchy.

Wildflowers are blooming in a paper cup in the middle of the table, next to a bowl of oranges. Two chairs at the table, also unsteady, are also dressed up with paisley fabric. A patterned rug underneath adds to the country-cozy ambiance. A narrow mattress rests a few feet beyond the table, covered with colorful toss pillows. A small crystal chandelier hangs from the ceiling over the table. The bulbs aren't on, so I can't tell by looking whether it's been added for function or style. Either way, it's an over-the-top accessory, seeing as how we're standing in the claustrophobic confines of a windowless metal box.

At least it's warmer out of the wind.

"Real Florida oranges," Bee Girl says, waving me toward one of the wobbly, fabric-covered chairs. "Crate came off one of the mayor's barges in the storm, and my scouts snagged it before Port noticed. Don't be afraid. Sit."

She takes the second chair herself, perching on the edge, shotgun laid across her skirted knees. "We weren't properly introduced first time around. I'm sorry for that. My name is Seraphine."

Tremblay and the girl with the sword have set up in front of the exit, standing elbow to elbow, disagreeable sentries.

I sit, taking the bottle of root beer Seraphine passes across the table. The lid's a twist off, and when it pops, a fine mist hangs for a moment in the air, smelling of sassafras. The first sip is like finally scratching that itch on the bottom of your foot that's been bugging you for twenty minutes because you're standing on the subway and can't reach the right spot through your shoe.

I don't think of the calories more than twice.

I won't pay two dollars for a stick of gum, but if I could get soda with real sugar on the black market, I'd probably blow all of my fortune.

"Was this on the mayor's barge, too?" I ask when my tongue stops tingling.

"No." Seraphine smiles. "These are special. We have five bottles. They're all yours, Hemingway, if you want. As a thank-you."

"A thank-you for what, exactly?" I smile right back. Neither of us mean it. "Your money was good. That's all the thanks I need. And although aggravated assault in a Bowling Green alley is a felony, the root beer almost makes up for it. Harboring a serial killer, on the other hand, is just not right."

Her smile crumples. "I don't know what you mean."

"Where's Grace?" I look past her at Tremblay. "I'm not interested in whatever sadistic game you think you're playing. Just give me my friend, and maybe I won't cut off your dick and cram it down your throat."

"Big words from a little man," Tremblay says. "You got a knife on you, eh? Because that baton you think you've got hidden in your coat isn't much use against someone like me."

"Who's Grace?" the girl with the sword on her back demands. "What's he talking about?"

Tremblay sighs and spreads his hands. I notice his blade has once again disappeared. "*Comment savoir*? How should I know? He was going on and on about the Ripper before he shot me in the chest with illegal personal self-defense merchandise." His mouth turns down at the corners in self-pitying moue.

I spring from my chair, almost overturning it in the process. "You stuck a knife in my back, threatened to make me a paraplegic, and called me a dumbass in French. Also, you broke my flower."

"You smashed it over my head!" It's not quite a howl, but it's close.

"You've been following me for days and hanging around my best friend. Now she's gone missing, and you're not fooling me, *toton*." I spit his own insult back at him with venom. "Central knows you're the Ripper. They know what you did to Christy Spears. They've got you on tape."

He crosses his arms over his chest. "I don't know what you're talking about."

"Sit down." Seraphine waves her hand. "Charlie, please help Hemingway back into his chair." Pink-haired girl rights my chair and glares until I relent and sit. Seraphine scrutinizes Tremblay over my shoulder. From the way her jaw flexes, she doesn't like whatever she sees.

"Jonathon's no killer," she says. "I'm sorry about your friend—Grace, is it?—but you've got the wrong idea. This city's been working to put Jonathon down for treason since he was fifteen. If the mayor wants to peg him for the Ripper, he's welcome to try, but it won't stick. You're making a mistake, Hemingway."

"I saw the tape. You and Spears in Morningside Park minutes before she vanished. And I've got a witness says you were chatting up Grace in Central Park Sunday morning—the same day *she* disappeared." The A&W has curdled behind my ribcage.

"I don't know Christy Spears except from the papers," Tremblay insists. "And, yeah, I like to walk a bit in the mornings when I can't sleep. I spend some time in Morningside; that's not a crime. I don't remember seeing her there." He flicks a quick, abashed glance Seraphine's way, then turns back to me. "I hung around some with your actor friend, but that was because of you. Gathering info, first, to see if you were the real thing. And then, hey—" He shrugs, Gallic and graceful. "—I liked her, okay. She's funny. She invited me to breakfast at the zoo, because she had to pick up something from the peddler for her old man. We were supposed to hang again Monday night after work, but she never showed. I didn't know she'd gone missing, honest to God. It has nothing to do with me."

In the resulting silence, I select an orange from the bowl just so I have something to do with my hands. I roll it against my palm, inhaling citrus. In that moment I hate Tremblay. I want to call bullshit, if only because the world seemed a little bit more tolerable when I thought I knew where Grace was, but the expression on his face is open, pained, like he needs me to believe him and not because he's afraid of being strung up from the mayor's front gates.

"If Central really thinks Jonathon's the notorious Ripper," Seraphine says softly, "why is he still walking around free? I promise you, Hemingway, they know exactly where to find us. It's no secret what's left of Rutch's following has taken up residence here, with me, on the Pier." She pats the barrel of the gun laid across her skirted knees.

"You weren't supposed to tell him that part," Tremblay mutters, startling me back to the present and the orange in my hand.

"I think these are unusual circumstances," Seraphine retorts. She's probably two years his junior, but she acts like she's scolding a favorite child. "Don't you?"

Tremblay walks around behind her chair so he's within my line of sight, but out of range of my fists. In the flowery setting, his lanky body seems even more awkward. He's taller than the chandelier, crowded by the container's low ceiling. His fingers flex on the back of Seraphine's chair. For a minute, he looks as guileless as he did when he first walked into Earnest Ink and asked, *Does it hurt?*

"I'm sorry," Tremblay says to me, again. "About Grace."

I set down the orange. I've peeled it halfway without even noticing.

"I don't give a shit about your difficulties with the mayor. The two of you were working together Friday." I hadn't given it much thought until just now. My skull had been full only of Grace. "What's the scam?"

"No scam," Seraphine promises. "I told you; I needed to see if you could really do what they said. Thaumaturgy is a tricky thing. Tremblay was there in case anything went wrong."

"Went wrong?" I let her see my skepticism. "It's a tattoo. I didn't notice either of you checking my autoclave for proper sterilization."

"Show him," Tremblay says flatly. "*Mon dieu*. I'm tired of this dance. Do it."

The dress Seraphine's wearing is high-necked, ruffled under her chin, run top to waist with small pearl buttons. It's very 1999 prairie chic. Eric would approve.

She unbuttons the front one-handed until things almost become uncomfortable, then pulls away the fabric, baring her collarbone and a tantalizing glimpse of white bra.

"I wasn't sure how long it would take," she tells me. "I've found drinking alcohol with my magic delays the change some, but I wasn't sure I'd had enough wine."

It takes me a moment to see. Then I gasp and recoil.

I'd inked her bumble bee in black and yellow, striped and fat, and when I finished, it was a whimsical archetype buzzing a few inches above her delicate clavicle. Art, animated. An outlandish accessory, an exotic talking point, magical and one of a kind. People pay good money for individuality.

It isn't that anymore. Black and yellow, yes, striped and fat. But no longer a stylistic rendering, and definitely not my design. The hornet squatting on Seraphine's shoulder is to my bumble bee as a wolf is to a Boston Terrier. It looks more solid than any of my other creations, capable of casting a shadow if we stepped out into the sunlight, capable of falling to a judicious swat.

I lean forward.

The hornet buzzes angrily as it lifts from Seraphine's collarbone. It flies a dizzying circle around the cargo container, making Charlie and Tremblay duck, before alighting once more on Seraphine's cheek, still humming furiously.

"What the hell is that?"

Seraphine reaches a fingertip up and strokes the length of the hornet's back, light as an air kiss. Its wings flutter, and the buzzing quiets.

"Yours and mine, Hemingway," she says. "Our creation. You gave it life; I gave it a boost."

"*That* has nothing to do with me. What I do is art. There's nothing pretty about that abomination."

"You planted the seed; I helped it grow into something better, something more. Let me show you. Jonathon?" She takes up my half-peeled orange, holds it out on her palm. Then she sets it on the middle of the table, near the wildflowers.

Tremblay presses his pointer finger to the crown of the orange. A small cobalt flame kindles, catches fire, smokes pungently as the flesh begins to burn blue. It's like one of those flambéed apples you used to see in fancy restaurants, only it stinks of smoked citrus.

"Are you watching?" Seraphine asks.

Before I can answer, she closes her eyes. A wrinkle appears on her forehead above her nose. Charlie takes a large step backward toward the door. Tremblay visibly braces.

Seraphine exhales.

The small flame bursts into an inferno, an arcing blue torch that touches the container ceiling and makes the rope holding the chandelier start to smoke. The wildflowers go up in a rush of flame; the table cover quickly catches. Bits of orange pulp smolder on the carpet, and then the carpet's burning, too, a small blue wildfire, spreading. Seraphine rises quickly to her feet, clutching the shotgun to her chest. The hornet is circling madly about her head.

I jump up from the table and away.

Blue fire races across the rug toward the mattress. The table's ablaze, a pyre.

"Out!" Tremblay grabs my elbow and shoves me toward the open end of the container. "Out, hurry!"

We tumble into safety, one after another, chased by smoke and tongues of blue flame. Tremblay slams the container doors shut behind us, heaving the locking bars into place. Charlie empties a bucket of water over the bottom of Seraphine's dress, putting out tiny cobalt fires. The hornet, infuriated, stings whatever bare flesh it can find within reach. Neither Seraphine nor Charlie slap it away, although Charlie muffles a sound of pain when it lands on her jaw.

She retreats, taking the empty bucket with her.

"Were you watching?" Seraphine asks me, breathing hard, while sting-welts rise on her face and neck. The hornet, calming at last, settles in her ponytail. "Did you see? I made it more—I made it better!"

There's a wildness in her expression that's too close to desperation, and I don't dare disagree out loud.

Smoke is billowing from seams in the cargo container in black clouds. It smells acrid. As I back away, hoping the thing's fireproof, three teens appear from beneath the shadows of the Pier carrying red fire extinguishers. They shoo the younger kids back and begin spraying the container up and down with retardant.

"That was only a demonstration." Seraphine strolls away from the commotion, expecting me to follow. Tremblay looms behind me, making sure I do. "Of what we might accomplish, working together."

"A wasp and a wildfire?" I cough, trying to clear smoke from my lungs. "I think I'll stick to ink. Safer. Less...totally insane."

She's leading me toward the parkade, but there's no way I'm walking right into their lair. I turn away at the last second, striding instead toward the gate in the fence. Tremblay jumps to block my way. Serious déjà vu, my forehead to his chin, only this time he doesn't draw the knife.

"Out of my way, creeper." I press my advantage, reaching. "I warned you: I'll take your dick off."

He blocks my hand, squeezing my fingers until bones grind. "First rule of self-defense: don't explain, just do." He squeezes harder. I stare at his chin until my eyes blur, but I refuse to back off. We breathe in sync.

Then I bring my knee up, quick and vicious.

He's too tall and I'm too short to do much good. He feints out of reach before I connect. Then he's back, blocking my way, and the gate is not any closer.

"Hemingway," Seraphine whispers in my ear. She's drifted up behind me. "The only difference between you and me is a cute little girl in a pink tutu and a photo gone viral." The hornet buzzes. Tiny legs tickle the back of my neck. "You're not exceptional at all."

"What do you want?" She's probably right—I'm less than exceptional—but I refuse to let her see she's hit a nerve. "All this—what do you want from me?"

"Only another tattoo, that's all." Her voice is sweet as molasses against the shell of my ear. "I've designed it myself; it's very unique." She sighs happily. "I'll make it worth your while, I promise."

"Kid." I shake my head, praying I don't earn a venomous sting. "Thanks to that viral photo, your money is not something I need."

"Not cash." Seraphine moves away, but Tremblay's still a wall at my front. Out of the corner of my eye, the girl with the sword closes in. "Although I admit that's what I had in mind at first. But now I see you're in need of my help as well. I'm not without connections in this city. Your friend is missing. I've no love for tragedy—I've seen enough loss to last a lifetime. Let me help you find her, your friend."

Shock makes me wrench around.

"I can find her for you," Seraphine pledges, practically vibrating with excitement. "My pack runs wild on this island. I have eyes and ears in places you'd never imagine, sources even the mayor can't imagine. If I want something or someone found"—she cocks her head to one side—"it happens."

She's not telling me the whole truth—I can practically smell deceit on her—but I want to believe her; I'm that desperate.

"Okay." It's my turn to get in her face, whisper in her ear. "Tell you what. Send your little Baker Street Irregulars out. They find Grace, then we'll talk favors. But right now, I'm done with you. I'm not listening to any more of this, and you can bet your ass I'm not leaving Grace's fate in your hands. I've got things to do. Now. Let. Me. Out."

The last is said over my shoulder, because I'm already walking away.

This time they don't chase me. Tremblay stands carefully out of reach, and even the spooky hornet stops buzzing around my head. It takes everything in me to keep from running toward that blue-wrapped gate, but I win the battle of nerves and manage a casual walk.

The kid in the grunt's helmet pops the bike lock and opens the gate.

I keep walking. I don't look back or around at the two grunts watching me from the other side of the street. One of them must still have Eric's pepper spray. He's going to be pissed that I lost it. And Thom's going to be pissed I snuck off without a word of warning or explanation after she made me promise not to.

As far as I'm concerned, the morning has been a total waste of time. Grace is still gone, and I'm pretty sure the one lead I thought I had just went up in smoke. Because Seraphine has a point—if Central really thinks Jonathon Tremblay is the East River Ripper, why's the punk still walking around free?

The wind off the Hudson sneaks under my coat and along my spine, so cold it numbs.

I wish I knew what to do next.

Chapter Thirteen

Assumptions

Emma's buttering a blueberry scone when I arrive, a tall glass of bubbled water garnished with lemon next to her plate. There are yellow orchid blooms among the white. I order green tea and wait while the barista makes it, trying to school emotion off my face. I haven't replaced my lost travel mug, so I take my tea to our table in one of the café's pottery mugs. I slouch, turning the mug between my hands. Emma pushes a yogurt parfait in my direction.

"Hello, Hemingway," she says. Her gray hair is up in a bun on the top of her head. Long turquoise earrings dangle from her earlobes. "I'm so glad you made it. When you called, I was concerned." Her cheeks dimple. "I don't think I've ever heard from you between sessions before."

I drop into the chair across from her. "Thanks for coming. You know, on short notice or whatever. I guess you're pretty busy."

"Not too busy for you," she promises. I can feel her assessing me as I sip steaming tea. Probably she can see things I'd rather she didn't, like guilt and anxiety and not enough sleep. "What happened to your face?"

I keep forgetting I'm wearing evidence of assault on my skin. I seize the opening with gratitude, launching into an abbreviated version of my kidnapping turned brawl, Grace's disappearances, and Central's interest in

Jonathon Tremblay. I leave out Tremblay's pyrotechnics and Seraphine's wacky thaumaturgy.

It's not that I feel I owe Tremblay or Seraphine my protection, but as far as I'm concerned Emma's as much witch-hunter as head-shrinker, and no matter how much I'm prepared to dislike Seraphine and her knife-wielding enforcer, I'm no Salem turncoat.

I hope Emma takes some of my hesitation for residual shock. Which she seems to, reaching across the table to squeeze my hand in sympathy. A lump rises in my throat, surprising me. I swallow a mouthful of tea too quickly. The hot liquid burns my tongue, making my eyes water. Emma takes the tears for distress.

"I'm so sorry, Hemingway," my therapist says gently. "What a terrible thing. How are you handling it?"

"Fine, okay. Eating"—because that's what she'll want to know first—"working, dreaming." I pause, because surely, she'll expect me to be affected. "I dreamed last night."

I don't have to say more. There's only one dream we ever talk about, only one dream that stays with me when I wake. Emma thinks I dream of drowning when I'm feeling especially overwhelmed by life. I think I dream of drowning because I grew up in Ketchum, Idaho, and never learned to swim.

Emma releases my hand and leans back in her chair. I dip a spoon into yogurt and nibble.

"I'm glad you called," she continues, switching from tender to brisk, friend to counselor. "Something like a mugging, Hemingway... Well, it makes sense that new violence might remind you of the old."

"Nobody got blown up," I point out. "Nobody died. It's not the same as Labor Day."

"Of course not," she agrees. She starts to say something else, then changes her mind, watching instead as I make a show of enjoying the yogurt. Probably I'm overdoing it because a wrinkle appears above her nose.

"We know your dream tends to reoccur in times of stress," she reminds me. "A mugging is certainly a stressful event." She returns to her scone, concentrating on scooping churned butter from the little café pot. "A troubled friend, too. Whether Grace is actually in danger or not, you're bracing yourself for loss. It's natural you're feeling very overwhelmed."

"You don't think Grace is in danger?"

Emma looks up, catches me staring in disbelief around a mouthful of yogurt. I gulp it down.

"I think your mind naturally jumps to worst-case scenario, Hemingway." She shakes her head. "And Thom's obsession with the Ripper only exacerbates the issue. Living day-to-day with murder is hardly what I'd recommend for someone suffering your particular type of PTSD. But you already know that." She sighs. "Grace is a hyperprotected young woman with authority issues, Hemingway. Teenagers run away all the time, for a variety of reasons. There's no reason to believe she's met with violence of any kind. In this day and age, in this city, she's safer than she would have been ten years ago and anywhere else in the world." She smiles. "Have you considered that her father isn't wrong? Grace wants to be a free spirit. You of all people should understand the need to stretch one's wings. It's been two days. Maybe give her a few more to turn up before you panic."

My mouth's fallen open. I shut it with a snap. "Central's taken an interest in her disappearance. Why would they do that if there's no reason to worry?"

Emma's dimples disappear when she frowns. "You should ask Thom how that came about. I think you'll find that without her interference, Grace's disappearance wouldn't have caught their attention at all."

"The Ripper—"

"Keeps a very methodical schedule. It's an essential part of his psychosis—a preoccupation with time. He's just finished with that poor girl from Morningside Heights. There's no reason at all to believe he's snatched another victim ahead of program. In fact, in my professional opinion, there's every reason to believe he has *not*." She pats my hand. "Maybe it's finally time to reassess your living arrangements, Hemingway. You've resisted in the past. I know you like Thom. But it's plain to me her presence in your life is doing more harm than good...unless there's something more you're not telling me?"

"No." I hope she takes the flush on my face for warmth off the tea. Honestly, I'm not sure what the truth is anymore—whether I should be frightened for Grace or angry at her, whether I should be blaming Thom for sleepless nights, or whether I should trust the knot of anxiety that's taken up residence in the back of my skull.

"Any other symptoms?" Emma inquires gently. "Agitation? Hyperarousal?"

Paranoia? I think sourly, though she doesn't say it out loud.

"Not really. I went to the zoo Sunday," I say by way of answer. "The crowd made me nervous at first. But I got over it. I mean, it went away. I'm fine now."

She nods. "And no thaumaturgical changes?"

"Nope. Did a koi fish on a wrist on Sunday. Client practically fainted when it became real, but he tipped me extra after. Nothing different." I've eaten the entire parfait, which should make Emma happy. "Why are they so afraid of me, anyway?"

"Who?" Emma makes a show of brushing crumbs from her shirt.

"Whoever it is you work for." I lean both elbows on the table. It wobbles. Antique, wrought-iron, café-style furniture, all curlicues and uneven table legs. "I'm not Rutch. I don't have any problem with the mayor or the state or...anything, really."

"Good," Emma says calmly. "For your sake, let's keep it that way."

A new suspicion squirms in my brain. "Don't suppose they sent you to 'look after' him, too, in the beginning? Maybe you showed up on Rutch's doorstep like you did mine and offered to keep *him* right?"

I can tell by the steel in her eyes that I've nailed it, which makes me sit up straight. "Shit, I'm right, aren't I? Wow. Well, that's disheartening."

"Rutch is a different person." Some of the gentleness has left her tone. "Even before the magic woke, that boy wanted what he couldn't have. There are things happening beyond our borders, Hemingway, frightening things, unreliable things. You know that. New York is a fortress in a dark wood. In order to keep danger out, we need stability within." She meets my eyes. "Of course they're afraid of you, and for you. You're a celebrity. That makes you powerful, more powerful even than thaumaturgy. But, like Rutch, you're young, and that makes you vulnerable."

"Relax." I tap my foot nervously against one table leg. The table shakes. The water in Emma's tall glass sloshes. "I'm not interested in power. Money's just fine."

Emma shakes her head, fond again, then changes the subject. "The zoo, you said? I thought you hated monkeys."

"That's Grace. She's afraid of anything with fur." I grab my bowl and mug, then reach for Emma's dish. "Look, thanks for the chat. I feel much better. About Thom—I'll think about it."

"Promise me." She walks me to the counter, standing just a little too close. "And keep me updated on Grace. I'm certain she'll show up in time for first rehearsals. She wouldn't miss that for the world."

"No," I agree. "She wouldn't."

Once around the corner, I hail a cab back to Earnest Ink. The cabbie does the usual double take when he sees my face but doesn't comment, and I'm grateful for the peace and quiet. The baton Thom gave me is still up my sleeve, pressing uncomfortably against my forearm, a physical reminder of her promise to keep me safe.

My peace and quiet doesn't last longer than the ride home. I should have guessed Tremblay wouldn't be so easy to shake—should have known he would take my challenge personally.

He's waiting in the hall when I step off the elevator, camped outside my charred door on his butt, two brown bottles and a plain white package balanced on his knees. The rainbow of bruises on his face is not improved by a new application of glitter paint, and there's a sprinkle of what looks suspiciously like ash still caught in his obnoxious hair.

"Took you long enough," he says without rising when I freeze in place. "Where the hell you been since this morning?"

"That belongs to me," I say, meaning the package. I don't like that he has his hands on it, or that he's probably read the return label.

"Brought it in for you," he says breezily. "Didn't think you'd want it sitting out in the weather, am I right? Root beer's yours, too, if you want it. A sort of peace offering, you understand. I saw how much you enjoyed it this morning."

"There was nothing enjoyable about this morning. How the hell did you get into my place—again?"

"Skeleton key," Tremblay confesses. "Borrowed from a friend. Happens it works well on an old building like yours."

I remember the long list of B and Es on his rap sheet, and I don't doubt him.

I slip the CEW out of my coat. There's no one but me and him in the hallway, and I've got absolutely zero patience left. "You're too stupid to be true."

"Wait, now." Tremblay looks genuinely pained. "Don't do anything you might regret. I've brought a peace offering."

"Even root beer isn't going to fix this."

"Not the soda! I think I know where Grace has got to!"

"What?" The baton sags in my hand.

He grins, cocky. "Don't look so surprised. Seraphine keeps me around because I'm just that good." He taps his head with one finger. "Wasn't all that difficult. See, after I got over the shock of your frankly disgusting accusations, I got to thinking."

"Not something you generally waste time on, I imagine."

He ignores me. "It wasn't just me and Grace at the zoo Sunday morning. That mousey theater kid—what's he called, Ang, somebody Ang. Henry? She met him during callbacks, and he's been her tagalong ever since. *Un petit garçon*, just barely old enough for the draft, but it's obvious he thinks Grace hung the stars. Hero worship, the sort of thing little kids do." He winks at me. "Also, pretty sure he was hoping I'd ask him out for tea. The modest ones always find me irresistible."

I frown. All this time I'd been so focused on Tremblay, I hadn't given Grace's other Sunday sidekick any thought at all. What had the peddler said?

"Shy kid with glasses?"

Tremblay nods. "Not my type. Far as I could tell, Grace treated him like a little brother, protective. She told me *Secret Garden*'s probably his last hurrah before he puts on the uniform and ships out. They were off to the theater together when I left on my own business. So I thought—maybe you should ask Ang a few questions, eh? And it happens I know exactly where to find him."

We lock eyes again there in the hall, another game of chicken. Only this time there's less posturing, more assessing. Tremblay doesn't back down. It's obvious he wants me to believe him, which doesn't mean he's not a psychopath. But for Grace's sake, I'm willing to take a chance.

"Move," I relent. "Unless you've already used your *highly illegal* skeleton key on my door."

"Of course not." He scrambles up. "What do you take me for?"

"An asshole," I spit out, unlocking the door. "And hard of hearing. I plainly said I want nothing to do with your girlfriend and her games."

"That's not all you said. A deal's a deal. I get the info you want; it's your turn to put out." He winks again. "Seraphine and I, we're on a deadline."

"I really couldn't care less. Give me that." I snatch my package from his hands. "Inside. Don't touch anything."

And just like that, against my better judgment, I let Jonathon Tremblay into my home. As he follows me over the threshold, I can't help thinking of vampires and invitations. Some superstitions are rooted in facts; it's never a good idea to give your enemy free access to your living room.

"Nice place." He sets the bottles of root beer on the kitchen counter and looks his fill of the high-end appliances, the mismatched furniture, the loft ceilings, and the map of Manhattan drawn onto brick, framing the dead faces. "Though that's a bit ghoulish, you ask me."

I leave him with the Ripper's victims and take my package into the bathroom where I pause to make sure he hasn't tampered with either the box or the contents. Testosterone cypionate, the synthetic hormone I've been injecting weekly since I moved to Manhattan and started transitioning, is still legal in New York, and since the manufacturing company that makes it happens to be in state, pretty easy for someone with a hefty bank account like mine to obtain.

But I can't help thinking, each and every time I find a box on my doorstep, that someday soon I'll have to go to the black market for T the way Miller does for his arthritis pills and Piano Jim does for his opiates.

When I come out of the bathroom, Tremblay's in the kitchen studying the murder wall. His hands spider restlessly on the counter surface. He glances my way, and I'm astonished to see that in a matter of minutes he's gone from unbearably cocky to subdued.

"Look," he says, turning from away from the wall. "Hemingway. I said it once, but I guess I need to say it again. I'm sorry." He glances briefly at my face, then shoves his hands in the back pockets of his baggy trousers. "I didn't mean to scare you like I did, or even, you know, bust you up a little. Sometimes I get carried away. And Seraphine—" He's studying the toes of his boots like the world's secrets are written on muddy leather. "—sometimes, when she wants something done, she has a way of making things..." He mutters something in French that I can't quite catch.

"More?" I suggest coldly, using Seraphine's own description.

He shakes his head, making the hoops in his ears shiver. "Worse," he says. He shrugs. "She's like adding a match to kerosene—not just her magic. Look, I'm really sorry, okay. But Jesus, you gave as good as you got." He touches his heart with one hand, then executes a strangely graceful and totally weird little bow, bending at the waist. I notice he's replaced his expensive wristwatch with a less flashy plastic Timex. "I'm sorry. I promise you it won't happen again."

"You bet your ass it won't."

Tremblay's got long, dark lashes. They flutter when he grimaces. "You actually thought I was the Ripper. That I could do...that." He shudders dramatically. "And still you came after me. *Vous avez de balles*, magic man."

"I'm still not sure you aren't." It's the truth, and probably I should be afraid, but all I feel is detachment, weary indifference, and general distrust. "Grace is my best friend. I'd do anything for her."

"Hey, I get that. I like her, too." He picks up a brown bottle. "So. Let's talk. Got a couple mugs or straight out of the bottle?"

Thom walks in as he's pouring, and all hell breaks out. She goes for his throat with her hands, and he goes for his knife, and I barely manage to get between them before blood spills. Even then it takes a good thirty seconds of shouting, shoving, and pleading before Thom agrees to back off and listen to what Tremblay has to say.

At first Thom doesn't believe him. Why would she? For years Thom's spent every free minute hunting Rafe's killer. She's studied the Ripper the way I study layers of color on a canvas: like it's the only thing that makes waking up in the morning worth doing. And Thom's as close to a forensics expert as she can get without an actual doctorate.

From the way she gets up again in Tremblay's glitter-painted face and calls him a liar and plenty of other nastier names, it's obvious Thom *wants* him to be the Ripper. She's inches away from taking him apart with fists and fury, wild faced and dangerous, and it's plain to me that Emma's guessed what I haven't seen: Thom's finally reached the end of her rope.

Five years of hunting her brother's killer has taken a toll. She needs closure, and she's not thinking clearly. Pent-up rage makes her shake and snarl. I almost don't recognize her when she shoves Tremblay right up against the murder wall.

Tremblay shouts right back—about jumping to conclusions and Central's vendetta against Rutch's followers and about faulty profiling. Even I can tell he's making a desperate kind of sense, but until Thom's ready to hear it, there's no point in speaking up. They're both swearing and sniping, but for all the noise, neither has bloodied the other yet, which means they probably won't—and I'm too tired to intervene again.

Instead I use Thom's mobile to order in pizza because there's nothing but cereal and bathtub gin in our pantry.

Then I leave them to it and go downstairs to watch pedestrians while I wait for delivery.

Thom's "friend" Fitz is hanging around, sweeping the pavement outside Earnest Ink, head bowed over his broom. Our sidewalk has got to be the cleanest five blocks either way.

"Hey," I say, settling on the stoop. "It's fine; you can take off." The cement beneath my hands is cold. The weather's changing, a low fog drifting in, filtering late-afternoon sun. The sky over Hell's Kitchen is the color of rainbow sherbet, the kind I used to get out of ice cream trucks in the summer, the kind that came in cardboard tubes.

Fitz squints doubtfully. "Not until Castillo says."

"Yeah, she sent me down here to say." Figuring he's waiting for payment, I fish out my wallet, but he turns my money down.

"No, sir. It's not like that. Castillo, she did me a big favor last year. Now I do her a few small ones in return." He tips his sweeper's hat in my direction. Underneath the brim his face is lined but merry. "Tell Castillo, call me if she needs me again tomorrow."

"Okay. What sort of favor?"

But Fitz is already on his way down Forty-Second, broom propped over one shoulder. Above his head the old sycamore trees rustle, catching fingers of fog in curling leaves. I watch him until he crosses the street and turns out of sight onto Ninth Avenue. People pass me by in fits and starts. Most pay me no mind. A woman takes a snap of the neon sign over my head, but either she doesn't make the connection or my scowl is working nicely because she leaves me alone.

I can hear Thom and Tremblay still going at it through my open window, but I can't tell what they're saying. It occurs to me that I should be more worried. I just can't muster up the energy to care.

My muscles are still protesting yesterday's adventure on Port's training mats. Anticipating pizza, my stomach growls. Slowly the sky turns from sherbet to cherry soda. A single, illicit bottle of root beer has me jonesing for sugar. I wonder if Seraphine has a line on Dr Pepper, then decide whatever price she'd ask in return is probably not worth it.

I stretch my legs out long, massaging my thigh, and think about Grace, realizing that since she moved out, we'd fallen into a very one-sided relationship routine. I'm biting my thumbnail, feeling guilty about my lack of perception, when the shouting three stories above my head finally stops.

A few minutes later, Tremblay joins me on the front stoop.

"Jesus, you look like your dog's just died," he says, sitting unceremoniously by my side, uncomfortably close. He's a rangy furnace against my shoulder, all heat and sinew. Involuntarily, I remember his skin against mine in a back-alley blind spot, and the jump of his pulse in the curve of his throat.

"What's wrong?" He shakes the pack of cigs out of his sleeve, knocks one out, offers it up. It's been a long time since I've indulged, but I take one anyway. It's just that sort of week. "Not afraid of a little noise, are you? It's just friendly yelling, that's all. Your lady's got backbone. Too bad about her brother."

Blue flame licks the tip of his thumb. He uses it to light our cigarettes. I take a long drag, choke, and try again until I find the rhythm of it. The smoke burns going down.

"She's not my lady. And these are crap cigarettes."

Tremblay shrugs. "Can't be choosy, these days, can you? Well, I guess *you* can, what with all that money sitting in your bank account." He blows smoke into the air, a practiced stream. "If yelling doesn't bother you, why are you sitting out on the street all by your lonesome, magic man?"

"Pizza," I say, then close my eyes to better enjoy the buzz of cheap tobacco. "You do realize I don't like you, not even a tiny bit?"

"That's okay. We only have to work together for a little while. And maybe I'll change your mind."

"'Work together,'" I repeat to the darkness behind my lids. "So you've convinced Thom you're not the Ripper?"

"Halfway there." He sounds smug. "She's not stupid, just still grieving. Maybe after you and me are done with business, I'll help her bring the real Ripper down. Couldn't hurt to have a girl like that on my side...so long as you don't mind."

"I told you, we're not like that." I open my eyes.

"Huh. Really? Your loss." He claps me on the shoulder with one large hand, then perks up visibly. "Hallelujah. Here comes lunch. I'm starved."

The delivery girl pulls up on a bicycle, an insulation box strapped to a rack on the back. Tremblay accepts the pizza while I pay. The girl blushes and stammers as she hands back my change, then works up enough courage to show me the skull and crossbones montage she's got on her ankle. The tat's small but well done. While I admire her choice of ink, she giggles nervously, and afterward she almost rides her bike smack into a small group of oncoming pedestrians when she leaves. They yelp and shout.

Tremblay stares after the delivery girl, frowning. "Do you suppose it's the thaumaturgy or your smile that's boiled her brain?"

Suspicious, I snatch my pizza from his hands. "What's wrong with my smile?"

"Nothing," he answers, still staring absently down the street. "It's fantastic when you use it. Can't be the magic," he muses. "No one on the Pier ever goes all stupid like that when I conjure fire. Mostly they just run away."

I blink, perplexed, trying to wrap my head around "fantastic when you use it."

"It's the being famous part," I mutter. "The being all over the internet and TV part. Probably also the being rich part."

We stare at each other over the warm pizza box. Filtered light softens the garish color in his hair and on his face, and mitigates the harsh lines of his nose. His petulant mouth is relaxed, smiling. He's almost attractive, except for the bruise on his cheek that reminds me he's a dick with a temper and a knife.

"Are we going upstairs?" Tremblay asks, gesturing at the studio door. "Do you think it's safe?"

"Aren't you leaving?" I suggest.

His shoulders shake when he laughs. "Hell, no. The day is short, and you and I've got work to do."

We nosh efficiently, Tremblay and Thom standing over the counter, me sitting in my armchair by the window with a plate on my knee and an empty shot glass in hand.

I pick at cheese and pepperoni, nibble crust. Bootleg gin makes Tremblay's happy eating sounds and Thom's icy detachment almost bearable.

Almost.

The pizza's good, my favorite basic pie from Thom's go-to hole-in-the-wall Italian joint. I chew methodically, trying to decide if the workout in Port's gym has earned me a second piece.

Tremblay eats four slices, one after another, licking sauce from his fingers after. Thom eats hers with a knife and fork because she doesn't like the texture of grease on her hands.

"You should cut him a break," Tremblay says to Thom instead of taking a fifth piece. "Even without the Grace thing, Hemingway would have come looking for us. He never had a choice, not really."

"Up yours." The gin bottle is on the floor by my chair. I refill the shot glass and dourly toast the city outside my window. "Why would I?"

"Like calls to like," Tremblay asserts. "That's what Rutch always said. Soon as you saw I've got the magic, too, you couldn't help yourself. Baited and hooked."

Thom sets down her knife and fork. She changed out of her uniform and showered while Tremblay and I were sitting on the stoop. She's wearing gray lounge pants and a baggie crew-neck T with "Big Apple" emblazoned across the front in red. Her short hair is still damp; the T-shirt is too big—it falls almost to her knees.

"What exactly is your connection to Rutch?" I ask Tremblay, hoping to distract everyone.

"I worked for him. Crowd control, that's all. Seraphine and I, at first we assumed we were the only ones, the only ones in the city who could do...things. Then one day this one—" He salutes me with two fingers. "—was all over the news, all over Twitter, in the Oval, in the magazines. And a week or two after, there was Rutch, and even better, Rutch was *here*, on the island, not some backwoods Idaho hick. And Rutch, he had big magic. He could heal people. Not just carnival tricks like blue flame or fancy three-dimensional tattoos. Rutch mattered. Rutch is *special*." He looks down at his plate. "I thought he was the miracle we needed."

"Maybe he's special," Thom allowed. When I glance over, she's scowling not at Tremblay, but at me. "But hardly intelligent. He had to know treason against the state wouldn't be tolerated. What did he think would happen when he started spouting off?"

Tremblay paces across the loft to the murder wall and back to the kitchen counter. I can tell by the way he walks—like he's got a stick up his ass and is afraid to step wrong—that he's angry and trying not to show it. He picks up a slice of pizza, then sets it back down in the greasy box.

"He took us in," Tremblay explains softly. "When even our families were afraid. He told us thaumaturgy was the universe's way of saving a world gone bad, fixing a century of mankind's interference, setting the world to rights again. Nature's solution, he called it."

"It's too late for that," I scoff. "The world will never be the same again. Half of it is rubble, and the rest is teetering on the edge. What good will *carnival tricks* do anyone *now*?"

"I don't know. Rutch, he was great at revving up the crowds, but not too keen on explanations."

"Rutch is on Rikers where he belongs." Thom's back in defensive posture, arms folded on her chest. "And not my problem. You, on the other hand, are. Even if you're telling the truth, and you're not the Ripper, you're a wanted man. Piracy and assault, robbery? Unregistered thaumaturgy added to the list? Well. You'll be joining your friend in prison, I think."

"Sure." Tremblay shrugs. "Turn me in. They'll happily hang me for murder. But your brother's killer, the real East River Ripper, will still be walking the streets. That sit easy with you?"

There's another uncomfortable silence. Thom closes the pizza box and takes it to the fridge. I resist another shot of gin and kick off my boots with a relieved sigh. Tremblay, showing smarts I wasn't sure he had, doesn't press either of us.

"You'll have been recorded entering Hemingway's building," Thom points out once the fridge is ordered to her satisfaction. "Sooner or later someone will twig to it. Sooner, probably. And it's my badge on the line."

"*Ma chère fille.* Don't worry your head. Nobody sees me if I don't want it."

"That's impossible."

Tremblay grins back at Thom. "Says you. *Secret Garden* rehearsals start today 'round four. I say we go talk to Ang."

A spark of hope flares. "Yes, good. Right." I peer through my fingers at Thom. "I need to sleep. I can't think straight. Give me an hour and then we'll go. One hour, no more."

Chapter Fourteen

Fog

I dream I'm sinking in deep water, my arms and legs useless, sunlight through ocean water a diminishing beacon overhead. I hold my breath to keep from choking on saltwater, but I know it's only a temporary solution. The water presses in all around me, and there are monsters in the depths, many-limbed creatures with large, bulging eyes and sharp, hooked tails. They watch me drown, swimming closer and closer as I sink. When a long, glistening feeler lassos my leg, I scream.

Elliot Bay fills my mouth, and then my lungs, to bursting. It's a flood of cold and salt and terror. I'd scream again if I had any air left to expel.

I wake choking, as I always do when I dream about the bay, and sit bolt upright on my mattress, shaking. I throw off confining blankets and stand up, stagger toward the window. I crank it open in search of fresh air and stick my head out into the evening to better see the city, but a pea-soup fog has settled over Hell's Kitchen, turning buildings opaque and the trees hazy.

The sound of ocean water is trapped in my ears. I shake my head to clear it, then slide down to sit on the floor, listening greedily to the muted sounds of the city.

A few minutes later, Thom slips into the room, wrapped in a tatty old cotton robe and carrying a glass of water.

"You were shouting," she says, handing me the glass. "It's been a while since you dreamed out loud."

I take the glass even though the last thing I want is water when I can still remember ocean bursting in my lungs. She watches me while I swallow, her face illuminated by street lights.

"Shouldn't you be getting ready for your shift?" I frown. "You're not skipping another on my account." We both know she's been walking a fine line lately, what with her misadventures on the Hudson, dismantling of government CCTVs, and now this mess with Tremblay. She's dangerously close to insubordination.

"Listen," Thom says, meeting my eyes, a thing she rarely does. "I know you think I'm wrong about Tremblay and the Ripper."

"I'm not sure what to think." I lean my head back against the window frame. Wisps of fog sneak in through the open casement before evaporating in the warmth of my room. "But he and Seraphine made a surprising amount of sense for a couple of whackos. And Emma—"

"You'd believe two complete strangers over me," Thom interrupts, gnawing her lower lip. She looks young and uncertain in the dark. I don't like it. Thom's the best and bravest person I know, and I hate that I'm questioning her judgment. "Maybe Tremblay's right—like calls to like."

I stand up, shivering now as sweat from the nightmare dries on my body. "This has nothing to do with thaumaturgy. The guy's an asshole and Seraphine's worse. But you've been chasing the Ripper for a long time, and maybe things in your head have gotten just a little mixed up." Tentatively, I pat her shoulder. The tatty robe is terry cloth, soft under my fingers. "And that's okay. I get it. But right now, I need to find Grace, make sure she's all right."

She shocks me by leaning forward, resting her forehead against mine, a small point of contact as intimate as any embrace. I freeze, my hand on her shoulder. She blinks rapidly, her face centimeters from my own.

"You'd rather believe anything than that the Ripper has her," she whispers. "*I* get that. I remember what it was like, when Rafe disappeared."

"It's fine," I promise softly. I don't want to scare her away. Warmth and affection pool in my stomach. "Or, it will be. Look, Tremblay and I will talk to this Ang kid and see what he knows. Probably he'll point us at the Four Seasons and say Grace's been holed up in luxury all this time."

"You're an awful liar, Hemingway." Thom's exhalation tickles my chin. "Your face always gives you away. I'm coming with you. Don't argue."

"What, you don't think I can Taser the dye right out of his hair if I need to?"

That startles a snort out of her.

"Tremblay's hiding something," she says. "Even if it's got nothing to do with Grace or the Ripper, he's keeping something back."

I squeeze her shoulder gently. "I know. And I'll be careful," I promise, grinning in the dark. "Relax. It's only a jaunt over to Fifty-Fifth. It's the City Center, for God's sake, and it's not even dark out yet."

"I'm relaxed." Thom steps away. "Because, like I said, I'm coming with you. Theater's not my thing, but I've always wondered how the sausage gets made backstage. Hurry up," she adds on the way out the door. "I don't like that kid hanging around our place."

Tremblay's waiting for us on the pavement outside Earnest Ink. Blue flame dances between the fingers of his right hand, a snake between branches. Wisps of fog wind about his bony form, turning him into a wraith, all color subdued but for the reflection of fire in his eyes.

"I've never met anyone able to elude Surveillance completely," Thom says, glancing up at the CCTV camera on a building across the street. "So you'll understand I'm wondering if you're an arrogant, stupid bastard who's full of shit."

"Not about this." Tremblay's nonchalant, too busy admiring the flames dancing between his fingers to give us his full attention. "Happens Rutch figured out early on my fireworks work really well as some sort of UV interference. So long as I'm kindled, and you stick close, we've got nothing to worry about. Just shows as a big blue blob on the feed."

"And how," Thom demands, chilly as the fog surrounding us, "did Rutch discover that?"

"He's a clever guy, Rutch. Maybe someday you'll have a chance to see for yourself." He smiles at me, blue flame jumping from his left hand to his right and back again. "Walk natural," he adds. "UV interference works on cameras, but not on any live grunts patrolling the streets, and I don't need you two drawing any attention my way."

I pull up my hood. The baton slides against my arm. Thom adjusts Rafe's beanie on her head. Side by side, we follow Tremblay away from Earnest Ink. The fog chases us all the way north out of Hell's Kitchen.

If you look up the New York City Center in one of those tourist booklets they sell at faded kiosks near Columbus Circle, the building's described as "venerable" and "an essential part of New York's cultural history." It's pretty, that much is true, all Moorish arches, tiled murals, and miles and miles of red velvet. Carnegie Hall's only a block away, and most tourists head there first, but in my opinion, they're missing out. Sure, Carnegie Hall's elegant, and the acoustics there are unbelievable, but if Carnegie Hall's a taste of champagne and caviar, the New York City Center is an entire feast for the eyes.

City Center has one large main stage, two smaller theaters, and several studios. At four o'clock the building's hopping with theater people: actors, musicians, stagehands, and all the other various and sundry support staff that help turn ideas into performance.

Standing just inside the front doors, looking around at all that hustle and bustle, I can see how Grace must fit in just fine. City Center exudes a frenetic, creative energy that makes me think important things are being accomplished with fanfare.

"How are we supposed to find one kid in all this mess?"

"Ask," Tremblay suggests, dodging a painted piece of cardboard prop precariously balanced between two laughing actors. I think the long prop is supposed to be part of a ship's mast. The actors are dressed in diaphanous, flowing white gowns and elaborate headpieces. They pay Tremblay no attention at all.

"Way ahead of you," Thom says, nudging my elbow. "*Secret Garden*'s running lines in one of the small studios. This way." She strides ahead, weaving her way through the beehive of color and sound, leaving Tremblay and I to follow as best we can.

It's a different sort of crowd than I suffered through at the zoo. The center is smaller, closer, with less air to breathe. But the costumes and stage dressing and bursts of instrumental noise make it seem so outlandish as to be unreal—a filmy, harmless dream circus set completely outside the mundane world.

I check myself for encroaching panic, but my pulse is steady, my palms dry, my brain too busy categorizing the theater's strange palette of light and color to remember anxiety.

The *Secret Garden* denizens are just gathering in a smaller theater labeled Stage II—fifteen or twenty thespians in small groups sit here and there on the floor or lean up against the wall, talking quietly, obviously waiting. It's a casual congregation; none of them are in costume. They all look up in surprise when Thom barrels through the door, but it's the sight of me that makes the space go dead quiet.

"Which of you is Henry Ang?" Thom booms into the startled silence. By my side Tremblay scans the group, then shakes his head.

"Henry's out today." A woman has come in behind us: small, almost as short as I am, frizzy black hair piled atop her head in a bun, pencil stuck behind one ear and a packet of paper tucked under one arm. The way she looks us up and down says "person in the know." Her examination pauses on my face, and her eyes widen. "What do you want with him?"

"He's a person of interest," Thom replies. Even out of her uniform she manages to exude *hard-core*. "In a missing person's case."

"I don't know about that." The woman takes the pencil from her ear. "Henry's out sick. His mom called in yesterday. Been a nasty cold going through the cast the last week or two. Henry must have picked it up." She shoves the pencil, and the script from beneath her arm, in my direction. "Sign that, will you? Maybe sketch a little something? I've got an autograph book, at home, and I collect all the big names. Mostly actors, but you'll do."

My fingers close automatically over the pencil before it drops. Immediately, everyone else in the room stands up and begins to press in my direction, talking excitedly:

"Like your style, man."

"So what's President Shannon really like? I hear she had her boobs done!"

"Hey, maybe can you draw something for my kid, too? I told her when she turns eighteen, she can get ink. Can't afford your stuff, of course, but..."

It's an enthusiastic overwhelming, a tide of starstruck ardor. I remind myself to keep smiling as I scrawl my name twenty times. Over the babble, I hear Thom demanding, "You said Ang and his mother live where? Chelsea? Where in—okay—and what about Grace Miller? When's the last time she was in?"

It's over as quickly as it began, but only because after I autograph the last scrap of paper, Tremblay grabs me by the arm and yanks me out of Stage II and into the theater hall. More people across the carpet are swarming our direction. Word's got out: there's a celebrity in the house.

Tremblay swears in French and uses his lanky body to shield me from reaching hands as we hurry toward the door. I glimpse Thom's face around his shoulder. She looks like she's swallowed a mouthful of something sour. I know she doesn't like masses of people any more than I do, but I guess maybe she's never really thought much about why I prefer to stay safely on my own turf.

We burst through the theater doors and into the foggy evening. I gasp in great lungfuls of chilly air. Thom glares back behind us at the doors. I wonder what she plans to do if the crowd follows us out, but they don't. They've remembered their manners just in time.

"Jesus Christ," Tremblay gasps. "Theater people. Everything has to be a scene."

I surprise myself by laughing and am startled again by Thom's explosive giggle. When I glance her way, she flashes me a rare grin.

"Now what?" I ask. "No Henry Ang."

"And no Grace," Thom says. "I got in a few questions while you were being mobbed. They haven't seen Grace, either, not since last week. But they know she had a big fight with her father a few days ago, and they think she's been camping out with the Angs ever since. Henry's mother is some sort of big-time theater donor. Apparently, Grace dotes on her, and Ms. Ang returns the favor."

"Mother issues," Tremblay says, nodding wisely. "I've got a few of those myself."

"Money issues," I amend. "Grace and a big, fat bank account always equal true love. Okay." An hour of sleep has restored my energy and optimism, or maybe it was Thom's brilliant grin. Maybe she's forgiven me for questioning her judgment. Maybe she's remembering that's what we do—keep each other balanced. "Let's go to Chelsea and meet the Angs."

Henry Ang and his mother live in a renovated brownstone off Twenty-Second Street. The brick is painted fuchsia pink, the door and window trim a soft cream. Boxes beneath the bottom windows are planted with fall flowers; the single scrawny maple on the parking strip is finally beginning to lose its leaves. In the sunshine the building is probably flamboyant and cheerful. Shrouded in fog, it's less welcoming. The dark brick looks gray, the cream trim washed out. The flowers crouch in their boxes, and the tree collects gloom in its branches. A porchlight burns above the door, throwing a pale and sickly light across the brownstone's front steps, picking out moisture beaded on a wrought-iron railing.

"Now what?" Tremblay inquires, climbing the steps. "Ring the bell?" He's playing snake-between-the-fingers with his flame, pretending boredom. "I'd say they're probably in the middle of dinner, but it's dark as a tomb in there. Looks like they're out."

A number of folded newspapers litter the top step, ink beginning to blur in the damp—several days' worth at least. Tremblay prods one with his foot. I ring the bell anyway and wait, gazing up at the brick facade, wondering if Grace is watching from behind any of the high, shuttered windows.

Surely if she were, she'd come down when she saw it was me. There's no reason I can think of that would cause Grace to hide from me. I stab the doorbell a second time, hold the button down. This time when I release it, I can hear a dog barking from inside the brownstone, a high, frenzied yapping.

"Window's open," Thom says, indicating a rectangular picture window up and to the right of the front door. The lower pane is partway open despite the increasing fog. The dog's barking grows frantic, shattering the tranquil evening.

"Hey!" A man sticks his head out the door of the neighboring brownstone. "Hey, you kids! The Angs aren't home, and you're disturbing my supper! Bloody deafening dog—you're only egging her on. Now get lost before I call you in!"

"Sorry," I say hastily. "You have any idea when they'll be back? The Angs, I mean?"

"Not soon enough! Good-for-nothing inbred mutt hasn't shut up all day! I'm counting to five, and if you're not gone, I'm calling in the nearest soldier, you understand?" He slams the door, making the dog behind the Angs' front window bark louder.

In response a grunt materializes out of the fog on the other side of the street, heading in our direction.

"That's our cue. We'll have to come back later," Thom says as Tremblay hops the wrought-iron railing and escapes down the street. Thom and I hurry after.

We've just caught up to him and—hopefully—ditched the inquisitive grunt, when one of Tremblay's cohorts pops up from behind a trash bin. It's sword girl, only sans sword. It's obvious she's been waiting for us.

"You're needed back at Earnest Ink," she tells Tremblay, shaking long pink fringe off her forehead. She peeks sideways at me. "Seraphine's not happy. Better hurry."

Eric raises both eyebrows and purses his lips when we bolt into the studio.

"Border breached?" he inquires mildly, setting aside his book. I recognize the book's abused cover from eighth-grade English: *Catcher in the Rye*. "Strange...I didn't hear the sirens."

He's being sarcastic. The border hasn't been breached for years, not by any force that matters. Virginia's pirates gave up long ago, and Jersey doesn't have an army left. Only the tired, poor, and yearning attempt Manhattan now, and they're easily turned away.

"What are you doing here?" I snap. "How'd you make it past the roadblock? Never mind. Studio's closed. Roads are locked down, or didn't you notice?"

Eric's eyebrows climb impossibly higher. He settles more solidly on his stool, arms crossed over a crisp Tom Ford button-down.

"Realized I'd left my book behind." He holds up *Catcher*. "Hate to be without a good read. Took the long way around, meant to take it with me to that café I like near Bryant Park. Best-laid plans and all that. I didn't realize we were expecting a guest.'"

"Hello, Hemingway," Seraphine says from where she's perched on my red velvet chaise, hands buried in the folds of a long black cape. "I trust Tremblay's been helpful?"

Thom locks the studio door. Then she hits the lever that lowers ancient metal shutters down over the storefront. The shutters haven't been used since I bought the place. They groan, shedding flakes of rust, as they fall into place.

"Someone's thinking." Seraphine appraises Thom, head tilted. "Move away from the shutters, Charlie. I don't like the look of that sweeper."

I peer between metal slats. Across the narrow alley, partially obscured by fog, Fitz is busy dusting a square of old brick cobblestone. Pink-haired Charlie moves to stand by Seraphine's side.

"Sweeper's with us," Thom says. "What are you doing here?"

Seraphine takes her hands from the folds of her cape. She's holding a small, plastic pistol. When she catches me staring, she awards us all one of her sweet-as-molasses smiles. Casually, she keeps the pistol's snub nose pointed in Eric's direction.

"I prefer the Remington," she confesses. "But it's just not practical for out and about. So, any luck? I know Jonathon's been working all his connections this afternoon—he's such a team player." She turns her smile on Tremblay and repeats, "Any luck?"

Tremblay's busy sniffing restlessly about my tools, squinting at ink bottles and machine tips. "Some," he says absently.

"Don't touch," I snap. "Those are sterile."

"And a good thing, too." Seraphine licks her lips. Then she turns to Thom. "I'm sure you've heard by now that Hemingway and I have a business agreement. Tremblay's spent the afternoon proving my worth; now it's Hemingway's turn to prove his."

"Grace is still missing," I point out coldly.

"Baby steps. This afternoon ought to demonstrate our good intent. Now demonstrate yours."

Thom shifts minutely. Eric, on his stool behind my counter, shakes his head. "Castillo, she's very capable of putting a hole in my chest before you can get in the way," he says quietly. "For all our sakes, please don't."

"I'm told an intricate tattoo can take several sessions to complete," Seraphine continues, ignoring both Thom and Eric. "I've decided it's in my best interest to begin tonight."

"Fine." With Tremblay, Charlie, and Seraphine's pistol in the room, it's clear we're outnumbered. Even Thom and Eric with their military training aren't impervious to bullets.

And there's no way in hell I'll risk either of them. I shrug out of my coat. I shake the CEW out of my sleeve and start to pass it to Thom, but Seraphine tuts loudly and Charlie snatches the Taser away.

"Get in the chair," I tell Seraphine, resigned.

Her laughter sounds like Christmas bells. "Oh, no, not me. I can't stand needles. No, Tremblay's your client." She pauses. "This doesn't change things, does it?" she asks, sweetness and light. "I know you and Jonathon have had your differences. But you've accepted his apology—haven't you?"

"Whatever." I hide surprise behind a sneer. I have accepted Tremblay's apology, mostly. I tolerated him in my home, let him eat my pizza. I'm 80 percent sure he's no serial killer. But that doesn't mean I trust him. Or that he doesn't make me uncomfortable, because he does.

"Believe me," Tremblay says, "it wasn't my first choice, either."

"Fine. Whatever. Let's get this over with." I hold up one finger, spin it around. "Oh, and, I need to get a copy of whatever you're passing as your curfew card for my records, because Eric there thinks you haven't hit puberty, and officially, I don't do anyone under eighteen."

Eric, still under Seraphine's watchful eye, snorts.

"Blow me," Tremblay says, but he shrugs out of his baggy shirt, baring a bony torso. "I'll be nineteen in December."

"If you say so." I smirk. "Get in the chair."

Chapter Fifteen

Gray Hours

Thaumaturgy may have made me rich, but the fat paycheck is not the only reason I stay open for business. I'm an artist, and I'm not talking about the half-completed landscapes in my room or the cityscapes hanging in Miller's gallery. Painting with brushes on canvas is a fine distraction and an interesting challenge. Painting on flesh with needle and ink is what makes me *me*, more even than the choices I've made, the people I hang out with, or my name inscribed in the studio window.

Before I was Hemingway, I was a kid haunting Tank Tattoo, stuck to Don's shadow, always observing, always asking questions. I worshipped Don, not just because he was fantastic at what he did, but because he didn't chase me away when I showed up on the daily. In fact, he was willing to teach me his trade. I scrubbed his worn counter, mopped the floor, sterilized tools, answered phones, and picked the background music. In return, Don let me practice with his machine on bananas off-hours, or trace stencils when he had a client in the chair. He showed me how to clean and maintain heads and needles, and how to take apart his machine and put it back together again, improved.

He didn't care that at twelve I was a cynical smartass trying to come to terms with a body that didn't fit, or that by letting me work behind the counter he was breaking child labor laws. It was a pretty safe bet that no one in Ketchum cared where I spent my time, so long as I was keeping out of trouble and not pissing off the middle school guidance counselor by skipping class.

I think my dad was just glad I'd found a safe place to channel my hectic energy. Don, despite his penchant for black leather and too many piercings, was well liked in town. He went to church every Sunday, volunteered at the animal shelter on his off day, and donated regularly to the Red Cross. He enjoyed good music and loud women and fly-fishing in Montana. He was patriotic, proud of Ketchum, proud of the United States, proud to have voted for our first female president. He probably would have been at the head of the line to volunteer for the draft if he hadn't been blown up.

Don gave me access to a world of color when most of my hours were gray; he gave me the gift of passion and helped nurture my uncertain skill to real, enviable talent. And in doing that he gave me the courage I needed to take those first small steps toward transitioning.

I think, if he were alive, Don would be proud of me. Baffled by the magical trick the universe decided to play on us, but proud. Probably, he'd insist on reminding me that ink is representation even before it comes alive, *especially* before.

"Don't rest on your laurels," he'd say. "Never give anything less than your best. And for Chrissake, never substitute diaper cream for petroleum jelly."

"What are you grinning about, magic man?" Tremblay asks. He's wiggled around on my chair, propped himself on one elbow, and is watching as I prepare my stencil. Seraphine, still with her pistol pointed at Eric, has settled cross-legged on my floor as far away from the chaise as possible. Her eyes reflect my lights. Eric's eyes are closed, but I doubt he's sleeping.

Thom and Charlie are standing on opposite sides of the room, glaring at each other like two dogs in a pissing match. It makes for an uncomfortable working environment, but I've handled worse. There were way more guns in the Oval when I tattooed President Shannon.

"Remembering a friend," I answer. "Lie down. Stop squirming, would you? I need you to be still."

According to Seraphine, the tattoo's meant to go on his back, so Tremblay stretches out on his stomach in my chair, arms folded beneath his chin. He's long enough that his feet hang over the edge. He wiggles them back and forth as I pull on my gloves and then use an alcohol wipe to scrub the skin on his back. His feet continue to twitch. I recognize a nervous tat virgin when I see one and remember how he'd watched me so carefully Friday morning—was it really less than a week ago?—and asked me *Does it hurt?*

"Make sure it's centered," Seraphine says from the floor. Eric shifts on the chaise, turning his face her way. She clears her throat and adds grudgingly: "Please."

I press my stencil carbon-down onto Tremblay's upper back, using his bony spine as a midpoint. I'd prepared the sheet in the last ninety minutes while they all watched, tracing Tremblay's baroque feathers into the backside of carbon paper, a sheet of greaseproof paper beneath. It was meant to be time-consuming, painstaking work, and I'd rushed it terribly, but in doing so I'd also come to appreciate Tremblay's artistic talent. It's possible it rivaled mine.

When she'd first withdrawn the stencil from beneath her cape and unrolled the paper across red velvet, I'd almost had a shit fit.

"You've got to be kidding me," I'd groaned, goggling between Seraphine and the design she laid out on my chaise. "You said unique, not rococo."

Seraphine's smile didn't waver. "A few feathers. I expect you can handle it."

"A few?" I recognized the artist's hand. I'd seen one of the lovingly sketched feathers before. Tremblay's work, and although this plumage was black ink on white paper, and not threatening to burst into blue flame, still it instilled a different sort of awe. "This isn't a few feathers. These are wings."

And not just the classical outline most clients are looking for in a quick angel-wing tat. Tremblay's wings were filled in, curve to tip, with elaborate plumage. As far as I could tell, no single feather was alike, each individual quill rendered in downy, one-of-a-kind detail.

I'd walked my fingers along the edges of the drawing, and it was like cupping two cupid's wings done in charcoal pencil. It's not a tattoo design at all; it's a baroque illustration.

"It's beautiful," Eric'd admitted warily from behind the counter, clicking his tongue. "But Hemingway's right—the stencil alone will take some time—"

"Which is why we start now," Seraphine had retorted. "Time is valuable."

"Relax," I say now when Tremblay flinches beneath my hands. He immediately stops wiggling. I smooth the greaseproof sheet with the palms of my hands, transferring the carbon from the paper to his flesh. "This is the easy part."

When I peel away the paper, Tremblay's design is left behind as a carbon outline. Black swirls and curls give his freckled skin dimension. The feathers stand out like eighteenth-century ink on ivory.

"Where did you learn to draw?" I ask as I smear a thin layer of petroleum jelly over his back, careful not to mar the lines. I'm stingy with the stuff, using only as much as needed. Petroleum jelly is a pain in the ass to find in the city and has to be shipped in from Texas, usually one single jarful at a time. "You're not bad."

Tremblay snorts into his folded arms. "I can't draw. I can copy pretty good, you know, if I have something to look at. Used to trace pictures from comics when I was little. Superman, Spider-Man, that sort of thing. Got okay at it, but never could draw anything from my head, original-like."

I turn from the chair to the counter, pausing to select the right machine head and needle from the options Eric has laid out. I choose a #10 Tight Liner's cluster, making sure the head is securely cranked before inserting the needle. When I test the power, pressing the foot pedal and making the head buzz, Tremblay gasps.

"Buck up." It would be cruel to laugh at his skittishness, and I'm not a cruel person, so I busy myself with squeezing black ink into a thimble-sized well. "Or, even better, just say 'no.' I've got plenty more important things to be doing right about now—just give me the word."

"The word is 'yes,'" Seraphine says. "It has to be you, Jonathon. You know it does."

Tremblay's shoulders rise and fall as he breathes, making the carbon feathers on his back ripple. I'm ready to go, my tools primed and at hand, but there's no way I'm going to ink a doubtful client. For all his posturing and over-the-top attitude, Tremblay's hardly more than a kid. Until I met Seraphine, I assumed he was a genuine asshole, even a murderer. Now I've begun to question just how much of an influence she has over his decisions.

More than I'm comfortable with, I decide, and start to strip off my gloves.

"I'm not doing this. Find a willing victim or no deal."

"No! No, wait." He snaps out a hand. "I'm good. I promise. I *want* to do this." He looks up at me, his usually petulant expression turned pleading. "Hell, I didn't even get drunk ahead of time, like *some people*. I'm good."

"*Êtes-vous sûr?*" asks Seraphine, with more kindness than I'd seen her show anyone yet.

Maybe I don't understand either of them. Maybe I'm wrong about her.

I'm not usually wrong.

"I'm sure," Tremblay replies. He's still looking up at me. "I'm good."

I glance Eric's way but get no help. He's playing a damn fine possum despite the gun pointed at his chest.

"Right." I snag a fresh pair of gloves. "But remember, I'll stop at any time. Just say."

"Yeah," Tremblay mutters, laying his head back down. "One thing you should know about me, magic man: I'm not a coward."

Tremblay holds still on my chair except for the clench and unclench of his fists—like he's squeezing water from an invisible sponge. Sweat has gathered on the back of his neck and around the edges of his hairline. I can't see his face, but a pulse is pounding again in the side of his throat. He smells warm, musky—not unwashed, exactly, but of perspiration and cigarette smoke and astringent.

"We can chat if you want." I take pity on him. "If you need distraction. Or take a break." I've only been at it thirty minutes. I can go another half hour before I need to stop and stretch the ligaments in my fingers and rest my leg. "Eric's CD player died a few weeks ago or I'd put on music."

He lifts his chin slightly. "Chat about what?"

I pause to reload ink. "Whatever." I glance Seraphine's way, but she's busy staring at Eric, possibly admiring his tight shirt. When the buzz of the machine starts up again, I take a gamble. "Why this design? Why wings?"

"Why do you think? I just really love birds." His sarcasm bites, but so does my needle, which makes us even.

"Funny. All those feathers. Guess you want to fly away?"

"Something like that." He turns his head in my direction. "You ever heard the story of that Greek nut, Icarus?"

"Sure. The boy who flew too close to the sun and, what, melted?"

"Crashed and burned, magic man. Him and his *père* wanted off Crete that badly. Only, Icarus, he let his new wings get to his head and *BAM* too late."

"You want off the island, Tremblay?" Hundreds of people every month try to cross the water from Jersey or Long Island, even Pennsylvania. Manhattan is all that remains of the way things used to be, an oasis.

Sort of.

There aren't very many people I know who want to leave, at least not the sane ones.

Tremblay doesn't answer. There's a buzzing around my head that has nothing to do with my machine; the hornet has come out from wherever it was hiding to circle my lights.

"Hemingway," Seraphine interrupts coldly, "is it true you used to be a girl?"

In the shadows beyond my bright lights, Thom stiffens.

My head's bent over a curl of black ink, Tremblay's skin so close I can see the blue veins beneath the dermis. I can count the individual knobs of his spine and glimpse the tiny dark hairs sprouting from stardust freckles. Seraphine's question make the muscles in his shoulders grow tight. I'm surprised. I expect Thom to take insult on my behalf, but not a glitterati street punk I've barely spent a whole day with.

"How old are you, really?" I ask Seraphine through gritted teeth.

"Old enough."

"Old enough to know better." I've been pelted with the same question more times than I can count, and it never gets easier. But it's been a long time since the person asking intended pain. More often, especially lately, people just don't understand.

Seraphine's smirk says she understands perfectly. She means to be cruel.

"It's only what I've read in the papers," she continues, as cloying as cinnamon sugar and donut crumbles. "It's really no secret that you used to be a girl before you moved to Manhattan."

"No." I wipe up black ink. Refill the ink reservoir. Work the pedal. "I was never a girl. AFAB, yeah. Assigned female at birth. But I never felt like a girl."

"So, what?" she drawls. "Born into the wrong body, that sort of thing? Liked, I don't know, toy trucks and guns instead of dolls from day one?"

I peek sideways at Thom and can tell by the deadpan expression on my roommate's face that if not for the dangerous little pistol, Seraphine would be out the door on her ass by now. I shake my head minutely. Seraphine's got a gun and a frankly explosive temper. Thom might be able to take her down before she blows a hole in one of us, but it's just not worth the risk.

Still, feelings are feelings, and I have to pause for a moment, breathing the sour ache in my gut away, before I'm ready to move on.

"Jesus, Seraphine," Tremblay mutters into his forearm. The back of his neck is turning pink. "Can you be anymore *inélégant*?"

"I'm not trying to be mean," she protests, although clearly she is. "I'm just curious, that's all. It's *interesting*. Like, science and all that." Each word drips enough sugar to make my teeth ache. "Did you go the whole way, do the surgeries? Cut off your boobs and... How do you—" Out of the corner of my eye, I catch her quick gesture in the direction of her crotch.

"Have sex?" I suggest, quieting my machine. I swivel Seraphine's way, let everyone in the room see I refuse to be rattled. "Or are you wondering whether I sit or stand to take a piss?"

She tosses her head, making fluorescent light dance on strands of copper-colored hair. She'd be pretty if not for the sharp edge to her smile and the obvious fact that she likes to watch people squirm. She starts to reply, but is interrupted when someone hammers on the studio shutters.

The sudden rattle makes me jump. Tremblay sits up, almost knocking the needle from my hand. Eric inhales sharply. Seraphine, seemingly unconcerned, eyes the shuttered glass panes.

"Someone's at your door," she says. Then, as the pounding increases, "Really, at this time of night?"

"Quiet!" Tremblay blurts at the same time I reply: "I get clients day and night. I'm just that popular. Eric, did we have someone booked?"

"Not that I recall," Eric muses. "Shall I see who it is and what they want?"

"No!" Tremblay springs off my chair, jaw set. I bet he's having premonitions of being hanged as a murderer from the mayor's front gate. Blue fire flickers around the blade now in his hand.

"Do *not*," I whisper, "stab anyone in my shop."

Charlie's already at the windows, peering through metal slats, my CEW clutched in one fist. Whatever she sees outside eases the tension in her shoulders. She holds up one hand, motioning for silence, then opens the shutters part way and unlocks my front door. A young street punk slips in with the fog.

"We've got trouble," he says past Charlie to Seraphine. "Down below." He jerks a thumb at the floor.

Tremblay's knife is gone again. I didn't see him put it away. "What sort of trouble?"

"Nothing for you to worry about," Seraphine tells Tremblay. "Charlie will handle it."

"Sorry, miss," the messenger says. He's missing his front teeth and wearing orange glitter paint. When he grimaces in sympathy, it's like looking at a jack-o'-lantern. "They've asked for you in particular."

Seraphine's expression turns thunderous. "Hemingway's barely started his work. How do I know he'll finish if I'm not here to make sure he does?"

Hackles rising, I open my mouth on an angry retort, but Thom beats me to it.

"Hemingway always finishes what he starts," she says coldly. "If he's said he'll do a thing, he will."

She doesn't mean it as a compliment but a fact. It's probably the nicest thing anyone's ever said about me and also the truest. I clear my throat, trying not to let my grin get out of hand.

"La-di-da," Seraphine sneers, but she rises slowly, offering Tremblay the pistol. "See he does," she orders.

"I don't need that." Tremblay makes a moue of disgust. "I've got everything under control."

I can tell she's furious by the way the hornet flits around the ceiling, dive-bombing its reflection in dark windowpanes.

"Go, *ma cherié*," Tremblay says soothingly. "You've stirred the pot enough already tonight. I'll be fine."

Seraphine's saccharine smile crumples to a scowl. The hornet leaves my windows and instead zips around Tremblay's head. Impressively, he doesn't react. The black insect, so different from the fat honeybee I brought to life, gives me the heebie-jeebies.

"Don't disappoint me," she cautions Tremblay, gaze sharp as any stinger. "Don't disappoint *us*."

Then she sweeps around, cape flaring, and ducks out into the night, pistol concealed in the folds of her skirt. Charlie and the kid with no teeth scurry after her. As soon as they're out the door, Thom dives across the studio and secures the door, checking it twice before she lowers the shutters.

"All right?" she asks Eric. "Did she hurt you?"

"Only my ego." Rising from behind the counter, he lifts his hands over his head, stretching until I can hear his spine crack. "Nasty piece of work. Someone should take her down a peg or two before she causes real harm."

"Too late for that," Tremblay says, dry as dust.

"Earned your overtime today," I tell Eric. A surge of unexpected affection makes me expansive. "Go home and get some rest."

But he settles on my chaise instead. "I'll stay," he decides. "Broadway's still closed and it's almost curfew. Besides, I'm afraid there's been a break-in. *Someone* stole the pepper spray from my drawer." Yawning, he closes his eyes. "I'm determined to see it doesn't happen again."

"About that—"

"Later. You can be sure we'll talk about it later." He rolls over onto his side. "But right now, I need a moment to recover from Annie Oakley and her plastic gun. Christ, I was sure she'd trigger it accidentally. Survive the Cascades only to bite it in a Hell's Kitchen tattoo parlor. What an inglorious way to go."

"Not just any tattoo parlor," I point out, mock-cheerful. "Earnest Ink."

Thom smothers a laugh. Eric, eyes still closed, lazily shoots me the bird.

I work until my fingers begin to ache. Tremblay's been mute for the last forty-five minutes, and I've been too busy tracing carbon feathers to give him much thought. I turn off my machine, set down my needle, and stretch, groaning. There's an ache in my leg where the shrapnel lodged that means I've been standing too long.

"That's enough for now."

Tremblay nods and unfolds himself slowly from my chair. The skin on his back where I've been working is pink and black, tender flesh flaming, black ink raised and angry under delicate skin. In three hours' solid work, I've completed not quite half of the intricate design; it's a longer session than I prefer, but still doable.

"Wait," I say when he begins to stand up. "Hang on."

I snatch up my jar of petroleum jelly, walk around the chair, and gently spread another thin layer over the fresh tattoo, then add a protective layer of plastic film. Tremblay sits on the edge of the chair, long legs dangling, head hanging, shoulders up around his ears. His skin is warm through my gloves. He's breathing slowly and deeply, caught in that stage in between sleeping and waking that sometimes grips a client after a long sitting.

I cap the jelly, take off my gloves, and hand him one of the pamphlets I keep on hand for first-timers.

"Read it," I say. "Even magical tats need good aftercare. You're going to be tender tonight and tomorrow."

He stirs and cranes his neck, trying to look over his shoulder.

"Has anything happened yet?"

"No." I scrub my hands with antibiotic gel. "It happens when it's ready, and half a tat doesn't count." Now that I'm coming back to myself, I'm exhausted again. The radiators are going gangbusters, snapping and popping. Fog has left frost in the corners of my windows, crystals catching the city lights through the slats in the shutters, reflecting red and white.

Tremblay's eager expression fades. "What's the point of that? I can kindle my fire whenever I want."

"Bully for you." I shut off my lights, leaving him sitting in the dark. Eric's snoring on the chaise. Thom, a silent steward, stands motionless by the door. She's missed another shift on my account. I'm pretty sure that's really bad news. "Now get lost. Come back tomorrow night, and we'll see about finishing up."

He starts to protest, but Eric stirs on the red velvet, and he changes his mind.

"*Merci*," he says instead. "Thank you."

"Fine, whatever, now go away. I'm spent."

Tremblay lets Thom escort him out the door. When he's gone, the studio's quiet except for Eric's hushed breathing. I need to clean my tools and start the autoclave, but my fingers and leg are cramping, and I figure Don's ghost will forgive me just this once.

"Upstairs?" Thom suggests in a whisper. We both look at Eric. He's on the cusp of snoring, and by unspoken, mutual consent, we leave him sleeping.

Thom leans against the mirrored elevator walls as it jerks toward the fourth floor. I stretch out my bad leg, massaging my thigh with aching fingers.

"About Henry Ang..." she begins.

"You and I both know that house was deserted," I reply, biting back a groan of pleasure as the knot in the muscle above my knee releases. "Did you see the newspapers on the front stoop? And the dog was barking up a shitstorm. Something's not right."

The ancient elevator bounces to stop, making me stagger. Thom catches my elbow until I steady. Embarrassed, I wave her off.

"You know what keeps buzzing around in my head?" I ask as we limp together over shag carpet. "Nagging like?"

"Tremblay's attachment to his nasty little knife?" Thom offers sourly. "Central's odd disinclination to haul him in? That vile, unholy insect you and Annie Oakley conjured up together?"

"Annie Oakley. I like that." Hysterical giggles erupt. It's my turn to lean against the wall as Thom turns the key in our door. "Eric's a card." Wagging my head, I turn somber. "Nope, not any of those. Grace's phone. It's Grace's phone that's bothering me. Ripper or not, she'd never willingly leave her phone behind for more than an hour or two. I mean, you and I both know she has her entire life in that thing. Everyone's digits, addresses, old snaps of her and her mom. She wouldn't leave those behind in a snit, no way."

"If you say so." It's cold inside the loft, even with the radiators working. Thom tilts her head in my direction. "So—back to Ang's, then? Right now?"

"Now," I agree, "while Annie Oakley is distracted."

Chapter Sixteen

Strong Tea

Grace and I fell in love quickly, over a pot of strong Assam, on a wintery day at the Flower Market on Twenty-Eighth Street. I was there with my sketchpad and pencils in search of chrysanthemums to draw for a client who wanted a bouquet done on his calf. He was my first client on the island—I hadn't yet found a studio and was renting a spot out of Anchor Art on the west side. There were three other artists at Anchor, and although they appreciated the rent, from their sideways glances and muted conversation, I could already tell it wasn't going to work out.

I needed a place of my own, in more ways than one. I was sick to death of living in a hotel, tired of being stared at every time I went out in public, and grudgingly missing Ketchum's open spaces. My fifteenth birthday was just around the corner, but I was friendless and lonely and—because so far November had been unusually cold and snowy—chilled through to the bone.

It didn't help that the sights and sounds of the market reminded me a little too strongly of overturned tulips in blood and shredded rubber beneath a Seattle sky.

I might not have been able to handle it at all, except the Flower Market was doing slow business; many of the vendors were off for the season, and the usual press of people was reduced to a trickle. Besides, I was determined to do well by my first city client; I was charging him a load of cash for two sessions in my chair, and I had to live up to the hype. I found chrysanthemums without any trouble: large, fragrant flowers with petals the color of fresh snow and garnets and pumpkins.

The shopkeeper was busy trying to keep warm near a propane heater under his awning and barely turned his head when I found a place out of the wind and began to sketch.

Time passed. The tips of my ears froze, and the end of my nose went numb. Fingerless gloves kept my hands warm enough to work, but I'd forgotten a hat. I'd found a thick scarf and a wool sweater in a secondhand shop near my hotel, but I was discovering denim jeans and motorcycle boots were pretty worthless in below-freezing temperatures.

It gets cold in Ketchum, but my first winter in New York was the kind that froze your snot to your nostrils as soon as you stepped outside and left you with goose bumps for a good half hour after you returned home. I'm not superstitious, but back then it was hard not to think of the cold snap as a bad omen.

Then a girl tapped my shoulder, interrupting my study of iced chrysanthemums, and things began to look up.

"Hey," she said, peeking around my arm at my sketchbook with a smile. "I don't want to interrupt, but you've been standing here for a really long time, and I hate to be the bearer of bad news, but your face is turning blue."

"Oh." I cleared my throat, licked frozen lips, and tried to smile back. "Thanks. I'm just...ah, working. I'm used to it."

"I don't think you are. You're not even wearing a hat."

She was dark eyed and delicate beneath a long winter coat, a knit cap protecting tendrils of dark hair from the wind, a silver ring in her nose. Taller than me by a few inches, but only because she was wearing boots with stacked heels. She was gorgeous and friendly and held a small bowl of steaming liquid in her hands. And she looked about my age.

"Here," she said, offering me the bowl. "I brought you something warm. It's tea from the shop across the street. Don't worry, it's good. Papa and I have tea there all the time when he's doing business; it's one of the best tea shops in Manhattan."

"Thanks." Bewildered, I closed my sketchbook and stuck it beneath one arm. Pocketing my pencils, I took the bowl of tea from her hands. Fragrant steam wreathed my face. The tips of my fingers throbbed as frozen nerves began to wake up.

"You're him, aren't you? Hemingway?" When I nodded, her grin stretched wider. "I knew it! Papa said no way, because someone like you wouldn't just be standing in the snow sketching flowers. But I knew it was you. No way."

"Thanks." The tea was bitter and very strong. It warmed the back of my throat and settled in my gut, a comfort. "It's good." I hadn't yet gotten used to drinking tea instead of coffee, but the specialty shops were sprouting up all over the city, and I could see how a person could become attached.

"Stupid to stand outside on a day like this. Why don't you just take the flowers home and draw them there?"

"I'm being careful with my money. Saving for a studio and maybe a place to live."

The girl's interest attracted the flower merchant away from his heater. He drifted closer, curious. When he caught sight of my face, his scrutiny sharpened. I finished the tea in a gulp, scalding my tongue, and returned the mug hastily to my new friend. But she stopped me before I could dodge the merchant's attention.

"Come inside," she urged. Snowflakes coated the top of her cap and her lashes. "It's boring as crap, waiting for Papa to finish his paperwork. But it's warm. I'll buy you more tea, and—look—a flower. Which do you want? Red or white or orange? No, all three." She fumbled in the pocket of her coat, producing a small coin purse. "I hate chrysanthemums. They remind me of my grandmother."

"You talk a lot," I managed as she cajoled the shopkeeper into wrapping my new flowers in paper.

"Nothing wrong with being friendly. I'm Grace." Transaction completed, flowers clutched against her chest, she wrapped a hand around my wrist and tugged me across the street. "Come on. I can't wait to tell Papa. He'll piss himself. We know plenty of brilliant people, but that's art-world famous—you know, dull. I've never met someone like you; I never thought I would. Someone magical."

She stopped and looked down at me, and her enthusiasm made the world seem suddenly warmer. She winked, and a bubble of happiness expanded behind my ribs, as unexpected as sunshine in a snowstorm.

We sat in that tea shop for hours, the chrysanthemums slowly wilting in their paper for lack of water, drinking Earl Grey after the Assam ran out. We talked of everything and nothing while Miller sat at a table in a corner, making notes on spreadsheets and occasionally glancing up to make sure we were still there. The man behind the counter let us linger because the increasing snowfall kept everyone else away, and because Grace had told the truth when she said she and her father were regular customers; they seemed on friendly terms with the barista.

"It's a chain," Grace confessed when she caught me eyeing up the masses of orchids on shelves along the walls. "There's one in the Financial District, another near the Met. Papa says Tea Toll in Harlem does a better Darjeeling, but I don't mind. I like the aesthetics here. I'm all about artistic presentation—I come from a *very* artistic family. The Millers have been in the business for generations." Under the table, her foot nudged against mine. From the way she bit her lower lip and smiled at me across our empty mugs, I was pretty sure the contact wasn't accidental.

"What about you?" she asked. "You must come from a long line of artists, to do what you do."

I shook my head, hiding traitorous blushes behind a hand. "Dad's a tree farmer, when he works at all. Mom was a kindergarten teacher." I shrugged. "She could draw, you know, stick figures and penguins and dinosaurs and things."

"What happened to her?" Grace scooted her chair around the table, leaning close. She'd taken off her cap, and her hair fell in loose waves around her shoulders. She was exactly the sort of girl I'd always imagined dating, when I let myself imagine dating girls at all. Bright, self-confident, and willing to fill my quiet spaces with chatter. "Your mom?"

"She ran off with her Pilates instructor when I was ten." It didn't bother me anymore, my mom's desertion.

Every other kid in Ketchum came from a split family; divorce was as common as deer ticks in the spring.

Grace bent even closer and deposited a kiss on my cheek. Her lips were dry and sticky with lip balm, and the kiss was brief but firm. "It happens all the time," she added, taking my hand. "Mine left us for the mayor's office. She's stopped coming home, she's so busy making sure things run smoothly. Sometimes she calls, but usually she's in a bad mood, and I'd rather not talk to her anyway. Politics are *so* pedestrian, don't you think?"

"Maybe." Her fingers linked with mine. I wondered if I was supposed to squeeze back. Outside the flower vendors were obscured by horizontal waves of snow. "President Shannon seemed all right."

Curiosity made her eyes bright. "Oh, I'd forgotten. You met her. Wow. What was that like? Was she nice? She looks nice. Could dress with more flare, but I guess it's important to look buttoned up when you're running a war." She sighed. "I wonder what it's like being the first and last female president of the United States?"

"I think..." I frowned, remembering the way President Shannon watched my tulip blossom on her wrist, like it was the most wonderful thing she'd seen in a very long time. "I think she wishes everyone wasn't always wondering what she is going to do next."

At his table in the corner Miller cleared his throat and rattled his papers. Grace let go of my hand and drew back. A tiny wrinkle had appeared between her perfectly arched brows.

"You know," she said in a stage whisper that carried in the small shop, "if you switched up your look a little, maybe went with a hoodie and sunglasses over basic black—well, this *is* Manhattan. You'd blend in."

"Really?" I'd been too busy trying to survive winter temperatures to give style much thought. Besides, in Ketchum, style was a clean pair of jeans.

"Definitely." Ignoring her father's narrow-eyed disapproval, Grace slapped one palm on the table, making the tea kettle shake. "Stick with me from now on, Hemingway. I know everything about anything that matters in this city. It's clear you need my help. Where are you staying?"

I named the small boutique hotel I'd chosen out of a group listed on a sign in the airport. The wrinkle over her nose grew deeper.

"That won't work," she said, then lowered her voice to an actual whisper, too soft for Miller or the barista to hear. "Tomorrow, noon. I'll meet you in the lobby. You're famous, Hemingway. You want to make the big bucks, get yourself a place? You want to cash in? You can't let people forget about you, not ever. Trust me. I know all about marketing, about presentation. I learned from the best." She smiled at me and tossed her hair, and with her kiss still burning on my cheek, I forgot all about bad omens.

Chapter Seventeen

Monsters

Thom and I bypass Eric's censure by climbing out my bedroom window and down the fire escape. Fog obscures the pavement only three stories below. I descend slowly, distrusting my bad leg, gripping the railing to keep from falling. The metal is slippery and cold in my grip.

We avoid the High Line, which Thom says is too well patrolled at night to risk. Instead we follow Tenth. Most of the way south we keep to the avenue and walk at an easy pace; the streets are quiet, the city tucked away for curfew. Three times Thom leads us off of Tenth, and then back again. I can't figure out why—I see no obvious sign of danger—but I don't question her decisions. Tremblay might be able to fool the CCTV cameras with his blue flame, but Thom's been hunting the Ripper day and night since before I met her, flitting from blind spot to blind spot, dodging detection with only her wits as camouflage. As far as I'm concerned, she knows Manhattan better than anyone in the city.

We're not the only ones out in the night. Tenth Avenue appears deserted, but it's not. There are shadows clinging to brick and glass, hovering just out of sight, hidden in the fog. They whisper among themselves, transacting private business, exchanging pleasantries, sharing secrets. Most turn their faces away as we pass. A few toss my roommate quiet greetings. It's apparent they know her well. She returns their hellos politely but doesn't stop to chat.

An occasional white cab ghosts north or south along the avenue.

Soldiers on patrol walk down Tenth Avenue in regular intervals but pay no notice to the shady business going on around them. Thom shrugs when I ask.

"You don't think Seraphine's the only one who's thought of bribing grunts?" she says quietly. "There's a whole night city runs on graft, and everybody likes it that way. Good for commerce and crime. Like the Ripper." She pauses before adding, "Also good for the evacs who make it past border patrols. For some of them, after dark is the only time it's safe to come out of hiding."

The Angs' brownstone looks even less inviting after sunset. The windows are dark. A streetlight flickers, barely illuminating the front steps and the scattered newspapers. If the dog is still inside, it's given up on barking; the house is silent.

"Window's still open." Together we slip up the front steps and try the front door. It's locked. "Ring the bell?"

"And wake the dog? No," Thom says. "No one's home. They haven't been for at least—" She counts folded newspapers. "—two days. Maybe three." Exactly as long as Grace has been missing. Chills creep down my spine; it's not the fog. "Stay out of the light. I'll go in."

"Not you. Me," I argue. "I'm small enough. I'll fit. You might not."

Thom scowls as she sizes up the window. It's open, all right, but not far enough for a full-sized adult to slip through. I might fit, if I suck in my rib cage and pray. Then again, I might get stuck halfway like goddamn Winnie the Pooh and his honey jar.

"Okay?" I prompt softly when Thom hesitates. Then she nods.

"Go straight in and around and unlock the front door," she orders. "Don't make any noise. And for Chrissake, be careful." She takes her baton from her belt, sets it in her hand: replacement for the CEW Charlie took with her when she left. "Come on, I'll give you a boost."

It's easier said than done. The window's far right of the steps, overhanging a small ground-level garden. Thom's strong, but she's not much taller than I am.

I hold the baton between my teeth. Probably not the smartest place for an electrified weapon, but risking electrocution may be the least lunatic thing I've done in the past week. Beneath the open window, Thom cups her hands for my foot. I put my foot in her hands.

"On three," she whispers. "Ready? One, two—"

Her muscles flex and she sends me up, up, and over her head. I catch the windowsill and barely manage to a solid grip. Also, I'm not a circus tumbler.

I start to fall, scrabbling with hands and feet. The soles of my boots catch on the facade. I bite back a yelp and try shimmying up the wall, using the seams in brick as toeholds. It's close, and I'm 100 percent sure I hear Thom suppress a giggle, but I manage to get my arms over the sill. After that it's not exactly easier, but workable. I wiggle up and over the window ledge—arms, elbows, then head and shoulders.

It's a close fit. The window's blocked open with a security latch, stuck in place. I'm nearly stuck—Winnie the Pooh and his honey pot—squirming between casement and sill. My heart lodges in my throat as I wiggle. I must be making a racket. Any moment a soldier on patrol will appear behind us, or maybe one of the Angs with a baseball bat, and I'm done for.

Then my hoodie rips free and I'm through, tumbling face-first through the opening onto scratchy carpet, knees and thighs scraping on the sill. The carpet muffles the thud I make when I fall. My jaw clenches painfully around the baton in my mouth.

I lie frozen for what feels like forever but must be only seconds. Everything is still: the room I'm sprawled out in and the night outside the window. Slowly, my eyes adjust and my pulse stops pounding in my ears. I've made it.

I'm in what must be a parlor, the room tastefully fussy and salted with expensive-looking antiques. A night-light in the shape of a stained-glass turtle shines fitfully on a writing desk against the far wall. It's barely enough light to see by, but it's better than nothing.

I spit the baton out into my hand and rise. The room reeks of lemon and dust and a metallic, sweet perfume that makes my skin crawl. I know what blood smells like; for days after Seattle I couldn't get that stink out of my nose.

My heart sinks into my gut. My first instinct is to curl up on the floor and cover my head. My second is to crawl right back out the window and run. Instead, I kick off my boots and carry them with me as I tiptoe across the parlor in my socks, remembering Thom's caution: *don't make any noise.*

It's only luck that saves me from stepping on a sea of broken glass. Luck, and the stained-glass turtle, because when I move, the gleam from the night-light reflects back at me from a multitude of shards scattered across the floor.

The glass is the first visible sign something's not right. I'm not sure where it's coming from, why the carpet is littered with it, what's broken. I pick my way painstakingly around the edge of the carpet, testing with socked toes before putting weight on each step, until I make the parlor door and the front hallway.

It's darker there than in the parlor, but not so black I can't see destruction. The space near the front door is in shambles, the entry rug pulled up off the ground, twisted to one side. A wooden console lies smashed on the bare floor, a pottery catchall shattered into pieces beneath it. An old grandfather clock lies near the console, sideways across the front door. Its cabinet door is smashed, and broken glass forms a sparkling river down the hall and into the parlor. The clock is at least eight feet tall and heavy. Its corpse is blocking the front door. I might be strong enough to push it away, but not without cutting my hands on the shards that still remain, gritted teeth along the edges of the smashed cabinet.

I can just make out Thom's shadowy figure through the sidelights flanking the front door. I don't dare call out to her.

In the end it's not a difficult decision. The violence in the hall and parlor is only further proof that something is terribly wrong, confirmation that where Grace is concerned, my instincts are always good. Something is very off, has been off for longer than I'd like to admit to myself. And even if that something has nothing to do with the East River Ripper, more than ever I'm certain my friend needs my help.

Gripping my baton in one hand and my boots in the other, I turn my back on the front door and start up the stairs.

They're dark. The light from the parlor behind me fades as I climb. My feet make no noise on the carpeted steps. The brownstone is eerily silent, waiting. Somewhere below me an appliance kicks on, hums briefly, kicks off. The stench of blood grows stronger as I climb. My skin is tight on my bones, itchy, anticipating attack from behind or above.

Halfway up the staircase, I find the Angs' dog. In the gloom it's difficult to make out more than a long body and floppy ears. It bares white teeth in a long snout, growling softly, but doesn't move from the rucked-up white dress shirt it's claimed in the corner of one step as shelter.

"Hush, now," I whisper. "You're okay. Stay."

I inch past, expecting the snap of teeth on my ankle, but the dog doesn't give chase. Its growls turn to soft snarls before it burrows further into the nest of fabric, hiding.

Good dog, I think. *You've got the absolute right idea.*

At the top of the stairs, I find more evidence of disorder. Someone's dropped a basket of laundry on the landing. Clothes are strewn all over the floor, vague piles in the dark. The basket is upside-down, and the top of its white plastic frame is splattered all over with something black. The carpet is tacky, stiff through my socks.

The blood smell is thick enough to choke me. My hand is shaking on Thom's baton, and I can hear the rasp of my panicked breathing in my ears.

"Grace?" I call softly. "Henry? Ms. Ang? Grace, are you here?"

There's no answer. There's a loud crash from below, and the sausage dog on the steps begins a terrified yapping.

I fumble along the wall at the top of the stairs for the light switch I know must be there. My fingers bump against a switch plate. Holding my breath, I flick the switch. Immediately light floods the second floor, blinding me. I blink through the dazzle, adrenaline pumping, and take a look around but not in time to fend off the monster waiting for me at the other end of the hall.

If the victims the Ripper discards in the East River resemble mummies, then the victim he's left alive is the spitting image of a horror film zombie but without all the juicy gore. Henry Ang—and I can only guess it's Henry because the poor kid's still wearing his thick-lensed glasses—shambles toward me, mouth hanging open, pink tongue protruding. The tongue's the only animated thing about him; the Ripper's magic has drained him to nothing but papery skin stretched tight over bones. His hands are gnarled claws, his bare feet no better. His clothes hang loose on his frame—whatever meat or muscle he had on his body is gone.

His short hair is so thin and white it's almost translucent, and his eyes behind the lenses of his glasses are sunken, colorless, staring. There's a makeshift bandage wrapped several times around his throat; it looks like part of a towel. Dried blood stains the edge.

"Jesus." I scramble backward as he lurches forward. "Jesus fucking Christ, Henry, how are you even still alive?"

The creature that was Henry Ang doesn't answer. He mumbles wordlessly, reaching both hands in my direction, but I'm not sure he knows I'm there. His head turns blindly from side to side, seeking. In a few more steps, he'll reach me, and the thought of those grasping claws on my flesh sends shudders up and down my body—visceral horror.

I thumb the button on Thom's baton. The CEW crackles to life.

"No," Thom says softly from behind me, climbing the last stair. "Don't hurt him. He's a witness." She's panting; she must have taken the stairs two at a time. "He's seen the Ripper and lived to tell about it."

Henry stops just out of reach, head wobbling, hands grasping. He looks right at me, but the expression of horror frozen on his withered face doesn't change.

"Barely," I say, sickened. Then I gulp. "There's a lot of blood." It's all over, on the walls in dried streaks, turning cream-colored carpet brown, ruining overturned laundry.

"Not his." Thom steps around me. "He's come from that room." She indicates a door down the hall. Several pairs of bloody footprints on the carpet lead in and out. She fishes in a pocket, hands me her phone. I have to drop my boots to take it. Ang shuffles vaguely in a circle, stumbles away back down the corridor. "Hemingway, I need you to go back downstairs and wake the neighbors. Call it in. We need backup."

"No. I'm not leaving you. The Ripper could still be anywhere." I'm starting to hyperventilate again. "And Grace." *Grace.*

"Call it in," Thom snaps in a whisper. Then she follows Ang.

I manage to dial with one hand, Taser at the ready in the other, as I hurry after, trying to avoid pools of dried blood. Central dispatch is talking in my ear, but I've forgotten what I'm supposed to say in return because we've reached the room at the end of the hall, Thom's flicked on the lights, and I'm pretty sure the tall woman curled like a comma on the king-sized bed used to be Ms. Ang.

"Jesus." I can't help the crack in my voice. "Is she still alive?"

But I can tell even from across the room that she's not. The gash across her throat is a bloodless leer. The gold-and-silver damask bed cover—what I can see of it—is clean, as is the faux-fur throw arranged over the desiccated corpse, presumably for modesty.

"He slit her throat at the top of the steps," Thom says, scanning the room, taking in the array of antique silver knickknacks arranged about the room, the open door to the master bathroom on our right, the ripped towel on the bathroom tile, the trail of blood on the floor. "Finished the job and arranged her on the bed after."

"Or someone did," I say, nodding at Ang where he hovers protectively between the bed and a nightstand cluttered with more silver. "He left them. Why did he leave them? *Did* he leave them?" I can't help but turn this way and that, seeking, just like Ang. "Is he still here?"

"Blood's at least two days old," Thom replies calmly. "The Ripper doesn't leave his victims behind. He gives them to the river. He was interrupted, didn't get to finish the job, left in a hurry, running from someone or something."

"Grace?" I see no sign of my friend anywhere in the gruesome room. Relief and terror tangle in my lungs, clogging them. "You were right all along."

"Maybe." Thom leans over the corpse on the bed, sniffing the air around the dead woman's face, careful not to touch. "We'll need to search the house top to bottom, but not until backup arrives. Roadblock on Broadway will slow them a little—they should be here soon. I wonder..."

She pauses, interest caught. I see it almost immediately: a flash of gold almost hidden in the tangled sheets, partially obscured by Mrs. Ang's mutilated corpse. Thom snatches a pencil from her pocket, uses the tip to carefully drag gleaming metal across damask.

An expensive watch, heavy gold links stained with drying blood. I recognize it immediately.

"Holy shit." My stomach flips.

"Tremblay's," Thom agrees grimly. "What did I tell you—"

"Look out!"

Ang has a silver candlestick in both hands, and he's moving much more quickly than seems possible given he's hardly more than a skeleton, aiming for Thom's bent head. I hear the crack of silver on flesh a heartbeat before I'm on Ang, arms wrapped around his emaciated middle. He's hardly more than parchment and determination—insubstantial as Tremblay's blue-fire feathers—and it takes nothing to bowl him over. We tumble to the floor. Ang releases a long sigh beneath me and goes still.

"Thom!" I scramble up. She's sprawled facedown on the mattress, inches from Ms. Ang's corpse. There's fresh blood in the room, on the back of Thom's head, on Rafe's beanie, on gold-and-silver damask. Despairing, I roll her over, call her name, press my brow to hers while searching for a pulse. My hands are too damp, my fingertips slip on her skin. There's a ringing in my ears.

But her chest is rising and falling. She groans. Her eyelids flutter when I cradle her in my lap and whisper reassurances against her matted curls. Her blood wets my fingers.

I should probably do something about the bleeding, staunch the wound, stop the *drip drip drip* of life escaping. I can't. I can't move. I'm locked in place, in time, in a moment, trapped in a memory.

I taste cinnamon sugar on my tongue and see Pike Place Market out of the corner of my eye.

Thom's eyes blink open. Her mouth moves.

"Answer it," she says. "Hemingway, you need to answer the phone."

The ringing in my ears is coming from the floor, from Thom's mobile where I've dropped it and the CEW baton, forgotten and useless in the face of danger because I'm an artist, not a fighter. And when it comes down to it, I'd rather attack with my fists and with my teeth.

I make myself climb off the bed and answer the phone, speak to dispatch on the other end. They're none too pleased with me, but after some prompting, I give them the Angs' address. Quickly help arrives in the form of hard-boiled, highly decorated soldiers carrying enough illicit ammo to start a second war. They're Central's best, and they're not playing around. They have absolutely zero patience to spare for me, especially when I contaminate the crime scene by blowing chunks in the Angs' master bath.

They tend to Thom immediately, cleaning and sealing the gash on the back of her head while they pepper her with questions. She's sitting up, Rafe's beanie clutched in her hand, fingers twisting in the red knit. She's gone the color of pea soup.

I'd go to her if I could, but I'm cornered against the wall by two very stern grunts, and they're not about to let me take a step until they've had approval from Central. They watch me from beneath their visors, hands on their weapons, and it's not hero worship I see in their eyes.

Against all odds, Henry Ang is still alive. A soldier with a medic's bag manages to find a vein in his shrunken arm and starts running fluids. Another slaps a monitor to his neck below the bandage on his throat. Ang is gasping shallowly, blind eyes rolled up in his skull. I thought I'd killed him by falling on him. I'm fiercely glad he's still alive.

"He was trying to protect his mother," Thom says as Ang is loaded onto a gurney and carried carefully out of the bedroom, trailed by a small army of guards. "He didn't mean any harm. I'm not sure he even understood she was dead."

Ms. Ang is beyond anyone's protection. Her corpse is loaded onto a second gurney, tidily covered, and toted out of the brownstone after her son.

The Angs' sausage dog slinks into the bedroom, tail tucked firmly between its back legs. The dog's tiny, no more than twelve pounds, dappled and long-eared with short, stubby legs. It makes a beeline in my direction, dodging heavy military boots. A grunt with a collection of medals on his chest is telling Thom she can choose between the hospital or the brig.

I pick the dog up, burying my nose in its short fur to block out the stink of death. The dog tolerates my sentiment and consents to swipe a wet tongue across my face, shivering.

Thom chooses the hospital, and she leaves the bedroom the same way as Ang and his mother, on a gurney. Her eyes are wide and apologetic when she turns her head in my direction. I show her my best reassuring smile, but from her crestfallen expression, I'm not sure I've got it right.

Then I'm alone in the bedroom except for my two guards and the dog. Central keeps me there as they search the Angs' brownstone floor by floor, nook and cranny, and closet by closet. I can hear their shouts—"Clear!"—as they storm each room. The racket of many heavy boots resounds through the old house. They're looking for more victims—*Grace*—or they're looking for the Ripper. Or maybe they think I'm the Ripper and my next stop is Riker's Island.

Eventually my bad legs gives out and I sit, the dog curled in my lap where Thom's head rested minutes—hours?—earlier. My guards don't seem to mind. Shock or grief makes my limbs heavy. My eyes drift shut. I'm drowsing when a familiar voice jolts me from the edge of oblivion.

"Hemingway," Emma says, kneeling on the floor in front of me. "Come with me. It's time to go now."

Of course, I realize. All along they were waiting for my watchdog, my government-appointed snitch.

"I can't leave," I protest, groggy. "I need to find Grace. I need to know if she was here."

"She was," Emma tells me. She lays a gentle hand on my cheek. "They found her things, in Henry's room: a duffle and a few other personal items. They'll have her father in to identify them, but there's little doubt."

I brace myself, squeezing the dog so hard it mutters protest, but Emma shakes her head.

"They haven't found her body," she says, her hand a brand against my icy cheek. "Not yet." Then she rises. "Come on."

"Where are we going?" It feels as if the night fog has crept through the open window and rooted between my ears. I can't think straight. I've been in shock before, but this is different—colder, duller. Maybe because nobody's offered drugs to take the edge off like they did after Labor Day.

"Home," Emma replies. "I'm taking you home."

Chapter Eighteen

Duplicity

I sleep for hours, at the mercy of my bruised mind and body, and surface reluctantly only when the murmur of voices outside my bedroom door becomes too persistent to ignore. The Angs' dog is curled under the covers near my feet. I smuggled her out under my jacket, Emma's arm a shield over my shoulders, and nobody so much as squeaked in protest. In the white cab on the way back to Earnest Ink, I checked the name on the dog's collar: Reba.

I throw on clean clothes and pad barefoot out into the kitchen, grinding sleep from my eyes with the heels of my hands. The dog follows reluctantly, claws tick-tacking on the wood floor. Eric and Emma are standing together at the kitchen counter, talking somberly over matching mugs of tea. The clock on the microwave says 7:00 a.m., and outside the loft windows, morning sun is doing its best to burn off the fog.

It's Tuesday. Day Three on the Ripper's calendar, if—in spite of his early and botched attack on the Angs' brownstone—he's kept Grace alive and is sticking to schedule.

Tremblay, I correct myself as I make a beeline for the bathroom. *Tremblay's* botched attack, *Tremblay's* schedule.

It hadn't taken long for Central to ID the watch through the snaps in Tremblay's file.

If I'd trusted Thom's instincts, Grace might be home safe, and Tremblay might be locked up on Rikers where he belongs instead of on the run, always one step ahead of Surveillance.

In the bathroom I take a piss, wash my face and hands, brush my teeth, and rinse out my mouth. I need to shave—rough stubble on my face and neck plus the hollows under my eyes and yesterday's wrinkled clothes make me look disreputable and debauched—but I don't have the time or patience.

When I come out of the bathroom, Eric hands me a mug of tea and joins me in front of Thom's murder wall. I suppose Ms. Ang's photo belongs up there now, and Henry Ang's if they haven't managed to stabilize him overnight.

"What are you going to do next?" Emma asks. She's putting water into a bowl for Reba. The dog laps it up eagerly. I'll have to remember to stop at the market for kibble. I've never had a pet before, unless you count the hens roaming our backyard in Ketchum, which I don't.

A dog around the house seems normal, cozy, regular. I wonder what that's like.

"Going to the hospital. I need to check on Thom and Ang." I put the tea on the kitchen counter untouched. I'm not the least bit hungry.

Emma gathers up her purse and her coat. There are new lines around her mouth, and her hair has escaped her braid in tendrils. Apparently, I'm not the only one who's had a long few days.

"I have appointments this morning," she explains apologetically, "or I'd go with you. Please let me know as soon as you hear."

When she's gone, Eric starts to speak, but I cut him off with a brisk shake of my head.

"How many appointments today?"

"Four," he reports reluctantly. He's dressed in stripes and shiny spats, fresh and bright-eyed. "First one's at eleven. But I can go with—"

"No. Open the shop. I left a mess last night. Clean everything up. I'll be back in time." I want to work. I need the comfort of ink and flesh, the reassurance of my machine in hand. "I'm going alone."

Fitz is sweeping the sidewalk outside Earnest Ink. He tips his hat at me when I step out into the morning. He's not the only one waiting for me. Pink-haired Charlie, a dirty blanket wrapped around her shoulders for warmth, detaches from the shadows of a building before I've made it to Tenth.

"Hey," she says in greeting. "You seen Tremblay?"

"No." I stare straight ahead. "I hope I never see him again. And you'd be smart not to go looking. Haven't you heard? Thom was right, Central was right, the rest of us were wrong. Tremblay's the East River Ripper."

"I heard. I heard this morning when they came for him with trucks and guns and gas and battered down our fence." Charlie ducks around in front of me so I'm forced to see the fear in her puckered frown. "You're wrong. Tremblay wouldn't hurt a fly. And now we're all scattered, them that didn't get away before Central bagged us as dodgers or evacs. The Pier's a wreck, and Seraphine needs somewhere safe to hole up."

"I don't care. As far as I'm concerned, all of you can go to hell."

Charlie scoffs and spits. The glob of saliva barely misses my front, spatters on the sidewalk instead. I step around it, increase my pace.

"You don't understand!" Charlie shouts. "Tremblay and Seraphine—they're all the family you got! The rest of this city, they might pay big money for your ink, magic man, but they still think you're a freak!"

Mount Sinai West used to be one of those hospitals that specialized in risky surgeries. Now the hospital caters to most of the west side, from head colds to war trauma, and everything in between. Outside, the glass and brick building is professional grade. Inside, the scuffed walls reflect threadbare desolation. Patients wander the halls or sit dejectedly in wheelchairs while they wait for treatment. Too many doctors and nurses have shipped out to the front line, and those who were lucky enough to evade the draft struggle to provide what care they can, plagued by out-of-date machinery and a severe shortfall of effective medication.

If you can afford it, you pay for private, in-home care and black-market remedies. If you can't, you end up at Mount Sinai West.

I catch a harried floor nurse near intake and charm him into disclosing Thom's room number. Fame has its perks, and Charlie's wrong: the nurse doesn't think I'm a freak. He hands me his digits on a piece of paper before he rushes off, swears up and down he gives the best massage in Manhattan. "You look like you could use a laying on of hands. Call me!"

I bin his number as I climb the stairs to the fifth floor, but I appreciate the sentiment.

Armed grunts patrol the entire fifth level and bracket the exits. Relief feels like a punch in the chest. So many soldiers can only mean that against all odds, Ang is still alive. That's miracle number one. Miracle number two occurs when the grunts let me pass without acknowledgment. The reason why meets me near the deserted fifth floor nurse's desk.

"Hemingway." Thom's chief shakes my hand with enough vigor to set the medals on his chest bouncing. "I'd hoped you might show. Good. Castillo's demanding I spring her. I want you to convince her to stay another night."

Central's put Thom and Ang in neighboring rooms. Ang's door is firmly shut. To my astonishment, Grace's father is loitering in the hall nearby. When he sees me, he bursts into tears. Scuttling across the worn vinyl floor, he catches me in a fierce embrace.

"My boy," he exclaims. "I'm so glad you're all right!"

I tolerate his emotional embrace as best I can. Snuffling, he drips onto my shoulder. At last I understand where Grace got her penchant for the dramatic.

"I'm not hurt," I say, thumping his shoulder awkwardly. I'm baffled. "Mr. Miller, what are you doing here?"

"They think the Ripper has my Gracie." He gulps down tears, casts a glance the chief's way, and wipes his upper lip with the back of his hand. "It turns out she was with Henry and Rose Ang, you see, all this time. We had an argument. Just a stupid argument. We have so many. I didn't realize she'd taken it to heart..." He trails off, looking again at the chief for confirmation.

"Ang's still unconscious," Thom's commanding officer tells me. "Hanging on by his fingernails, and God knows, he'll never be the same again. But the mayor's flown in the best doctors the free world has to offer. It's possible if—when—Ang wakes, he'll have some answers."

I doubt it. The pitiful creature we encountered in the Angs' brownstone seemed incapable of thought, much less coherent speech.

"I hope so." I endure a second, wet hug from Miller. "Sir, I hope they find Grace soon."

Day Three, I think again, as the chief escorts me away from Grace's father and into Thom's hospital room.

He gives us privacy, which is nice, although with the unspoken agreement I do my best to convince Thom she needs another night in hospital attached to obsolete machines.

She's dozing, the blankets tucked tight around her body and underneath her armpits. The doctors have shaved her curls at the crown of her head and I can see a row of angry black sutures against her scalp. She stirs when I lean over the cot, counting stitches, and wakes with a scowl on her face.

"Fifteen," I report. "Impressive. Who'd have thought Ang had it in him?"

"Candlestick was pure silver," Thom replies, voice rough as sandpaper. "With sharp edges."

There's a chair drawn up by the side of the cot. I sink into it.

"You look like shit," Thom says. "Is Ang talking yet?"

"He's still out." I catch myself chewing the inside of my cheek. "Do you really think he'll wake?"

Thom shrugs against the mattress. "He's stubborn," she says. "A fighter. Bandaged his own cut throat with bathroom towels and stood guard over his mother's corpse even with most of his vitals sucked dry." She pauses. "Grace is a fighter, too."

Thom's left hand is small and dark on white hospital sheets. I take it lightly in my own. She doesn't protest, and when she squeezes my fingers, it's the best feeling in the world, even better than the kiss of tattoo needle on skin.

"I want to go home," she says. "It's cold and loud and dirty and too loud here. Will you take me home?"

"Man with the medals says you have a concussion on top of the gash. Heavy silver with sharp edges, and all that. They want to keep an eye on you just a little longer, make sure your head doesn't swell any bigger."

She huffs, and winces at the effort, and closes her eyes against the bright fluorescent lights. "Have they found Tremblay yet?"

"No."

"They will. It's just a matter of time. He can't hide forever, now Central's finally in the game."

"I should have listened to you."

"Yeah." Thom's mouth curls faintly. "You should have."

"You're the smartest person I know. The most capable. Kind. Not afraid to stick to your guns and that Hung Gar thing you do with your hands and feet—I wish you'd teach me that." I bring our linked hands up to my mouth, brush her knuckles with my lips.

"Careful." But Thom's smile deepens. "Don't want my head to swell further."

"Let me sketch you," I cajole against her knuckles. Her hand is rough, calloused from hard work, strong.

"No," Thom says. "But you can stay for a while. Will you?" I can hear uncertainty beneath detachment, and I want to promise her the world.

But I won't insult her by guaranteeing impossibilities, so I give her the only promise I can keep.

"I'll stay until they kick me out. Now try and get some sleep."

I use a phone at the nurses' station to call Eric check in and discover he's made the dubious decision of working in another client before our eleven o'clock.

"Sorry," he says. "But it's Lincoln Roe, just in town for the day. Publicity on that's worth the time, Hemingway. You know it."

Lincoln Roe's the king of Wall Street, probably richer than I am, and at the moment I could care less. But Eric hangs up before I can protest, and I'm too tired to call him back and pitch a fit.

Early morning passes uneventfully. Thom spends most of it in fitful sleep. I half expect Central to haul me off to Rikers for aiding and abetting Tremblay's mischief, but for the most part the grunts on the fifth floor ignore my presence. The room next door is quiet. If Ang hasn't roused to consciousness, at least it appears he hasn't yet succumbed to Tremblay's attack, either.

Eventually the chief shoos me out with promises he'll send word when Thom's ready to be discharged. Miller's nowhere to be seen. I leave the hospital room intending to shower and eat before I have to face Lincoln Roe. The fog has melted away; the sun is shining in a cold autumn sky.

Work turns out to be a relief, a break from the clamor of alarm that seems to have set up permanent residence in the front of my head. I turn preparation into a ritual. Feeding ink to my well, testing my machine, encouraged by its friendly buzzing. Checking my tools for proper sterilization, apologizing to Roe for arriving late to our appointment while I disinfect the spot on his skinny bicep where he wants me to tattoo a stag midcharge.

The guy's an easier client than I predicted, asking for a selfie or two before I get started, but otherwise sitting quietly in my chair.

Eric is engrossed in his book behind the register. The studio door is propped open to let in the crisp afternoon air. Pedestrians roam back and forth on the street, stopping occasionally to peek in. Time slows to a crawl. I'm in my element again, my safe space, the only quarter of my life where I know for sure each move I make is the right one.

I'm finishing up, putting the last touches on the buck's lowered antlers, when Eric's mobile rings from inside the register. He pops the drawer and answers. Whatever he hears on the other end makes his brows climb.

"He's with a client. Can he call you back? Yes, okay. Ten minutes. Yes, I promise." He ends the call and flicks a finger my direction. "Thom," he relays, "needs to speak to you soon as you're finished. Must be ready for discharge." He slides his vintage Nokia along the counter in my direction.

Roe reacts with grave appreciation when the stag on his upper arm comes to life and gallops, snorting, in circles around his bicep. He counts a stack of bills into Eric's waiting hand, poker-faced, and leaves Earnest Ink with the self-possession of someone who witnesses small miracles every day.

"Wow," I say, grudgingly impressed. I've never before seen such a pleased nonreaction to my talents.

"Commodities traders," Eric replies as the phone on the counter starts ringing again. "Nothing rattles them anymore."

I snatch up the phone, take it with me to the front door, shutting out street noise. "Thom? You ready? I'll order up a cab."

"Ang's awake," Thom interjects over static on the line.

"You're shitting me." I stare blindly out at the sidewalk. "Is he talking?"

"Not yet, but the chief says any moment now. I want to sit in on the interview, Hemingway, if they'll let me. I think you should come."

She's still talking, but I've lost track of what she's saying because just then I notice two unexpected things at once.

One: there's a commotion on down the block, people running this way and that, fleeing before a too-tall punk with ugly indigo hair and blue fire in his hands. It's the flame they're running from, the shower of cobalt embers spitting at their heels.

"Hemingway?" Thom's frustration is a distant concern, one I can't possibly address, because...

Two: Eric's left his perch on the stool behind the counter. His reflection looms in the windowpane behind my own as he bends over my shoulder. I can't see his expression, but his hand on my arm is a vice, and when he presses the blade of his folding knife against my carotid artery, it's a winsome caress, nothing at all like Tremblay's ham-handed jabs.

"Give me the phone," he says, reaching around to lock the front door. He presses the lever, and the metal shutters come down much too quickly. Tremblay's still half a block away. I think our eyes meet through the glass, but maybe it's only my imagination. The shutters crash into place and I'm trapped.

"Hemingway?" Thom's calling down the line. Eric plucks his mobile out of my grasp, disconnecting the call. His blade is a promise beneath my chin.

"Well," he says. "Isn't that disappointing. Waking up, is he? I'd hoped he wouldn't. I thought I'd have more time."

"What?" I stare from the mobile in his hand to his face. "Eric, what the hell?" My body realizes before my brain catches on. Adrenaline floods my system, and my mouth goes dry, a fight-or-flight reaction to sudden danger.

"Sorry, darling," he says softly, and although his face is creased in a familiar, fond smile, his eyes are dark and flat and alien. Then he grabs me.

I struggle, of course I do, twisting in his grasp, striking out with fist and feet but maybe not with everything I've got, because I can't believe he means me any harm. The knife scrapes but doesn't slice. He tolerates my fists and dodges my feet and swears when I bite a chunk out of his hand.

"I survived World War III, Hemingway," he says grimly, holding me at arm's length. He's much stronger than I realized, steel and sinew beneath pretend indolence. All this time I've been taking his stolid protection for granted, not thinking too deeply about what lies within. "You can't touch me. You'll only make things worse by trying."

When he grows tired of my struggling, he cuts me down. Not with the knife. He takes me with magic, fingertips cold against the back of my neck. Ice spreads in my veins as he steals all liveliness from my body cell by cell.

It's not like dying should be, like going to sleep or just stopping. It's deeply painful, a rending, but I've lost the ability to scream out. The studio floor comes up to meet me as Eric tears from me everything I didn't know was precious until too late.

Turns out, "the Ripper" is a suitable sobriquet after all.

"Come on, Hemingway," Grace pleads over the cheerful pop of radiator pipes hard at work. "Open your eyes. Come on, babe. You've got this."

She pats at my cheek. I wish she'd stop. My skin smarts worse than the time I spent a whole day in July rafting Alturas Lake without sunscreen. I'd felt feverish for days after and then shed skin in huge patches a week later.

"Ouch. Stop." I bat her hand away, keep my eyes stubbornly closed. "Go away." Waking up can be a bitch even on good days, and from the ache in my head, I've had a rough night. I can't remember starting in on the gin, but sometimes it's like that.

I also can't recollect the last time I've gone on a blackout bender, which means something truly awful must have set me off.

"Go away," I repeat, curling knees to nose, wincing when my skin protests. The sounds of the old building are intimate, comforting, but when I passed out, I must have missed my mattress—and the hard wood floor does nothing for my tender bones. Everything hurts, from my fingernails to the roots of my hair. "Jesus. Just a little while longer."

"He needs water," Grace says to someone who is not me. "For fuck's sake, you son of a bitch, just a few swallows."

It's true my tongue is sandpaper against my teeth, and now that I'm surfacing, I'd kill for a cold glass of water. I don't think I've ever been so miserably thirsty in my life.

"Not yet. Ms. Harcourt's at the corner store, and she could come back any minute. Today of all days I don't have the patience to endure her stares. I swear, some days it's like talking to a brick wall—she wouldn't know small talk if fell on her head. Waste of space and air."

"Why don't you just kill her then?" Grace's fury rings false to my ears; she's tugging at my shirt collar a little too insistently. "Drop her in the river like everyone else who pisses you off?"

Eric chuckles. "You've got it backward, sweetheart. That old lady doesn't deserve distinction. Hemingway, stop moping. Rise and shine. You're not hurt. I barely took anything from you at all."

Just like that everything comes rushing back: Grace's disappearance, the peddler in Central Park, Seraphine's creepy interference, Christy Spears and Central's CCTV Morningside snaps, Emma's dubious concern, the Angs' brownstone, Thom lying injured in my lap, Miller's tears outside her hospital room.

I bolt upright. My skin tugs painfully at my bones, but that torment is nothing compared to the pain inflicted by Eric's smug grin. He's sitting only inches away, settled atop a square wooden crate, ever-present book open on his lap. A finger marks his place between pages. His eyes flick eagerly back and forth between Grace and me, anticipating. He's wearing a long cashmere coat over a purple shirt and striped socks under neatly pressed trousers.

"Surprise!" he says, shamming elation. "She's been under your nose all along, Sherlock Holmes. Literally within shouting distance—as if I'd ever be careless enough to let *that* happen, right, Grace?"

She doesn't dignify him with an answer. Instead she pulls me close in a halting embrace and buries her face in my shoulder.

"Grace?"

She's weightless, a collection of bird bones and shrunken skin. When I cup the back of her head, hanks of dry hair comes away between my fingers. The curve of her skull trembles in my palm.

"Oh, God. Grace."

"Don't look," my best friend says into my shirt. Unlike her father, she doesn't shed any tears. "He's made me ugly. I can't be ugly."

"You're alive." Exhilaration makes me hug her tight. A gasp of pain escapes her.

"Didn't you hear what I said?" She rears back. "He's made me ugly. I'd rather be dead!"

In the flickering fluorescent light, I can see the full extent of the Ripper's dismantling. She's not quite reached the zombie horror levels Henry Ang endured, but she's close. Desiccated, shriveled. Parchment skin stretched too tight on stark bone. Spine hunched, bony protuberances visible through the cotton of her shirt. The bridge of her nose is a hatchet, her chin acute, her eyes colorless, wandering orbs.

She's alive, but I can't think how, or that she will be for much longer. She must be only one step away from Ang's blind unintelligibility, two steps away from becoming a mummy in the East River.

I pull her close again, rock her gently, trying to sooth without bruising. It hurts us both, but I don't let go.

"Day Four," says Eric, meeting my gaze over the top of her skull. "Make the most of it."

"Why are you doing this?"

He closes his book and sets it down on the crate beside him. "By 'this' do you mean all of it, or just the part that inconveniences you?" He spreads his hands. "Although, I suppose you could argue it's always been an inconvenience on your part, though you were too self-absorbed to notice. If you'd bothered to look up and around sometime in, say, the last half decade, you might have charged me rent."

I look up and around now. I know where we are—how could I not? The third-floor layout is exactly the same as the fourth was before I cut it apart and made it into my living space. The same old floors, the same brick shell divided into tiny 1980s-era apartments, the bubbling radiators, and the off-white appliances. Ms. Harcourt had been my building's only resident when I signed the purchase documents. I'd let her stay and left the rest of the residences empty except for a few I'd used to store the boxes in which I kept the remnants of my old life.

"I needed a place," the East River Ripper explains, still smiling, "to store my treasures. My books and...other things. Couldn't use my home, too dangerous. Imagine my delight when I saw you had all this unused space just a short elevator's ride up from work. And you just handed me the key with my employment papers. You really are naïve, Hemingway."

Grace is limp in my arms, as if she used up all the strength she had left shaking me awake. I need to get her help. I need to get us both help. I remember Tremblay darting down the street toward the studio, pedestrians scattering out of his way. But how much time has passed since Thom phoned to say Ang was awake? Day Four, Eric said. Has Tuesday become Wednesday?

"I trusted you. I *admired* you."

"Exactly," Eric agrees sadly. He rolls his shoulders. "Maybe you didn't have a choice. What was it the street punk said? Like calls to like? I think he might be right."

Anger rises at last, a weak flicker of rage growing steadily stronger. It's good to know shock or the Ripper's magic hasn't smothered my ability to feel.

"You were listening!"

"I'm always listening. Earnest Ink isn't just your castle. It's mine, too. And you and I, we've got to protect the important things, right?" Eric hops off the storage crate and secures his book under one arm. "Ms. Harcourt should be back and all tucked in by now. I'll get you that drink of water now. Don't bother yelling. The walls in this unit are soundproof—I saw to that myself. Besides, it's not like that old biddy will take any notice—she's deaf in one ear."

"Thom—"

"Is busy chasing the wrong suspect, thanks to some cleverly staged evidence. By the time she realizes she's made a mistake—again—I'll be long gone, and you'll be in my river. I'm sorry, Hemingway. You and I were good together. If Grace hadn't been so nosy, it wouldn't have to end this way. But things are heating up, and I can't think of any other way out."

He leaves the room, closing the door behind him. I hear the snick of more than one lock being turned and the thump of something being pushed up against the outside of the door.

Chapter Nineteen

Regret

As soon as we're alone, I ease Grace from my embrace and stretch her carefully on the floor. Her eyes are shut, lids shivering, but she opens them when I lay her down.

"Don't go. I've been so lonely and scared. Hemingway, I'm cold."

"Hush." I press a tender kiss to the top of her head. "I'm just going to look around. Maybe there's a blanket, or something I can use to get us out of here."

"I looked and looked. There's nothing." Her milk-white eyes track me as I stand, but she makes no effort to rise. "He's smart. Who would have thought—Eric, the East River Ripper? I always thought he was some kind of war hero. Isn't that what he said?"

"Yes." My joints protest when I start to move. I look down at my hands, expecting claws and papery skin, but they look the same as always. Small, competent, ink-stained. Artist's hands. "That's what he said. Now I'm not so sure."

The unit's not very big, but it's large enough. I walk the periphery slowly, glad of the uncertain fluorescent light, determined not to miss anything important. A jumble of packing boxes take up most of the floor space, the majority made of cardboard, a few of them wood. For the most part, they're crammed with books. I pick up a paperback, come away with dust on my hands when I put it back down.

I find at least one cardboard box containing clothing: vintage '90s couture. I dig out a heavy velvet overcoat and use it to cover Grace's wasted body.

"He'll take it away when he comes back," she confides wistfully, plucking at the velvet nap. "He doesn't let me keep them. He always takes the good things away."

"No," I promise. "I won't let him."

A second circuit around the room and I see what Eric meant about soundproofing. Behind the packing crates, the walls are covered floor-to-ceiling with acoustic paneling. I walk my fingers along the thick felt, searching for seams or nails, but come up empty. Even the space where I know the windows should be is covered over. He's turned the unit into a felt-lined box, leaving only the wooden floor unaltered. I stamp my feet hard on the planking, which only results in Grace sitting up in alarm.

"Don't do that!" she says. "It just makes him mad!"

On cue the locks click and Eric comes through the door clutching two tall glasses of water. My thirst returns in a wave, dizzying in its intensity. Grace scrambles to her hands and knees and then upright, charging Eric like a dog after fresh meat.

"Easy now." But he passes her one of the glasses. She clutches it in both hands, drinks with a desperation that leaves water slopping onto the floor. "You, too, Hemingway. You'll feel better."

More than anything I want to refuse him, but I can't. My depleted body knows what it needs, and the compulsion is too strong. I snatch the glass from his hand and drink. It must be water from the tap downstairs, but it's the sweetest thing I've tasted in all my life. My head swims with the pleasure of it.

Too quickly, the glass is drained.

"You've been exploring," Eric observes. "Nice coat. See anything else you like?"

"No." Water gone, Grace has returned to her spot on the floor, like a frightened animal to her burrow. She pulls the overcoat around her shoulders, baring her teeth at Eric.

"Hemingway says I can keep it." My heart breaks a little for the picture she makes, hardly more than a skeleton swathed in velvet, defiance in the jut of her pointed chin.

"Who am I to argue with the boss?" But he's not pleased. His mouth folds into a flat line. "Hemingway, have you found my treasures yet? No, not the books. Look, there, in that box. I like to keep them close at hand."

If it means Grace gets to keep her wrap, I'm willing to play along. I look in the box Eric indicates and catch my breath when I realize what's inside. Not treasures: souvenirs.

"The bracelet belonged to Christy Spears. Car keys belonged to Blake Andrews. Javier Smith: the money clip. Richard Yuen: that was my first, his curfew card. He almost caught me lifting it. Richards and Nour: they belong to the wristwatches. I like a nice timepiece. I enjoyed lifting Tremblay's Rolex. It was wasted on him. But what I really think you'll enjoy—" He ghosts close, and I brace myself for the brush of his fingers and the pain that comes with his touch. "—is that scarf, there. Ring a bell?"

The scarf he means is tattered and red, worn through in spots from too much use. I know at once it's half of a set. The other half is a beanie.

"Rafe Castillo," Eric confirms. "I scout them out ahead of time, understand? The ones I think might be worth taking. Watch them for weeks. Months. And then I'll take something home with me, to keep close for a while, just to be sure. To be sure I've made the right choice. I learned how to pick pockets in the army, same place I learned how to kill."

"You're mental," Grace cries. "I hate you!"

"If you'd kept your nose out of my business instead of following me up here Sunday morning, we wouldn't be in this predicament," Eric retorts viciously. "You'd be happily preparing for your debut as *Mary*, I wouldn't be looking for a way off this island, and Hemingway would be none the wiser. I should cut your throat now and leave you here in the dust. You don't deserve the river."

"No." Grace cowers. "I'm sorry. Please don't."

Rafe Castillo's scarf is soft in my hands. I pull it through my fingers, testing the knit, trying to ignore the sting in my eyes as I think of Thom. Then I drop it back into the box with the rest of the Ripper's souvenirs and turn around.

"Stay away," I warn. "Just leave her alone."

Eric's shoulders slump. "I've canceled your appointments for the rest of the week," he reports. "Miksail's wrangling up an exit visa, but it's not cheap. I've taken what I need from the cash drawer. You don't mind, do you, Hemingway? You've got plenty in reserve. Not that you'll be needing it now, thanks to Grace."

"I don't mind," I say, as I concentrate on nursing fury from a flicker to a roar. "Take all you want. Only, will you tell me something?"

"Sure. I guess. Maybe. What is it?"

"Was it thaumaturgy that made you like this? Or have you always been a killer?"

"I told you." Eric shakes his head, disappointed. "War made me a killer. War turned me into a monster. Murder is penitence; magic keeps the pain away. Without thaumaturgy, I'd be dead and buried like the rest of my patrol, and I'm just not ready to die. I pay the river's price, and the magic keeps me safe."

"I don't understand." If I can keep him talking, distract him long enough, maybe I can make a run for the open door.

"You should," Eric says. "It's kept you safe, too. Without thaumaturgy, you'd be nothing but a backwoods rube struggling to make a living in some closet tattoo shop while everyone you know goes off to war, or retreats into the brush, or worse. You'd go dead inside from the tedium, and eventually you'd go looking for your daddy's hunting rifle or his skinning knife and you'd just be dead. Like most of the rest of the world." He smirks, but it doesn't reach his eyes. "The magic *chose* you for bigger things, Hemingway. It's kept you safe."

I grind my teeth because if I open my mouth, I'll start howling. Eric just stands there in front of the door, watching me. The disgust I'm feeling must be clear as crystal because eventually, he shrugs.

"Kept you safe until now," he adds. He takes a small packet from his back pocket and drops it on the floor by the toes of his shiny loafers. "Sandwiches," he explains. "Slightly squished, I'm afraid. Eat up, both of you. I need your strength. I'll be back after sunset, and we'll take a little walk. Pay the river's price one last time."

Grace screams when I leap. It's a dumb move, because he's read my intentions on my treasonous face and catches me easily. He lets me land a few blows around his chest and neck before he does the Ripper thing, reminding me that if he wanted, he could easily turn me into nothing but a lifeless husk.

He takes just enough to leave me groaning at his feet, fireworks bursting behind my eyes. I scrabble weakly, trying to find the strength to rise, but my muscles aren't interested in cooperating.

"Don't try that again," Eric says. "It's embarrassing for both of us." He slams the door as he leaves. Grace begins to make dry, wretched noises.

"It's fine," I gasp. Talking feels like swallowing sand. My cells are on fire again; I half expect to see smoke rising from my skin. "I'm fine. We're fine." The last is a blatant lie, but I figure I get points for optimism.

I drag myself to standing against the door and try the knob, just in case he's forgotten to lock us in. He hasn't, so I pound on the frame and on the wall, until agony forces me to stop. Then I slump, forehead against the door, and listen to my heart pound in my ears.

"It's no use," Grace says, from where she's hiding under her coat. "I screamed for days and no one came. No one heard me, not even you, and you were right downstairs. Trying just makes things worse."

I roll against the door so I'm facing the room. Again I'm pathetically grateful for the lights. Idly, trying to distract myself from the pain arching from nerve to nerve, I take inventory: books, boxes, clothes, dust, and the Ripper's souvenirs.

"Take a walk, he said. He didn't kill them here. There's no blood anywhere."

"I don't think there's much blood left inside by the end." Grace sticks her head out from beneath her shelter. To my credit I don't flinch. It's hard to see anything left of the girl I fell in love with behind the ghoulish mask.

"Besides, didn't you pay attention to anything I said? Typical Hemingway. Everyone knows he cuts their throats right before he tosses them in. Has to do with the way the blood doesn't coagulate on the wound, or something. The coroner can tell."

"The coroner's an idiot, but okay." I make myself move away from the door, farther into the room. Each step is like shards of glass rubbing against my skin. "That means we've got a chance. We're not gonna die in here."

"What are you doing?" Grace swivels, keeping me carefully in sight. More than anything, she must have been disconsolate, tucked away up here all by herself. Grace hates to be alone with her own thoughts. She'll always choose distraction over introspection.

I crouch by one of the crates, walk my hands along the edges. The box isn't huge, but it's solid wood, held together by nails as long as my thumb. I grimace in satisfaction.

"Preparing."

"You can't fight back. I tried!"

"C'mon, Grace," I cajole. "Where's that fuck-you attitude I know and love? You're not alone anymore. It's us now. Together, we can do anything."

It's much harder to take the box apart than I expected. Without a hammer or screwdriver it's almost impossible. I tear my fingertips to bloody nubs scratching at the nail heads until eventually I realize it's easier just to kick the crate apart. And then I'm glad for Eric's soundproofing because I'm not the Karate Kid, able to land a single catastrophic kick. I make a shit ton of ugly noise trying to break the thing apart.

I have no idea how much time passes, but it seems like forever before the box explodes in a blowout of lumber and paperback books. Grace squeals in triumph. She's been alternating between dozing and deriding my antics. I'm glad I can provide her with suitable distraction.

"Now what?" she asks, crawling forward. I squat on the floor, sorting through pieces of wood until I find the one I want. The slat is sturdy, but more importantly, it's got reach, and there are four wicked-looking nails sticking point first out of one end.

"When he comes back, you hit him with this. Again and again. And don't let him touch you. Just distract him."

Grace takes the slat from me. She turns it over, ruined hands quivering. Both of us are wondering if she has the strength to hang onto the thing, let alone swing it, but neither of us say so out loud. Her dead eyes widen in deep sockets as she studies the devilishly pointed nails.

"And what will you do?"

"Finish the job."

I conceal the broken crate behind a pile of books and boxes, then hide the piece of wood under Grace's overcoat. We wait. Grace dozes, and I pace the room, poking at boxes until my energy falters and I'm forced to sit down. My thirst has returned in force. It's hard to think straight past parched longing. There's a kitchen sink in the unit buried beneath stacks of books, and I make myself get up and try the taps. But when I twist the handles, nothing happens. The pipes are dry, disconnected.

I don't sleep; I can't. I'm too angry. There's nothing left in me but rage and the thirst. I rewind the years over and over again in my head, examining everything Eric said, replaying every move he made, looking for any sign that I should have known what he was. But there's nothing. He was an excellent employee and more than that a friend and mentor. Starting a business is no easy thing; starting a business when you're a minor and new in town is unthinkable.

Without Eric I might have failed in the beginning, when I had no real idea what I was doing, and definitely no interest in the day-to-day tedium of enterprise. I'd wanted only to create, and to make money. I'd been able to do that in spades, thanks to thaumaturgy, but also thanks to Eric's ability to manage every other detail that kept Earnest Ink's doors open, all the while making me feel safe in an uncertain world.

He'd been my partner in all but name. More than that, he'd been a friend.

I don't want to believe it's all been a sham, meant nothing. I want to wake up from this nightmare, roll out of bed to the noise of tea brewing, and start a new day.

But I can't, so I do the next best thing and brace myself for what's coming.

"Get up." Eric bursts through the door, making me jump. I hadn't heard the locks click; I must have been closer to sleep than I'd thought. "It's time to go." He has a backpack over his shoulder and his butterfly knife, folded shut, in one hand.

"What's happening?" I don't have to pretend to be woozy. My head feels like a hornet-filled balloon and my hands are on fire. I keep them out of sight as I rise. The tips are bloody and torn from fighting with the box.

"Time to go," he repeats, brittle and too bright. He's changed into a suit and tie, more stripes, and silly, polka-dotted socks. He's so much my Eric that I can almost forget he's also the Ripper. "Things are happening. Big things. I do love Thom, Hemingway, but she's like a schnauzer with a hambone."

"She's figured you out," I guess. Too late for Grace and me, maybe, but still I'm delighted. "She'll catch you yet."

"No. I won't let that happen. Dammit, Grace, you're not as helpless as you pretend. I've been very careful. Get up! Here, for Chrissake, Hemingway, help me get her up."

He's tugging at Grace's overcoat, and she's whimpering, clinging to its cover, trying to escape his hands. The door's open behind Eric, and I know I could make a dash for it, maybe even get as far as Ms. Harcourt on second floor, but I won't leave Grace.

"Don't hurt her!" The floor seems to rock back and forth beneath my feet, a ship on angry water, as I cross the room. My hair had started falling out overnight, clumps of white and black into my lap. I'm hardly as vain as Grace, but I don't like mirrors even on a good day, and I'm pretty sure I'd faint if I saw my reflection now.

"Come on, Grace." I grab the hem of the coat and tug. "Let's go. I don't want to die here. You'll feel better in fresh air."

Grace has always had a taste for the dramatic, and she doesn't disappoint me now. She comes up out of her shelter caterwauling, swinging with all her might. Eric shouts. Grace slams him directly in the knees with the nail end of her stick, and he falls, howling. That's when I jump on him from behind, Rafe Castillo's scarf wrapped around both hands. I loop the scarf around Eric's throat as tight as I possibly can and twist.

Fury and fear make me strong. The force of my attack knocks Eric on top of me. We're lying prone on the floor, me on my back, strangling Eric, who is on my chest, gasping. He pulls at the scarf, trying to get air, but I only twist harder. Grace is still hitting him with her piece of wood, doing a fine impersonation of a banshee. Blood splatters.

Good for you, Grace, I think. *Let him have it.*

Eric gives up on the scarf and reaches for me instead. I expected this; I knew it was coming. He presses his fingers into my wrists. His magic tears into me, invading and then draining. I close my eyes and try my best to endure, outlast. I don't expect to win. I'm half Eric's size, and I don't have his training. I just need to hold on a long enough for Grace to make her escape.

But it doesn't happen the way I planned. Someone else is screaming. I turn my head, trying to see. It's Ms. Harcourt, in the hallway, a kitchen knife in one hand, Thom close behind her, and Tremblay on Thom's heels. Ms. Harcourt's yelling into a phone while she waves the knife vaguely our direction. Thom pushes her aside and rushes the room. Tremblay's brandishing Seraphine's shotgun, but he's holding it like it's a snake and he's worried it might bite him. I think I hear sirens, or maybe it's my eardrums giving out under the Ripper's assault. There's a film growing across my eyes. Could be it's only tears. Pain is my new best friend.

I can't hold on much longer. Lucky for me, I don't need to. Eric stops fighting exactly one heartbeat before I do. The floor shakes as he breathes out for the last time. An army of grunts are charging down the hallway, screaming instructions. We're saved.

Maybe too late for me.

Thom falls to her knees at my side, clutching at my hands. Her fingers on mine hurt worse than shrapnel in bone, but I can't tell her that because my tongue's useless, dry and swollen in my mouth.

For the second time in my life, I leave a crime scene in an ambulance. But this time I'm awake to appreciate the experience.

Turns out the Eric's magic doesn't work on me like it does on other people. Could be it's because I have magic of my own, could be because I come from hardy Idaho farm stock. Either way, after half a day of continuous hydration, the only thing I'm left with to prove that I took on the Ripper is an embarrassing streak of white in what's left of my hair and an ache like I've just survived a nasty bout with the flu.

They keep me overnight anyway. I don't protest because they've put Grace next door, and I want to keep an eye on her. She's fared worse than I have by a long shot, but she's got more kick left in her than Ang did, which gives me hope.

Thom won't leave my side, even when I point out that someone had better check and make sure Reba the sausage dog isn't chewing up all our shoes.

"Ms. Harcourt said she'd feed her." Thom scowls. The uncomfortable plastic hospital chair isn't doing her posture any favors. "I can't believe it—*Eric*. He'd been in our faces all this time. If not for Tremblay, I might never have figured it out. He swore up and down you were in trouble and wouldn't shut up about it even when I shot him with my CEW."

"Ouch."

"Yeah. He probably saved your life." Thom screws up her nose in sympathy. She exhales. "I'm a shit detective."

"Afraid so." I wink to soften the truth. "But the way I see it, you're pretty excellent at saving lives."

Chapter Twenty

Evolution

I can almost forget I've killed a man. Not just a man. Someone I trusted, a friend. I can almost forget the way the Eric looked when we left him still and battered on the floor, blood pooling around his body. I can almost forget the relief I'd felt when he was dead, relief that was dangerously close to celebration.

Tremblay's been drinking, but I don't call him on it—there's no point. I suppose it's not easy evading Central. He may not be the East River Ripper, but he's still high on the mayor's shit list with no secure place to call home. Pier 88's in shambles, and I'm guessing it will be quite a while before Seraphine and her punks put it back together again.

At least bathtub gin relaxes him in my chair. We chat about nothing for an hour as I transform his flesh. Seraphine sits on my chaise, observing. She's brought her gun, which is rude, but I'm pretty sure she doesn't plan to shoot me at this stage of the game.

The hornet sleeps on the crook of her jaw, waiting.

"I like you, Hemingway," Tremblay confesses as I trace the lines on his back with my needle. "I've liked you from the beginning, since you fought back. You're cute. And you've got plenty of balls, for a short guy."

"You, too," I reply absently. "For a stork with purple hair."

"I'm sorry you had to kill him. I should have done it instead. Could have done it, if I'd got there in time." He shakes his head. "*Mon dieu*, we were looking for you everywhere. In the building all along, when I thought somehow he'd snuck you out the back."

Thom says the same thing, over and over again, when I wake up yelling from a new nightmare, one in which I'm choking on air instead of water and Eric's watching me drown. Then she clutches me close until I stop shivering. And drying the tears and sweat on my cheeks with her breath, she murmurs in my ear, promising me I'll never have to hurt anyone again.

It's a promise Thom probably can't keep, but I don't tell her that.

The feathers are a baroque painting on Tremblay's skin, beautiful, spreading from his spine. They begin to flutter as I work: almost finished. I wonder if he can feel them moving, but he gives no sign.

"Have you ever killed anyone?"

"No," Tremblay answers. He nods, and then shakes his head but doesn't elaborate. I don't press. Some things are too private to share.

Tremblay's feathers are the color of old ivory and soft as the falling snow. He moves them uncertainly, a grounded fledgling, and I clap my hand over my mouth to keep from laughing. Tremblay's wings are a gorgeous example of living rococo and possibly my best work yet, but they're also much too small for his lanky body, and undeniably silly.

"Cut it out," he tells me, craning to see over his shoulder. The wings flap uncertainly against his spine. It's adorable. "*Tas toi*, magic man."

"They're very nice," I say around helpless giggles. "At Earnest Ink, we aim to please."

He awards me with a scathing glare, then pivots on Seraphine. "We'll do it now. No more waiting."

"You're not ready." She walks in circles around him, studying the new wings with avid attention. "You need to build up muscle. Besides, I didn't bring anything to cover them." Sweet as black-market sugar, she adds: "They're really very good, Hemingway. Beyond expectation." She runs her fingers through white down, but Tremblay jerks away.

"Now," he insists. "I can't build up muscle with these stubby things. I need to practice or it will never work."

"What will never work?" I ask, although of course I've suspected some of it all along, ever since the blue conflagration in the cargo container, ever since I watched the hornet sting and bite.

"Outside," Seraphine relents. "Kindle your flame so the cameras don't see."

Tremblay leads the way out back. I follow, admiring the way my feathers ruffle in the cold air. Snow dusts Tremblay's hair and shoulders. White flakes dissolve when they drift too near his flame. The cold makes the air catch in my lungs.

"Here is fine," Seraphine says, glancing around the alley. "Quickly, now. Take my hand."

They link hands. I expect I'm there as a reluctant witness, but Tremblay reaches out suddenly and grabs my elbow, then slides his hand down my arm until our fingers are linked. Before I can protest, Seraphine exhales.

Her magic courses through us all, an electric arc. It jars. We're a closed circuit, racing toward overflowing, approaching combustion. I bite my tongue to keep from shouting. My heart is beating in an unfamiliar rhythm; I think it might be Seraphine's.

The white feathers on Tremblay's back shade to gray and then black, from swan to raven, snow to ash. They grow as his wings expand, just like the blue-fire feather hanging in the air over Roosevelt Island, only much more substantial. He groans and doubles over as the wings grow to twice their size, and then again, and again. By the time the tips of his pinions touch the ground, he's on his knees in the alley, gasping.

"Stop!" he cries.

I'm frightened Seraphine won't, but she releases his hand immediately.

"Oh, look," she says, eyes shining. "Hemingway, look what we've done!"

I look, and like the hornet buzzing about our heads, Tremblay's new wings are wrong. They're alluring, yes, blue-black as good ink and shiny. But they're all wrong.

He struggles to flex the muscles beneath as he rises; the wings twitch feebly.

"How do they look?" Tremblay asks, and all at once, he's an insecure kid wondering about a new haircut. "They're so heavy. Will they work?"

"Of course they will," Seraphine promises. "I told you, you need to practice. They're perfect. Just perfect."

I want to be away from the alley, away from them both. Snow gathers on black feathers. I shiver, not because of the cold.

"We're finished, right?" I say pointedly. "It's over, our bargain? Because I don't want anything to do with whatever the hell you two are up to. I'm out for good, understand? I have Grace to think of now."

"And yourself, as usual," Seraphine retorts.

"As usual," I agree. "Now get lost, the both of you. And don't come back. Earnest Ink is closed to you."

Tremblay's face falls. I've never seen him forlorn before. I hurry back into the building before he can say anything that might change my mind, throwing the bolt firmly behind me.

It's a month before I catch wind of Tremblay and Seraphine again, and even then, it's only tangential. I'm sitting in Grace's hospital room sketching her withered hands for practice while she watches the old black-and-white television affixed to the wall across the room. It's showing a documentary about polar bears—not quite up to Signals' standards, but the bears are almost as cute as *Ailurus fulgens*. When Central breaks in with a news bite, we both go still.

"Impenetrable" fortress breached! the grainy, scrolling banner reads. *Multiple underground explosions reported! Thaumaturge missing, feared escaped!* A snap of Rikers flashes onscreen, followed by Rutch's picture, equally monotone. The snap was taken while he addressed a crowd; he's caught midwave, an unremarkable young man with the beginnings of a beard on his round chin.

Birdman sighted overhead! the scroll continues in dramatic font. *Some fatalities expected!*

"Birdman." I slap my forehead. "Tremblay will love that."

Grace blinks. "Do I want to know?"

"No," I say, smiling into the CCTV camera above our heads. "Absolutely not."

He comes for us the next day, that unremarkable young man from the television. He's dressed in a doctor's coat, a paper mask obscuring much of his face. It's an elementary disguise, but apparently it works, because no one kicks up a fuss when he walks into Grace's room and closes and locks the door.

"Hello, Hemingway," he says, crossing the floor and pulling curtains across the window. "Fantastic to finally meet you." He yanks down the paper mask so I can see his grin.

"Can't say the same about you," I reply, helping Grace into a more comfortable sitting position so she doesn't have to stare up at our unwelcome visitor. "What are you doing here?"

"Tremblay says I owe you my freedom." His disguise is complete with a stethoscope. He plays distractedly with the end, all the while keeping the back of his head to the CCTV on the ceiling. "Which means in the near future, the State of New York will also owe you its freedom."

"I want nothing to do with that," I declare. "I'm an artist, not a politician. I just want to lie low and do my own thing. Go the fuck away before I call security."

The corners of his mouth curl. "Good show," he murmurs. "Keep it up, but don't be afraid. There are more of us out there than even I know. Magic is rising, as it should. Look how technology has failed us."

Grace is reaching for the call button. Rutch stops her, grabbing her hand. Grace releases a sound of surprise, then another of distinct pleasure.

"Hey!" I jump up, press into Rutch's space. "Leave her alone!"

I can see why Seraphine likes him; there's a patronizing tilt to his smile as he backs away. "My debt is paid," he says simply. "Be smart, Hemingway. When the time comes, choose wisely."

The doctor's coat swirls as he makes his exit, theater at its best. I hope to God I never see his smug face again. But when I turn back to Grace, I change my mind. Shock almost sends me to the sticky hospital floor.

Grace is sitting up in bed, but not just sitting up, propped on pillows and surrounded by sling and machinery. She's sitting up on the *edge* of the bed, legs dangling over the side, bare knees flexing, bare feet swinging gently. Vitality restored, eyes bright and shining, life returning to her withered body in increments as I watch.

"I think..." she ventures. "I think he's fixed me." And then she laughs, loud and full of unfettered joy, and I know it's the most beautiful sound I've ever heard.

Piano Jim is playing Gershwin outside my window. It's late in the season for a private concert. There's a fine layer of snow on the sidewalk, and usually by late October Jim's packed it up for the winter season.

I'm fairly certain he's trying to catch my attention. I haven't left my apartment much in the last few weeks, so his pocketbook is probably running empty. No doubt he's jonesing for a fix and decided it's time to come calling in person.

I ignore "Rhapsody in Blue" while I daub cheerful yellow flecks of acrylic paint onto a small, square canvas. My room is crowded with new blank canvases and stretcher bars. Paint fumes make me light-headed, even with the window cracked. I whistle tunelessly as I create, a raucous counterpoint to Jim's music. A field of yellow sunflowers grows beneath my brush, turning their faces toward a nonexistent sun, filling the canvas to bursting. Reba, the sausage dog, snores loudly between my bare feet. Henry Ang is still confined to his hospital room; the last I heard, they're not sure he'll ever walk or talk again. The Ripper took too much from him, and unlike Grace, he didn't have Rutch to give it back.

When I'm satisfied I've filled in the final detail, I switch out brushes, trading thick yellow for slender black. I sign the left-hand corner of the canvas where I've left a patch of clean white: Hemingway.

As soon as I finish the curve of the Y, I grab the canvas and take it with me to the window.

"Hey, Jim," I shout, leaning out over the sill, canvas in hand.

Still playing, he tilts his head around and up in acknowledgment.

"Good morning, Hemingway," he answers. "How's it hanging?"

I turn the painting upside down. Sunflowers erupt from canvas: long stems, green leaves, and yellow petals explode into thin air, smelling of fertile fields and honey. I shake the upside-down canvas, and the flowers rain down on Jim and on his piano and onto the sidewalks alongside.

Gershwin stumbles to silence. Pedestrians braving the cold morning look around in amazement.

"Good morning, Jim," I call cheerfully. "As it happens, things are fantastic."

About the Author

Sarah Remy/Alex Hall is a nonbinary, animal-loving, proud gamer geek. Although Sarah reads widely across the adult genre, their passion is SFF (in all its forms, epic to urban, angst to fluff) and LGBTQ+ fiction. Their work can be found in a variety of cool places, including HarperVoyager, EDGE, and NineStar Press.

Email:madisonplacepress@gmail.com

Twitter:@sarahremywrites

Website: www.sarahremy.com

Also Available from NineStar Press

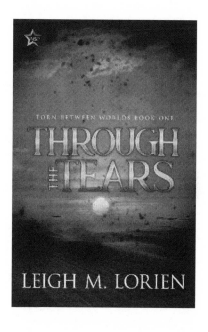

Connect with NineStar Press

www.ninestarpress.com

www.facebook.com/ninestarpress

www.facebook.com/groups/NineStarNiche

www.twitter.com/ninestarpress

www.tumblr.com/blog/ninestarpress